I0762928

BROTHERS
GRIMM

EDITED BY EDGAR TAYLOR AND MARIAN EDWARDES
ILLUSTRATIONS BY WALTER CRANE, CAROLINE S. KING,
AND EDWARD HENRY WEHNERT

Published by Harper Muse, an imprint of HarperCollins Focus LLC, 501 Nelson Place, Nashville, TN 37214, USA.

ISBN 9781400355716 (HC)

HarperCollins Publishers, Macken House, 39/40 Mayor Street Upper, Dublin 1, D01 C9W8, Ireland (https://www.harpercollins.com)

Printed in Vietnam

26 27 28 29 30 31 32 33 34 35 36 37 38 / RRD / 16 15 14 13 12 11 10 9 8 7 6 5 4 3 2 1

Grimm's Fairy Tales, originally titled Children's and Household Tales (Kinder- und Hausmärchen), is a famous collection of stories by the Brothers Grimm, Jacob and Wilhelm.

First published in 1812, the first edition featured eighty-six tales written for adults and wasn't necessarily suited for children. It included academic commentary and stories that addressed darker themes, such as death, betrayal, and violence. By altering the content and adding illustrations in later versions, the Grimms succeeded in appealing to a wider audience. Their Kleine Ausgabe ("small edition"), published in 1825, was specifically aimed at children and went through ten editions. By the seventh edition in 1857, their collection grew to include two hundred fairy tales and ten legends.

Grimm's Fairy Tales has endured for over two centuries, captivating readers of all ages. While early versions of the tales were shadowed by hardship and complexity, their enduring charm lies in their ability to transport us to magical worlds, teach moral lessons, and entertain with imaginative twists. Today, the collection remains one of the most treasured literary works of all time.

The Golden Bird

A certain king had a beautiful garden, and in the garden stood a tree which bore golden apples. These apples were always counted, and about the time when they began to grow ripe it was found that every night one of them was gone. The king became very angry at this, and ordered the gardener to keep watch all night under the tree. The gardener set his eldest son to watch; but about twelve o'clock he fell asleep, and in the morning another of the apples was missing. Then the second son was ordered to watch; and at midnight he too fell asleep, and in the morning another apple was gone. Then the third son offered to keep watch; but the gardener at first would not let him, for fear some harm should come to him: however, at last he consented, and the young man laid himself under the tree to watch. As the clock struck twelve he heard a rustling noise in the air, and a bird came flying that was of pure gold; and as it was snapping at one of the apples with its beak, the gardener's son jumped up and shot an arrow at it. But the arrow did the bird no harm; only it dropped a golden feather from its tail, and then flew away. The golden feather was brought to the king in the morning, and all the council was called together. Everyone agreed that it was worth more than all the wealth of the kingdom: but the king said, "One feather is of no use to me, I must have the whole bird."

Then the gardener's eldest son set out and thought to find the golden bird very easily; and when he had gone but a little way, he came to a wood, and by the side of the wood he saw a fox sitting; so he took his bow and made ready to shoot at it. Then the fox said, "Do not shoot me, for I will give you good counsel; I know what your business is, and that you want to find the golden bird. You will reach a village in the evening; and when you get there, you will see two inns opposite to each other, one of which is very pleasant and beautiful to look at: go not in there, but rest for the night in the other, though it may appear to you to be very poor and mean."

But the son thought to himself, "What can such a beast as this know about the matter?" So he shot his arrow at the fox; but he missed it, and it set up its tail above its back and ran into the wood. Then he went his way, and in the evening came to the village where the two inns were; and in one of these were people singing, and dancing, and feasting; but the other looked very dirty, and poor. "I should be very silly," said he, "if I went to that shabby house, and left this charming place"; so he went into the smart house, and ate and drank at his ease, and forgot the bird, and his country too.

Time passed on; and as the eldest son did not come back, and no tidings were heard of him, the second son set out, and the same thing happened to him. He met the fox, who gave him the good advice: but when he came to the two inns, his eldest brother was standing at the window where the merrymaking was, and called to him to come in; and he could not withstand the temptation, but went in, and forgot the golden bird and his country in the same manner.

Time passed on again, and the youngest son too wished to set out into the wide world to seek for the golden bird; but his father would not listen to it for a long while, for he was very fond of his son, and was afraid that some ill luck might happen to him also, and prevent his coming back. However, at last it was agreed he should go, for he would not rest at home; and as he came to the wood, he met the fox, and heard the same good

counsel. But he was thankful to the fox, and did not attempt his life as his brothers had done; so the fox said, "Sit upon my tail, and you will travel faster." So he sat down, and the fox began to run, and away they went over stock and stone so quick that their hair whistled in the wind.

When they came to the village, the son followed the fox's counsel, and without looking about him went to the shabby inn and rested there all night at his ease. In the morning came the fox again and met him as he was beginning his journey, and said, "Go straight forward, till you come to a castle, before which lie a whole troop of soldiers fast asleep and snoring: take no notice of them, but go into the castle and pass on and on till you come to a room, where the golden bird sits in a wooden cage; close by it stands a beautiful golden cage; but do not try to take the bird out of the shabby cage and put it into the handsome one, otherwise you will repent it." Then the fox stretched out his tail again, and the young man sat himself down, and away they went over stock and stone till their hair whistled in the wind.

Before the castle gate all was as the fox had said: so the son went in and found the chamber where the golden bird hung in a wooden cage, and below stood the golden cage, and the three golden apples that had been lost were lying close by it. Then thought he to himself, "It will be a very droll thing to bring away such a fine bird in this shabby cage"; so he opened the door and took hold of it and put it into the golden cage. But the bird set up such a loud scream that all the soldiers awoke, and they took him prisoner and carried him before the king. The next morning the court sat to judge him; and when all was heard, it sentenced him to die, unless he should bring the king the golden horse which could run as swiftly as the wind; and if he did this, he was to have the golden bird given him for his own.

So he set out once more on his journey, sighing, and in great despair, when on a sudden his friend the fox met him, and said, "You see now what has happened on account of your not listening to my counsel. I will still, however, tell you how to find the golden horse, if you will do as I bid you. You must go straight on till you come to the castle where the horse stands in his stall: by his side will lie the groom fast asleep and snoring: take away the horse quietly, but be sure to put the old leathern saddle upon him, and not the golden one that is close by it." Then the son sat down on the fox's tail, and away they went over stock and stone till their hair whistled in the wind.

All went right, and the groom lay snoring with his hand upon the golden saddle. But when the son looked at the horse, he thought it a great pity to put the leathern saddle upon it. "I will give him the good one," said he; "I am sure he deserves it." As he took up the golden saddle the groom awoke and cried out so loud, that all the guards ran in and took him prisoner, and in the morning he was again brought before the court to be judged, and was sentenced to die. But it was agreed, that, if he could bring thither the beautiful princess, he should live, and have the bird and the horse given him for his own.

Then he went his way very sorrowful; but the old fox came and said, "Why did not you listen to me? If you had, you would have carried away both the bird and the horse; yet will I once more give you counsel. Go straight on, and in the evening you will arrive at a castle. At twelve o'clock at night the princess goes to the bathing house: go up to her and give her a kiss, and she will let you lead her away; but take care you do not suffer her to go and take leave of her father and mother." Then the fox stretched out his tail, and so away they went over stock and stone till their hair whistled again.

As they came to the castle, all was as the fox had said, and at twelve o'clock the young man met the princess going to the bath and gave her the kiss, and she agreed to run away with him, but begged with many tears that he would let her take leave of her father. At first he refused, but she wept still more and more, and fell at his feet, till at last he consented; but the moment she came to her father's house the guards awoke and he was taken prisoner again.

Then he was brought before the king, and the king said, "You shall never have my daughter unless in eight days you dig away the hill that stops the view from my window." Now this hill was so big that the whole world could not take it away: and when he had worked for seven days, and had done very little, the fox came and said, "Lie down and go to sleep; I will work for you." And in the morning he awoke and the hill was gone; so he went merrily to the king, and told him that now that it was removed he must give him the princess.

Then the king was obliged to keep his word, and away went the young man and the princess; and the fox came and said to him, "We will have all three, the princess, the horse, and the bird."

"Ah!" said the young man, "that would be a great thing, but how can you contrive it?"

"If you will only listen," said the fox, "it can be done. When you come to the king, and he asks for the beautiful princess, you must say, 'Here she is!' Then he will be very joyful; and you will mount the golden horse that they are to give you, and put out your hand to take leave of them; but shake hands with the princess last. Then lift her quickly on to the horse behind you; clap your spurs to his side, and gallop away as fast as you can."

All went right: then the fox said, "When you come to the castle where the bird is, I will stay with the princess at the door, and you will ride in and speak to the king; and when he sees that it is the right horse, he will bring out the bird; but you must sit still, and say that you want to look at it, to see whether it is the true golden bird; and when you get it into your hand, ride away."

This, too, happened as the fox said; they carried off the bird, the princess mounted again, and they rode on to a great wood. Then the fox came, and said, "Pray kill me, and cut off my head and my feet." But the young man refused to do it: so the fox said, "I will at any rate give you good counsel: beware of two things; ransom no one from the gallows, and sit down by the side of no river." Then away he went. "Well," thought the young man, "it is no hard matter to keep that advice."

He rode on with the princess, till at last he came to the village where he had left his two brothers. And there he heard a great noise and uproar; and when he asked what was the matter, the people said, "Two men are

THE
GOLDEN-BIRD
"- THE FOX SAID,
NOW WHAT WILL YOU GIVE ME
FOR MY REWARD?"

going to be hanged." As he came nearer, he saw that the two men were his brothers, who had turned robbers; so he said, "Cannot they in any way be saved?" But the people said, "No," unless he would bestow all his money upon the rascals and buy their liberty. Then he did not stay to think about the matter, but paid what was asked, and his brothers were given up, and went on with him towards their home.

And as they came to the wood where the fox first met them, it was so cool and pleasant that the two brothers said, "Let us sit down by the side of the river, and rest awhile, to eat and drink." So he said, "Yes," and forgot the fox's counsel, and sat down on the side of the river; and while he suspected nothing, they came behind, and threw him down the bank, and took the princess, the horse, and the bird, and went home to the king their master, and said, "All this have we won by our labour." Then there was great rejoicing made; but the horse would not eat, the bird would not sing, and the princess wept.

The youngest son fell to the bottom of the river's bed: luckily it was nearly dry, but his bones were almost broken, and the bank was so steep that he could find no way to get out. Then the old fox came once more, and scolded him for not following his advice; otherwise no evil would have befallen him: "Yet," said he, "I cannot leave you here, so lay hold of my tail and hold fast." Then he pulled him out of the river, and said to him, as he got upon the bank, "Your brothers have set watch to kill you, if they find you in the kingdom." So he dressed himself as a poor man, and came secretly to the king's court, and was scarcely within the doors when the horse began to eat, and the bird to sing, and the princess left off weeping. Then he went to the king, and told him all his brothers' roguery; and they were seized and punished, and he had the princess given to him again; and after the king's death he was heir to his kingdom.

A long while after, he went to walk one day in the wood, and the old fox met him, and besought him with tears in his eyes to kill him, and cut off his head and feet. And at last he did so, and in a moment the fox was changed into a man, and turned out to be the brother of the princess, who had been lost a great many, many years.

Hans in Luck

Some men are born to good luck: all they do or try to do comes right, all that falls to them is so much gain, all their geese are swans, all their cards are trumps—toss them which way you will, they will always, like poor puss, alight upon their legs, and only move on so much the faster. The world may very likely not always think of them as they think of themselves, but what care they for the world? what can it know about the matter?

One of these lucky beings was neighbour Hans. Seven long years he had worked hard for his master. At last he said, "Master, my time is up; I must go home and see my poor mother once more: so pray pay me my wages and let me go." And the master said, "You have been a faithful and good servant, Hans, so your pay shall be handsome." Then he gave him a lump of silver as big as his head.

Hans took out his pocket handkerchief, put the piece of silver into it, threw it over his shoulder, and jogged off on his road homewards. As he went lazily on, dragging one foot after another, a man came in sight, trotting gaily along on a capital horse. "Ah!" said Hans aloud, "what a fine thing it is to ride on horseback! There he sits as easy and happy as if he was at home, in the chair by his fireside; he trips against no stones, saves shoe leather, and gets on he hardly knows how."

Hans did not speak so softly but the horseman heard it all, and said, "Well, friend, why do you go on foot then?"

"Ah!" said he, "I have this load to carry: to be sure it is silver, but it is so heavy that I can't hold up my head, and you must know it hurts my shoulder sadly."

"What do you say of making an exchange?" said the horseman. "I will give you my horse, and you shall give me the silver; which will save you a great deal of trouble in carrying such a heavy load about with you."

"With all my heart," said Hans: "but as you are so kind to me, I must tell you one thing—you will have a weary task to draw that silver about with you." However, the horseman got off, took the silver, helped Hans up, gave him the bridle into one hand and the whip into the other, and said, "When you want to go very fast, smack your lips loudly together, and cry "Jip!"

Hans was delighted as he sat on the horse, drew himself up, squared his elbows, turned out his toes, cracked his whip, and rode merrily off, one minute whistling a merry tune, and another singing,

"No care and no sorrow,
A fig for the morrow!
We'll laugh and be merry,
Sing neigh down derry!"

After a time he thought he should like to go a little faster, so he smacked his lips and cried "Jip!" Away went the horse full gallop; and before Hans knew what he was about, he was thrown off, and lay on his back by the roadside. His horse would have ran off, if a shepherd who was coming by, driving a cow, had not stopped it. Hans soon came to himself, and got upon his legs again, sadly vexed, and said to the shepherd, "This riding is no joke, when a man has the luck to get upon a beast like this that stumbles and flings him off as if it would break his neck. However,

I'm off now once for all: I like your cow now a great deal better than this smart beast that played me this trick, and has spoiled my best coat, you see, in this puddle; which, by the by, smells not very like a nosegay. One can walk along at one's leisure behind that cow—keep good company, and have milk, butter, and cheese, every day, into the bargain. What would I give to have such a prize!"

"Well," said the shepherd, "if you are so fond of her, I will change my cow for your horse; I like to do good to my neighbours, even though I lose by it myself."

"Done!" said Hans, merrily. "What a noble heart that good man has!" thought he. Then the shepherd jumped upon the horse, wished Hans and the cow good morning, and away he rode.

Hans brushed his coat, wiped his face and hands, rested awhile, and then drove off his cow quietly, and thought his bargain a very lucky one. "If I have only a piece of bread (and I certainly shall always be able to get that), I can, whenever I like, eat my butter and cheese with it; and when I am thirsty I can milk my cow and drink the milk: and what can I wish for more?" When he came to an inn, he halted, ate up all his bread, and gave away his last penny for a glass of beer. When he had rested himself he set off again, driving his cow towards his mother's village. But the heat grew greater as soon as noon came on, till at last, as he found himself on a wide heath that would take him more than an hour to cross, he began to be so hot and parched that his tongue clave to the roof of his mouth. "I can find a cure for this," thought he; "now I will milk my cow and quench my thirst": so he tied her to the stump of a tree, and held his leathern cap to milk into; but not a drop was to be had. Who would have thought that this cow, which was to bring him milk and butter and cheese, was all that time utterly dry? Hans had not thought of looking to that.

While he was trying his luck in milking, and managing the matter very clumsily, the uneasy beast began to think him very troublesome; and at last gave him such a kick on the head as knocked him down; and there he lay a long while senseless. Luckily a butcher soon came by, driving a pig in a wheelbarrow. "What is the matter with you, my man?" said the butcher, as he helped him up. Hans told him what had happened, how he was dry, and wanted to milk his cow, but found the cow was dry too. Then the butcher gave him a flask of ale, saying, "There, drink and refresh yourself; your cow will give you no milk: don't you see she is an old beast, good for nothing but the slaughterhouse?"

"Alas, alas!" said Hans, "who would have thought it? What a shame to take my horse, and give me only a dry cow! If I kill her, what will she be good for? I hate cow beef; it is not tender enough for me. If it were a pig now—like that fat gentleman you are driving along at his ease—one could do something with it; it would at any rate make sausages."

"Well," said the butcher, "I don't like to say no, when one is asked to do a kind, neighbourly thing. To please you I will change, and give you my fine fat pig for the cow."

"Heaven reward you for your kindness and self-denial!" said Hans, as he gave the butcher the cow; and taking the pig off the wheelbarrow, drove it away, holding it by the string that was tied to its leg.

So on he jogged, and all seemed now to go right with him: he had met with some misfortunes, to be sure; but he was now well repaid for all. How could it be otherwise with such a travelling companion as he had at last got?

The next man he met was a countryman carrying a fine white goose. The countryman stopped to ask what was o'clock; this led to further chat; and Hans told him all his luck, how he had so many good bargains, and how all the world went gay and smiling with him. The countryman then began to tell his tale, and said he was going to take the goose to a christening. "Feel," said he, "how heavy it is, and yet it is only eight weeks old. Whoever roasts and eats it will find plenty of fat upon it, it has lived so well!"

"You're right," said Hans, as he weighed it in his hand; "but if you talk of fat, my pig is no trifle." Meantime the countryman began to look grave, and shook his head.

"Hark ye!" said he, "my worthy friend, you seem a good sort of fellow, so I can't help doing you a kind turn. Your pig may get you into a scrape. In the village I just came from, the squire has had a pig stolen out of his sty. I was dreadfully afraid when I saw you that you had got the squire's pig. If you have, and they catch you, it will be a bad job for you. The least they will do will be to throw you into the horse pond. Can you swim?"

Poor Hans was sadly frightened. "Good man," cried he, "pray get me out of this scrape. I know nothing of where the pig was either bred or born; but he may have been the squire's for aught I can tell: you know this country better than I do, take my pig and give me the goose."

"I ought to have something into the bargain," said the countryman; "give a fat goose for a pig, indeed! 'Tis not everyone would do so much for you as that. However, I will not be hard upon you, as you are in trouble." Then he took the string in his hand, and drove off the pig by a side path; while Hans went on the way homewards free from care. "After all," thought he, "that chap is pretty well taken in. I don't care whose pig it is, but wherever it came from it has been a very good friend to me. I have much the best of the bargain. First there will be a capital roast; then the fat will find me in goose grease for six months; and then there are all the beautiful white feathers. I will put them into my pillow, and then I am sure I shall sleep soundly without rocking. How happy my mother will be! Talk of a pig, indeed! Give me a fine fat goose."

As he came to the next village, he saw a scissor grinder with his wheel, working and singing,

"O'er hill and o'er dale
So happy I roam,
Work light and live well,
All the world is my home;
Then who so blythe, so merry as I?"

Hans stood looking on for a while, and at last said, "You must be well-off, master grinder! you seem so happy at your work."

"Yes," said the other, "mine is a golden trade; a good grinder never puts his hand into his pocket without finding money in it—but where did you get that beautiful goose?"

"I did not buy it, I gave a pig for it."

"And where did you get the pig?"

"I gave a cow for it."

"And the cow?"

"I gave a horse for it."

"And the horse?"

"I gave a lump of silver as big as my head for it."

"And the silver?"

"Oh! I worked hard for that seven long years."

"You have thriven well in the world hitherto," said the grinder, "now if you could find money in your pocket whenever you put your hand in it, your fortune would be made."

"Very true: but how is that to be managed?"

"How? Why, you must turn grinder like myself," said the other; "you only want a grindstone; the rest will come of itself. Here is one that is but little the worse for wear: I would not ask more than the value of your goose for it—will you buy?"

"How can you ask?" said Hans; "I should be the happiest man in the world, if I could have money whenever I put my hand in my pocket: what could I want more? there's the goose."

"Now," said the grinder, as he gave him a common rough stone that lay by his side, "this is a most capital stone; do but work it well enough, and you can make an old nail cut with it."

Hans took the stone, and went his way with a light heart: his eyes sparkled for joy, and he said to himself, "Surely I must have been born in a lucky hour; everything I could want or wish for comes of itself. People are so kind; they seem really to think I do them a favour in letting them make me rich, and giving me good bargains."

Meantime he began to be tired, and hungry too, for he had given away his last penny in his joy at getting the cow.

At last he could go no farther, for the stone tired him sadly: and he dragged himself to the side of a river, that he might take a drink of water, and rest awhile. So he laid the stone carefully by his side on the bank:

but, as he stooped down to drink, he forgot it, pushed it a little, and down it rolled, plump into the stream.

For a while he watched it sinking in the deep clear water; then sprang up and danced for joy, and again fell upon his knees and thanked heaven, with tears in his eyes, for its kindness in taking away his only plague, the ugly heavy stone.

"How happy am I!" cried he; "nobody was ever so lucky as I." Then up he got with a light heart, free from all his troubles, and walked on till he reached his mother's house, and told her how very easy the road to good luck was.

Jorinda and Jorindel

There was once an old castle, that stood in the middle of a deep gloomy wood, and in the castle lived an old fairy. Now this fairy could take any shape she pleased. All the day long she flew about in the form of an owl, or crept about the country like a cat; but at night she always became an old woman again. When any young man came within a hundred paces of her castle, he became quite fixed, and could not move a step till she came and set him free; which she would not do till he had given her his word never to come there again: but when any pretty maiden came within that space she was changed into a bird, and the fairy put her into a cage, and hung her up in a chamber in the castle. There were seven hundred of these cages hanging in the castle, and all with beautiful birds in them.

Now there was once a maiden whose name was Jorinda. She was prettier than all the pretty girls that ever were seen before, and a shepherd lad, whose name was Jorindel, was very fond of her, and they were soon to be married. One day they went to walk in the wood, that they might be alone; and Jorindel said, "We must take care that we don't go too near to the fairy's castle." It was a beautiful evening; the last rays of the setting sun shone bright through the long stems of the trees upon the green underwood beneath, and the turtledoves sang from the tall birches.

Jorinda sat down to gaze upon the sun; Jorindel sat by her side; and both felt sad, they knew not why; but it seemed as if they were to be parted from one another for ever. They had wandered a long way; and when they looked to see which way they should go home, they found themselves at a loss to know what path to take.

The sun was setting fast, and already half of its circle had sunk behind the hill: Jorindel on a sudden looked behind him, and saw through the bushes that they had, without knowing it, sat down close under the old walls of the castle. Then he shrank for fear, turned pale, and trembled. Jorinda was just singing,

"The ring dove sang from the willow spray,
Well-a-day! Well-a-day!
He mourn'd for the fate of his darling mate,
Well-a-day!"

Then her song stopped suddenly. Jorindel turned to see the reason, and beheld his Jorinda changed into a nightingale, so that her song ended with a mournful jug, jug. An owl with fiery eyes flew three times round them, and three times screamed:

"Tu whu! Tu whu! Tu whu!"

Jorindel could not move; he stood fixed as a stone, and could neither weep, nor speak, nor stir hand or foot. And now the sun went quite down; the gloomy night came; the owl flew into a bush; and a moment after the old fairy came forth pale and meagre, with staring eyes, and a nose and chin that almost met one another.

She mumbled something to herself, seized the nightingale, and went away with it in her hand. Poor Jorindel saw the nightingale was gone—but what could he do? He could not speak, he could not move from the spot where he stood. At last the fairy came back and sang with a hoarse voice:

"Till the prisoner is fast,
And her doom is cast,
There stay! Oh, stay!
When the charm is around her,
And the spell has bound her,
Hie away! away!"

On a sudden Jorindel found himself free. Then he fell on his knees before the fairy, and prayed her to give him back his dear Jorinda: but she laughed at him, and said he should never see her again; then she went her way.

He prayed, he wept, he sorrowed, but all in vain. "Alas!" he said, "what will become of me?" He could not go back to his own home, so he went to a strange village, and employed himself in keeping sheep. Many a time did he walk round and round as near to the hated castle as he dared go, but all in vain; he heard or saw nothing of Jorinda.

At last he dreamt one night that he found a beautiful purple flower, and that in the middle of it lay a costly pearl; and he dreamt that he plucked the flower, and went with it in his hand into the castle, and that everything he touched with it was disenchanted, and that there he found his Jorinda again.

In the morning when he awoke, he began to search over hill and dale for this pretty flower; and eight long days he sought for it in vain: but on the ninth day, early in the morning, he found the beautiful purple flower; and in the middle of it was a large dewdrop, as big as a costly pearl. Then he plucked the flower, and set out and travelled day and night, till he came again to the castle.

He walked nearer than a hundred paces to it, and yet he did not become fixed as before, but found that he could go quite close up to the door. Jorindel was very glad indeed to see this. Then he touched the door with the flower, and it sprang open; so that he went in through the court, and listened when he heard so many birds singing. At last he came to the chamber where the fairy sat, with the seven hundred birds singing in the seven hundred cages. When she saw Jorindel she was very angry, and screamed with rage; but she could not come within two yards of him, for the flower he held in his hand was his safeguard. He looked around at the birds, but alas! there were many, many nightingales, and how then should he find out which was his Jorinda? While he was thinking what to do, he saw the fairy had taken down one of the cages, and was making the best of her way off through the door. He ran or flew after her, touched the cage with the flower, and Jorinda stood before him, and threw her arms round his neck looking as beautiful as ever, as beautiful as when they walked together in the wood.

Then he touched all the other birds with the flower, so that they all took their old forms again; and he took Jorinda home, where they were married, and lived happily together many years: and so did a good many other lads, whose maidens had been forced to sing in the old fairy's cages by themselves, much longer than they liked.

The Travelling Musicians

An honest farmer had once a donkey that had been a faithful servant to him a great many years, but was now growing old and every day more and more unfit for work. His master therefore was tired of keeping him and began to think of putting an end to him; but the donkey, who saw that some mischief was in the wind, took himself slyly off, and began his journey towards the great city, "For there," thought he, "I may turn musician."

After he had travelled a little way, he spied a dog lying by the roadside and panting as if he were tired. "What makes you pant so, my friend?" said the donkey.

"Alas!" said the dog, "my master was going to knock me on the head, because I am old and weak, and can no longer make myself useful to him in hunting; so I ran away; but what can I do to earn my livelihood?"

"Hark ye!" said the donkey, "I am going to the great city to turn musician: suppose you go with me, and try what you can do in the same way?" The dog said he was willing, and they jogged on together.

They had not gone far before they saw a cat sitting in the middle of the road and making a most rueful face. "Pray, my good lady," said the donkey, "what's the matter with you? You look quite out of spirits!"

"Ah, me!" said the cat, "how can one be in good spirits when one's life is in danger? Because I am beginning to grow old, and had rather lie at my ease by the fire than run about the house after the mice, my mistress laid hold of me, and was going to drown me; and though I have been lucky enough to get away from her, I do not know what I am to live upon."

"Oh," said the donkey, "by all means go with us to the great city; you are a good night singer, and may make your fortune as a musician." The cat was pleased with the thought, and joined the party.

Soon afterwards, as they were passing by a farmyard, they saw a cock perched upon a gate, and screaming out with all his might and main. "Bravo!" said the donkey; "upon my word, you make a famous noise; pray what is all this about?"

"Why," said the cock, "I was just now saying that we should have fine weather for our washing day, and yet my mistress and the cook don't thank me for my pains, but threaten to cut off my head tomorrow, and make broth of me for the guests that are coming on Sunday!"

"Heaven forbid!" said the donkey, "come with us Master Chanticleer; it will be better, at any rate, than staying here to have your head cut off! Besides, who knows? If we care to sing in tune, we may get up some kind of a concert; so come along with us."

"With all my heart," said the cock: so they all four went on jollily together.

They could not, however, reach the great city the first day; so when night came on, they went into a wood to sleep. The donkey and the dog laid themselves down under a great tree, and the cat climbed up into the branches; while the cock, thinking that the higher he sat the safer he should be, flew up to the very top of the tree, and then, according to his custom, before he went to sleep, looked out on all sides of him to see that everything was well. In doing this, he saw afar off something bright and shining and calling to his companions said, "There must be a house no great way off, for I see a light."

"If that be the case," said the donkey, "we had better change our quarters, for our lodging is not the best in the world!"

"Besides," added the dog, "I should not be the worse for a bone or two, or a bit of meat." So they walked off together towards the spot where Chanticleer had seen the light, and as they drew near it became larger and brighter, till they at last came close to a house in which a gang of robbers lived.

The donkey, being the tallest of the company, marched up to the window and peeped in. "Well, Donkey," said Chanticleer, "what do you see?"

"What do I see?" replied the donkey. "Why, I see a table spread with all kinds of good things, and robbers sitting round it making merry."

"That would be a noble lodging for us," said the cock.

"Yes," said the donkey, "if we could only get in"; so they consulted together how they should contrive to get the robbers out; and at last they hit upon a plan. The donkey placed himself upright on his hind legs, with his forefeet resting against the window; the dog got upon his back; the cat scrambled up to the dog's shoulders, and the cock flew up and sat upon the cat's head. When all was ready a signal was given, and they began their music. The donkey brayed, the dog barked, the cat mewed, and the cock screamed; and then they all broke through the window at once, and came tumbling into the room, amongst the broken glass, with a most hideous clatter! The robbers, who had been not a little frightened by the opening concert, had now no doubt that some frightful hobgoblin had broken in upon them, and scampered away as fast as they could.

The coast once clear, our travellers soon sat down and dispatched what the robbers had left, with as much eagerness as if they had not expected to eat again for a month. As soon as they had satisfied themselves, they put out the lights, and each once more sought out a resting place to his own liking. The donkey laid himself down upon a heap of straw in the yard, the dog stretched himself upon a mat behind the door, the cat rolled herself up on the hearth before the warm ashes, and the cock perched upon a beam on the top of the house; and, as they were all rather tired with their journey, they soon fell asleep.

But about midnight, when the robbers saw from afar that the lights were out and that all seemed quiet, they began to think that they had been in too great a hurry to run away; and one of them, who was bolder than the rest, went to see what was going on. Finding everything still, he marched into the kitchen, and groped about till he found a match in order to light a candle; and then, espying the glittering fiery eyes of the cat, he mistook them for live coals, and held the match to them to light it. But the cat, not understanding this joke, sprang at his face, and spat, and scratched at him. This frightened him dreadfully, and away he ran to the back door; but there the dog jumped up and bit him in the leg; and as he was crossing over the yard the donkey kicked him; and the cock, who had been awakened by the noise, crowed with all his might. At this the robber ran back as fast as he could to his comrades, and told the captain how a horrid witch had got into the house, and had spat at him and scratched his face with her long bony fingers; how a man with a knife in his hand had hidden himself behind the door, and stabbed him in the leg; how a black monster stood in the yard and struck him with a club; and how the devil had sat upon the top of the house and cried out, "Throw the rascal up here!" After this the robbers never dared to go back to the house; but the musicians were so pleased with their quarters that they took up their abode there; and there they are, I dare say, at this very day.

Old Sultan

A shepherd had a faithful dog, called Sultan, who was grown very old, and had lost all his teeth. And one day when the shepherd and his wife were standing together before the house the shepherd said, "I will shoot old Sultan tomorrow morning, for he is of no use now." But his wife said, "Pray let the poor faithful creature live; he has served us well a great many years, and we ought to give him a livelihood for the rest of his days."

"But what can we do with him?" said the shepherd, "he has not a tooth in his head, and the thieves don't care for him at all; to be sure he has served us, but then he did it to earn his livelihood; tomorrow shall be his last day, depend upon it."

Poor Sultan, who was lying close by them, heard all that the shepherd and his wife said to one another, and was very much frightened to think tomorrow would be his last day; so in the evening he went to his good friend the wolf, who lived in the wood, and told him all his sorrows, and how his master meant to kill him in the morning. "Make yourself easy," said the wolf, "I will give you some good advice. Your master, you know, goes out every morning very early with his wife into the field; and they take their little child with them, and lay it down behind the hedge in the shade while they are at work. Now do you lie down close by the child, and pretend to be watching it, and I will come out of the wood and run away with it; you must run after me as fast as you can, and I will let it drop; then you may carry it back, and they will think you have saved their child, and will be so thankful to you that they will take care of you as long as you live." The dog liked this plan very well; and accordingly so it was managed. The wolf ran with the child a little way; the shepherd and his wife screamed out; but Sultan soon overtook him, and carried the poor little thing back to his master and mistress. Then the shepherd patted him on the head, and said, "Old Sultan has saved our child from the wolf, and therefore he shall live and be well taken care of, and have plenty to eat. Wife, go home, and give him a good dinner, and let him have my old cushion to sleep on as long as he lives." So from this time forward Sultan had all that he could wish for.

Soon afterwards the wolf came and wished him joy, and said, "Now, my good fellow, you must tell no tales, but turn your head the other way when I want to taste one of the old shepherd's fine fat sheep."

"No," said the Sultan; "I will be true to my master." However, the wolf thought he was in joke, and came one night to get a dainty morsel. But Sultan had told his master what the wolf meant to do; so he laid wait for him behind the barn door, and when the wolf was busy looking out for a good fat sheep, he had a stout cudgel laid about his back, that combed his locks for him finely.

Then the wolf was very angry, and called Sultan "an old rogue," and swore he would have his revenge. So the next morning the wolf sent the boar to challenge Sultan to come into the wood to fight the matter. Now Sultan had nobody he could ask to be his second but the shepherd's old three-legged cat; so he took her with him, and as the poor thing limped along with some trouble, she stuck up her tail straight in the air.

The wolf and the wild boar were first on the ground; and when they espied their enemies coming, and saw the cat's long tail standing straight in the air, they thought she was carrying a sword for Sultan to fight with;

and every time she limped, they thought she was picking up a stone to throw at them; so they said they should not like this way of fighting, and the boar lay down behind a bush, and the wolf jumped up into a tree. Sultan and the cat soon came up, and looked about and wondered that no one was there. The boar, however, had not quite hidden himself, for his ears stuck out of the bush; and when he shook one of them a little, the cat, seeing something move, and thinking it was a mouse, sprang upon it, and bit and scratched it, so that the boar jumped up and grunted, and ran away, roaring out, "Look up in the tree, there sits the one who is to blame." So they looked up, and espied the wolf sitting amongst the branches; and they called him a cowardly rascal, and would not suffer him to come down till he was heartily ashamed of himself, and had promised to be good friends again with old Sultan.

The Straw, the Coal, and the Bean

In a village dwelt a poor old woman, who had gathered together a dish of beans and wanted to cook them. So she made a fire on her hearth, and that it might burn the quicker, she lighted it with a handful of straw. When she was emptying the beans into the pan, one dropped without her observing it, and lay on the ground beside a straw, and soon afterwards a burning coal from the fire leapt down to the two. Then the straw began and said: "Dear friends, from whence do you come here?"

The coal replied: "I fortunately sprang out of the fire, and if I had not escaped by sheer force, my death would have been certain—I should have been burnt to ashes."

The bean said: "I too have escaped with a whole skin, but if the old woman had got me into the pan, I should have been made into broth without any mercy, like my comrades."

"And would a better fate have fallen to my lot?" said the straw. "The old woman has destroyed all my brethren in fire and smoke; she seized sixty of them at once, and took their lives. I luckily slipped through her fingers."

"But what are we to do now?" said the coal.

"I think," answered the bean, "that as we have so fortunately escaped death, we should keep together like good companions, and lest a new mischance should overtake us here, we should go away together, and repair to a foreign country."

The proposition pleased the two others, and they set out on their way together. Soon, however, they came to a little brook, and as there was no bridge or foot plank, they did not know how they were to get over it. The straw hit on a good idea, and said: "I will lay myself straight across, and then you can walk over on me as on a bridge." The straw therefore stretched itself from one bank to the other, and the coal, who was of an impetuous disposition, tripped quite boldly on to the newly built bridge. But when she had reached the middle, and heard the water rushing beneath her, she was after all, afraid, and stood still, and ventured no farther. The straw, however, began to burn, broke in two pieces, and fell into the stream. The coal slipped after her, hissed when she got into the water, and breathed her last. The bean, who had prudently stayed behind on the shore, could not but laugh at the event, was unable to stop, and laughed so heartily that she burst. It would have been all over with her, likewise, if, by good fortune, a tailor who was travelling in search of work, had not sat down to rest by the brook. As he had a compassionate heart he pulled out his needle and thread, and sewed her together. The bean thanked him most prettily, but as the tailor used black thread, all beans since then have a black seam.

The Sleeping Beauty

A king and queen once upon a time reigned in a country a great way off, where there were in those days fairies. Now this king and queen had plenty of money, and plenty of fine clothes to wear, and plenty of good things to eat and drink, and a coach to ride out in every day: but though they had been married many years they had no children, and this grieved them very much indeed. But one day as the queen was walking by the side of the river, at the bottom of the garden, she saw a poor little fish, that had thrown itself out of the water, and lay gasping and nearly dead on the bank. Then the queen took pity on the little fish, and threw it back again into the river; and before it swam away it lifted its head out of the water and said, "I know what your wish is, and it shall be fulfilled, in return for your kindness to me—you will soon have a daughter." What the little fish had foretold soon came to pass; and the queen had a little girl, so very beautiful that the king could not cease looking on it for joy, and said he would hold a great feast and make merry, and show the child to all the land. So he asked his kinsmen, and nobles, and friends, and neighbours. But the queen said, "I will have the fairies also, that they might be kind and good to our little daughter." Now there were thirteen fairies in the kingdom; but as the king and queen had only twelve golden dishes for them to eat out of, they were forced to leave one of the fairies without asking her. So twelve fairies came, each with a high red cap on her head, and red shoes with high heels on her feet, and a long white wand in her hand: and after the feast was over they gathered round in a ring and gave all their best gifts to the little princess. One gave her goodness, another beauty, another riches, and so on till she had all that was good in the world.

Just as eleven of them had done blessing her, a great noise was heard in the courtyard, and word was brought that the thirteenth fairy was come, with a black cap on her head, and black shoes on her feet, and a broomstick in her hand: and presently up she came into the dining hall. Now, as she had not been asked to the feast she was very angry, and scolded the king and queen very much, and set to work to take her revenge. So she cried out, "The king's daughter shall, in her fifteenth year, be wounded by a spindle, and fall down dead." Then the twelfth of the friendly fairies, who had not yet given her gift, came forward, and said that the evil wish must be fulfilled, but that she could soften its mischief; so her gift was, that the king's daughter, when the spindle wounded her, should not really die, but should only fall asleep for a hundred years.

However, the king hoped still to save his dear child altogether from the threatened evil; so he ordered that all the spindles in the kingdom should be bought up and burnt. But all the gifts of the first eleven fairies were in the meantime fulfilled; for the princess was so beautiful, and well behaved, and good, and wise, that everyone who knew her loved her.

It happened that, on the very day she was fifteen years old, the king and queen were not at home, and she was left alone in the palace. So she roved about by herself, and looked at all the rooms and chambers, till at last she came to an old tower, to which there was a narrow staircase ending with a little door. In the door there was a golden key, and when she turned it the door sprang open, and there sat an old lady spinning away very busily. "Why, how now, good mother," said the princess; "what are you doing there?"

"Spinning," said the old lady, and nodded her head, humming a tune, while buzz! went the wheel.

"How prettily that little thing turns round!" said the princess, and took the spindle and began to try and spin. But scarcely had she touched it, before the fairy's prophecy was fulfilled; the spindle wounded her, and she fell down lifeless on the ground.

However, she was not dead, but had only fallen into a deep sleep; and the king and the queen, who had just come home, and all their court, fell asleep too; and the horses slept in the stables, and the dogs in the court, the pigeons on the housetop, and the very flies slept upon the walls. Even the fire on the hearth left off blazing, and went to sleep; the jack stopped, and the spit that was turning about with a goose upon it for the king's dinner stood still; and the cook, who was at that moment pulling the kitchen boy by the hair to give him a box on the ear for something he had done amiss, let him go, and both fell asleep; the butler, who was slyly tasting the ale, fell asleep with the jug at his lips: and thus everything stood still, and slept soundly.

A large hedge of thorns soon grew round the palace, and every year it became higher and thicker; till at last the old palace was surrounded and hidden, so that not even the roof or the chimneys could be seen. But there went a report through all the land of the beautiful sleeping Briar Rose (for so the king's daughter was called): so that, from time to time, several kings' sons came, and tried to break through the thicket into the palace. This, however, none of them could ever do; for the thorns and bushes laid hold of them, as it were with hands; and there they stuck fast, and died wretchedly.

After many, many years there came a king's son into that land: and an old man told him the story of the thicket of thorns; and how a beautiful palace stood behind it, and how a wonderful princess, called Briar Rose, lay in it asleep, with all her court. He told, too, how he had heard from his grandfather that many, many princes had come, and had tried to break through the thicket, but that they had all stuck fast in it, and died. Then the young prince said, "All this shall not frighten me; I

THE
SLEEPING
BEAUTY
"AT LAST HE CAME TO THE
TOWER & OPENED THE DOOR
OF THE LITTLE ROOM WHERE
ROSAMOND LAY."

will go and see this Briar Rose." The old man tried to hinder him, but he was bent upon going.

Now that very day the hundred years were ended; and as the prince came to the thicket he saw nothing but beautiful flowering shrubs, through which he went with ease, and they shut in after him as thick as ever. Then he came at last to the palace, and there in the court lay the dogs asleep; and the horses were standing in the stables; and on the roof sat the pigeons fast asleep, with their heads under their wings. And when he came into the palace, the flies were sleeping on the walls; the spit was standing still; the butler had the jug of ale at his lips, going to drink a draught; the maid sat with a fowl in her lap ready to be plucked; and the cook in the kitchen was still holding up her hand, as if she was going to beat the boy.

Then he went on still farther, and all was so still that he could hear every breath he drew; till at last he came to the old tower, and opened the door of the little room in which Briar Rose was; and there she lay, fast asleep on a couch by the window. She looked so beautiful that he could not take his eyes off her, so he stooped down and gave her a kiss. But the moment he kissed her she opened her eyes and awoke, and smiled upon him; and they went out together; and soon the king and queen also awoke, and all the court, and gazed on each other with great wonder. And the horses shook themselves, and the dogs jumped up and barked; the pigeons took their heads from under their wings, and looked about and flew into the fields; the flies on the walls buzzed again; the fire in the kitchen blazed up; round went the jack, and round went the spit, with the goose for the king's dinner upon it; the butler finished his draught of ale; the maid went on plucking the fowl; and the cook gave the boy the box on his ear.

And then the prince and Briar Rose were married, and the wedding feast was given; and they lived happily together all their lives long.

The Dog and the Sparrow

A shepherd's dog had a master who took no care of him, but often let him suffer the greatest hunger. At last he could bear it no longer; so he took to his heels, and off he ran in a very sad and sorrowful mood. On the road he met a sparrow that said to him, "Why are you so sad, my friend?"

"Because," said the dog, "I am very, very hungry, and have nothing to eat."

"If that be all," answered the sparrow, "come with me into the next town, and I will soon find you plenty of food."

So on they went together into the town: and as they passed by a butcher's shop, the sparrow said to the dog, "Stand there a little while till I peck you down a piece of meat." So the sparrow perched upon the shelf: and having first looked carefully about her to see if anyone was watching her, she pecked and scratched at a steak that lay upon the edge of the shelf, till at last down it fell. Then the dog snapped it up, and scrambled away with it into a corner, where he soon ate it all up.

"Well," said the sparrow, "you shall have some more if you will; so come with me to the next shop, and I will peck you down another steak." When the dog had eaten this too, the sparrow said to him, "Well, my good friend, have you had enough now?"

"I have had plenty of meat," answered he, "but I should like to have a piece of bread to eat after it."

"Come with me then," said the sparrow, "and you shall soon have that too." So she took him to a baker's shop, and pecked at two rolls that lay in the window, till they fell down: and as the dog still wished for more, she took him to another shop and pecked down some more for him. When that was eaten, the sparrow asked him whether he had had enough now. "Yes," said he; "and now let us take a walk a little way out of the town."

So they both went out upon the high road; but as the weather was warm, they had not gone far before the dog said, "I am very much tired—I should like to take a nap."

"Very well," answered the sparrow, "do so, and in the meantime I will perch upon that bush." So the dog stretched himself out on the road, and fell fast asleep. Whilst he slept, there came by a carter with a cart drawn by three horses, and loaded with two casks of wine. The sparrow, seeing that the carter did not turn out of the way, but would go on in the track in which the dog lay, so as to drive over him, called out, "Stop! stop! Mr Carter, or it shall be the worse for you."

But the carter, grumbling to himself, "You make it the worse for me, indeed! what can you do?" cracked his whip, and drove his cart over the poor dog, so that the wheels crushed him to death.

"There," cried the sparrow, "thou cruel villain, thou hast killed my friend the dog. Now mind what I say. This deed of thine shall cost thee all thou art worth."

"Do your worst, and welcome," said the brute, "what harm can you do me?" and passed on. But the sparrow crept under the tilt of the cart, and pecked at the bung of one of the casks till she loosened it; and then all the wine ran out, without the carter seeing it. At last he looked round, and saw that the cart was dripping, and the cask quite empty. "What an unlucky wretch I am!" cried he.

"Not wretch enough yet!" said the sparrow, as she alighted upon the head of one of the horses, and pecked at him till he reared up and kicked. When the carter saw this, he drew out his hatchet and aimed a blow at the sparrow, meaning to kill her; but she flew away, and the blow fell upon the poor horse's head with such force, that he fell down dead. "Unlucky wretch that I am!" cried he.

"Not wretch enough yet!" said the sparrow. And as the carter went on with the other two horses, she again crept under the tilt of the cart, and pecked out the bung of the second cask, so that all the wine ran out. When the carter saw this, he again cried out, "Miserable wretch that I am!"

But the sparrow answered, "Not wretch enough yet!" and perched on the head of the second horse, and pecked at him too. The carter ran up and struck at her again with his hatchet; but away she flew, and the blow fell upon the second horse and killed him on the spot. "Unlucky wretch that I am!" said he.

"Not wretch enough yet!" said the sparrow; and perching upon the third horse, she began to peck him too. The carter was mad with fury; and without looking about him, or caring what he was about, struck again at the sparrow; but killed his third horse as he had done the other two. "Alas! miserable wretch that I am!" cried he.

"Not wretch enough yet!" answered the sparrow as she flew away; "now will I plague and punish thee at thy own house." The carter was forced at last to leave his cart behind him, and to go home overflowing with rage and vexation. "Alas!" said he to his wife, "what ill luck has befallen me! My wine is all spilt, and my horses all three dead."

"Alas! husband," replied she, "and a wicked bird has come into the house, and has brought with her all the birds in the world, I am sure, and they have fallen upon our corn in the loft, and are eating it up at such a rate!" Away ran the husband upstairs, and saw thousands of birds sitting upon the floor eating up his corn, with the sparrow in the midst of them.

"Unlucky wretch that I am!" cried the carter; for he saw that the corn was almost all gone.

"Not wretch enough yet!" said the sparrow; "thy cruelty shall cost thee thy life yet!" and away she flew.

The carter seeing that he had thus lost all that he had, went down into his kitchen, and was still not sorry for what he had done, but sat himself angrily and sulkily in the chimney corner. But the sparrow sat on the outside of the window, and cried "Carter! thy cruelty shall cost thee thy life!" With that he jumped up in a rage, seized his hatchet, and threw it at the sparrow; but it missed her, and only broke the window. The sparrow now hopped in, perched upon the window seat, and cried, "Carter! it shall cost thee thy life!" Then he became mad and blind with rage, and struck the window seat with such force that he cleft it in two: and as the sparrow flew from place to place, the carter and his wife were so furious, that they broke all their furniture, glasses, chairs, benches, the table, and at last the walls, without touching the bird at all. In the end, however, they caught her: and the wife said, "Shall I kill her at once?"

"No," cried he, "that is letting her off too easily: she shall die a much more cruel death; I will eat her." But the sparrow began to flutter about, and stretch out her neck and cried, "Carter! it shall cost thee thy life yet!" With that he could wait no longer: so he gave his wife the hatchet, and cried, "Wife, strike at the bird and kill her in my hand." And the wife struck; but she missed her aim, and hit her husband on the head so that he fell down dead, and the sparrow flew quietly home to her nest.

The Twelve Dancing Princesses

There was a king who had twelve beautiful daughters. They slept in twelve beds all in one room; and when they went to bed, the doors were shut and locked up; but every morning their shoes were found to be quite worn through as if they had been danced in all night; and yet nobody could find out how it happened, or where they had been.

Then the king made it known to all the land, that if any person could discover the secret, and find out where it was that the princesses danced in the night, he should have the one he liked best for his wife, and should be king after his death; but whoever tried and did not succeed, after three days and nights, should be put to death.

A king's son soon came. He was well entertained, and in the evening was taken to the chamber next to the one where the princesses lay in their twelve beds. There he was to sit and watch where they went to dance; and, in order that nothing might pass without his hearing it, the door of his chamber was left open. But the king's son soon fell asleep; and when he awoke in the morning he found that the princesses had all been dancing, for the soles of their shoes were full of holes. The same thing happened the second and third night: so the king ordered his head to be cut off. After him came several others; but they had all the same luck, and all lost their lives in the same manner.

Now it chanced that an old soldier, who had been wounded in battle and could fight no longer, passed through the country where this king reigned: and as he was travelling through a wood, he met an old woman, who asked him where he was going. "I hardly know where I am going, or what I had better do," said the soldier; "but I think I should like very well to find out where it is that the princesses dance, and then in time I might be a king."

"Well," said the old dame, "that is no very hard task: only take care not to drink any of the wine which one of the princesses will bring to you in the evening; and as soon as she leaves you pretend to be fast asleep."

Then she gave him a cloak, and said, "As soon as you put that on you will become invisible, and you will then be able to follow the princesses wherever they go." When the soldier heard all this good counsel, he determined to try his luck: so he went to the king, and said he was willing to undertake the task.

He was as well received as the others had been, and the king ordered fine royal robes to be given him; and when the evening came he was led to the outer chamber. Just as he was going to lie down, the eldest of the princesses brought him a cup of wine; but the soldier threw it all away secretly, taking care not to drink a drop. Then he laid himself down on his bed, and in a little while began to snore very loud as if he was fast asleep. When the twelve princesses heard this they laughed heartily; and the eldest said, "This fellow too might have done a wiser thing than lose his life in this way!" Then they rose up and opened their drawers and boxes, and took out all their fine clothes, and dressed themselves at the glass, and skipped about as if they were eager to begin dancing. But the youngest said, "I don't know how it is, while you are so happy I feel very uneasy; I am sure some mischance will befall us."

"You simpleton," said the eldest, "you are always afraid; have you forgotten how many kings' sons have already watched in vain? And as for this soldier, even if I had not given him his sleeping draught, he would have slept soundly enough."

When they were all ready, they went and looked at the soldier; but he snored on, and did not stir hand or foot: so they thought they were quite safe; and the eldest went up to her own bed and clapped her hands, and the bed sank into the floor and a trapdoor flew open. The soldier saw them going down through the trapdoor one after another, the eldest leading the way; and thinking he had no time to lose, he jumped up, put on the cloak which the old woman had given him, and followed them; but in the middle of the stairs he trod on the gown of the youngest princess, and she cried out to her sisters, "All is not right; someone took hold of my gown."

"You silly creature!" said the eldest, "it is nothing but a nail in the wall." Then down they all went, and at the bottom they found themselves in a most delightful grove of trees; and the leaves were all of silver, and glittered and sparkled beautifully. The soldier wished to take away some token of the place; so he broke off a little branch, and there came a loud noise from the tree. Then the youngest daughter said again, "I am sure all is not right—did not you hear that noise? That never happened before."

But the eldest said, "It is only our princes, who are shouting for joy at our approach."

Then they came to another grove of trees, where all the leaves were of gold; and afterwards to a third, where the leaves were all glittering diamonds. And the soldier broke a branch from each; and every time there was a loud noise, which made the youngest sister tremble with fear; but the eldest still said, it was only the princes, who were crying for joy. So they went on till they came to a great lake; and at the side of the lake there lay twelve little boats with twelve handsome princes in them, who seemed to be waiting there for the princesses.

One of the princesses went into each boat, and the soldier stepped into the same boat with the youngest. As they were rowing over the lake, the prince who was in the boat with the youngest princess and the soldier said, "I do not know why it is, but though I am rowing with all my might we do not get on so fast as usual, and I am quite tired: the boat seems very heavy today."

"It is only the heat of the weather," said the princess: "I feel it very warm too."

On the other side of the lake stood a fine illuminated castle, from which came the merry music of horns and trumpets. There they all landed, and went into the castle, and each prince danced with his princess; and the soldier, who was all the time invisible, danced with them too; and when any of the princesses had a cup of wine set by her, he drank it all up, so that when she put the cup to her mouth it was empty. At this, too, the youngest sister was terribly frightened, but the eldest always silenced her. They danced on till three o'clock in the morning, and then all their shoes were worn out, so that they were obliged to leave off. The princes rowed them back again over the lake (but this time the soldier placed himself in the boat with the eldest princess); and on the opposite shore they took leave of each other, the princesses promising to come again the next night.

When they came to the stairs, the soldier ran on before the princesses, and laid himself down; and as the twelve sisters slowly came up very much tired, they heard him snoring in his bed; so they said, "Now all is quite safe"; then they undressed themselves, put away their fine clothes, pulled off their shoes, and went to bed. In the morning the soldier said nothing about what had happened, but determined to see more of this strange adventure, and went again the second and third night; and everything happened just as before; the princesses danced each time till their shoes were worn to pieces, and then returned home. However, on the third night the soldier carried away one of the golden cups as a token of where he had been.

As soon as the time came when he was to declare the secret, he was taken before the king with the three branches and the golden cup; and the twelve princesses stood listening behind the door to hear what he would say. And when the king asked him, "Where do my twelve daughters dance at night?" he answered, "With twelve princes in a castle underground."

And then he told the king all that had happened, and showed him the three branches and the golden cup which he had brought with him. Then the king called for the princesses, and asked them whether what the soldier said was true: and when they saw that they were discovered, and that it was of no use to deny what had happened, they confessed it all. And the king asked the soldier which of them he would choose for his wife; and he answered, "I am not very young, so I will have the eldest." And they were married that very day, and the soldier was chosen to be the king's heir.

The Fisherman and His Wife

There was once a fisherman who lived with his wife in a pigsty, close by the seaside. The fisherman used to go out all day long a-fishing; and one day, as he sat on the shore with his rod, looking at the sparkling waves and watching his line, all on a sudden his float was dragged away deep into the water: and in drawing it up he pulled out a great fish. But the fish said, "Pray let me live! I am not a real fish; I am an enchanted prince: put me in the water again, and let me go!"

"Oh, ho!" said the man, "you need not make so many words about the matter; I will have nothing to do with a fish that can talk: so swim away, sir, as soon as you please!" Then he put him back into the water, and the fish darted straight down to the bottom, and left a long streak of blood behind him on the wave.

When the fisherman went home to his wife in the pigsty, he told her how he had caught a great fish, and how it had told him it was an enchanted prince, and how, on hearing it speak, he had let it go again. "Did not you ask it for anything?" said the wife, "we live very wretchedly here, in this nasty, dirty pigsty; do go back and tell the fish we want a snug little cottage."

The fisherman did not much like the business: however, he went to the seashore; and when he came back there the water looked all yellow and green. And he stood at the water's edge, and said:

"O man of the sea!
Hearken to me!
My wife Ilsabill
Will have her own will,
And hath sent me to beg a boon of thee!"

Then the fish came swimming to him, and said, "Well, what is her will? What does your wife want?"

"Ah!" said the fisherman, "she says that when I had caught you, I ought to have asked you for something before I let you go; she does not like living any longer in the pigsty, and wants a snug little cottage."

"Go home, then," said the fish; "she is in the cottage already!" So the man went home, and saw his wife standing at the door of a nice trim little cottage.

"Come in, come in!" said she; "is not this much better than the filthy pigsty we had?" And there was a parlour, and a bedchamber, and a kitchen; and behind the cottage there was a little garden, planted with all sorts of flowers and fruits; and there was a courtyard behind, full of ducks and chickens.

"Ah!" said the fisherman, "how happily we shall live now!"

"We will try to do so, at least," said his wife.

Everything went right for a week or two, and then Dame Ilsabill said, "Husband, there is not near room enough for us in this cottage; the courtyard and the garden are a great deal too small; I should like to have a large stone castle to live in: go to the fish again and tell him to give us a castle."

"Wife," said the fisherman, "I don't like to go to him again, for perhaps he will be angry; we ought to be easy with this pretty cottage to live in."

"Nonsense!" said the wife; "he will do it very willingly, I know; go along and try!"

The fisherman went, but his heart was very heavy: and when he came to the sea, it looked blue and gloomy, though it was very calm; and he went close to the edge of the waves, and said:

"O man of the sea!
Hearken to me!
My wife Ilsabill
Will have her own will,
And hath sent me to beg a boon of thee!"

"Well, what does she want now?" said the fish.

"Ah!" said the man, dolefully, "my wife wants to live in a stone castle."

"Go home, then," said the fish; "she is standing at the gate of it already."

So away went the fisherman, and found his wife standing before the gate of a great castle. "See," said she, "is not this grand?" With that they went into the castle together, and found a great many servants there, and the rooms all richly furnished, and full of golden chairs and tables; and behind the castle was a garden, and around it was a park half a mile long, full of sheep, and goats, and hares, and deer; and in the courtyard were stables and cow houses.

"Well," said the man, "now we will live cheerful and happy in this beautiful castle for the rest of our lives."

"Perhaps we may," said the wife; "but let us sleep upon it, before we make up our minds to that." So they went to bed.

The next morning when Dame Ilsabill awoke it was broad daylight, and she jogged the fisherman with her elbow, and said, "Get up, husband, and bestir yourself, for we must be king of all the land."

"Wife, wife," said the man, "why should we wish to be the king? I will not be king."

"Then I will," said she.

"But, wife," said the fisherman, "how can you be king. The fish cannot make you a king."

"Husband," said she, "say no more about it, but go and try! I will be king." So the man went away quite sorrowful to think that his wife should want to be king. This time the sea looked a dark grey colour, and was overspread with curling waves and the ridges of foam as he cried out:

"O man of the sea!
Hearken to me!
My wife Ilsabill
Will have her own will,
And hath sent me to beg a boon of thee!"

"Well, what would she have now?" said the fish.

"Alas!" said the poor man, "my wife wants to be king."

"Go home," said the fish; "she is king already."

Then the fisherman went home; and as he came close to the palace he saw a troop of soldiers, and heard the sound of drums and trumpets. And when he went in he saw his wife sitting on a throne of gold and diamonds, with a golden crown upon her head; and on each side of her stood six fair maidens, each a head taller than the other.

"Well, wife," said the fisherman, "are you king?"

"Yes," said she, "I am king." And when he had looked at her for a long time, he said, "Ah, wife! what a fine thing it is to be king! Now we shall never have anything more to wish for as long as we live."

"I don't know how that may be," said she; "never is a long time. I am king, it is true; but I begin to be tired of that, and I think I should like to be emperor."

"Alas, wife! why should you wish to be emperor?" said the fisherman.

"Husband," said she, "go to the fish! I say I will be emperor."

"Ah, wife!" replied the fisherman, "the fish cannot make an emperor, I am sure, and I should not like to ask him for such a thing."

"I am king," said Ilsabill, "and you are my slave; so go at once!"

So the fisherman was forced to go; and he muttered as he went along, "This will come to no good, it is too much to ask; the fish will be tired at last, and then we shall be sorry for what we have done." He soon came to the seashore; and the water was quite black and muddy, and a mighty whirlwind blew over the waves and rolled them about, but he went as near as he could to the water's brink, and said:

"O man of the sea!
Hearken to me!
My wife Ilsabill
Will have her own will,
And hath sent me to beg a boon of thee!"

"What would she have now?" said the fish.

"Ah!" said the fisherman, "she wants to be emperor."

"Go home," said the fish; "she is emperor already."

So he went home again; and as he came near he saw his wife Ilsabill sitting on a very lofty throne made of solid gold, with a great crown on her head full two yards high; and on each side of her stood her guards and attendants in a row, each one smaller than the other, from the tallest giant down to a little dwarf no bigger than my finger. And before her stood princes, and dukes, and earls: and the fisherman went up to her and said, "Wife, are you emperor?"

"Yes," said she, "I am emperor."

"Ah!" said the man, as he gazed upon her, "what a fine thing it is to be emperor!"

"Husband," said she, "why should we stop at being emperor? I will be pope next."

"O wife, wife!" said he, "how can you be pope? there is but one pope at a time in Christendom."

"Husband," said she, "I will be pope this very day."

"But," replied the husband, "the fish cannot make you pope."

"What nonsense!" said she; "if he can make an emperor, he can make a pope: go and try him."

So the fisherman went. But when he came to the shore the wind was raging and the sea was tossed up and down in boiling waves, and the ships were in trouble, and rolled fearfully upon the tops of the billows. In the middle of the heavens there was a little piece of blue sky, but towards the south all was red, as if a dreadful storm was rising. At this sight the fisherman was dreadfully frightened, and he trembled so that his knees knocked together: but still he went down near to the shore, and said:

"O man of the sea!
Hearken to me!
My wife Ilsabill
Will have her own will,
And hath sent me to beg a boon of thee!"

"What does she want now?" said the fish. "Ah!" said the fisherman, "my wife wants to be pope."

"Go home," said the fish; "she is pope already."

Then the fisherman went home, and found Ilsabill sitting on a throne that was two miles high. And she had three great crowns on her head, and around her stood all the pomp and power of the Church. And on each side of her were two rows of burning lights, of all sizes, the greatest as large as the highest and biggest tower in the world, and the least no larger than a small rushlight. "Wife," said the fisherman, as he looked at all this greatness, "are you pope?"

"Yes," said she, "I am pope."

"Well, wife," replied he, "it is a grand thing to be pope; and now you must be easy, for you can be nothing greater."

"I will think about that," said the wife. Then they went to bed: but Dame Ilsabill could not sleep all night for thinking what she should be next. At last, as she was dropping asleep, morning broke, and the sun rose. "Ha!" thought she, as she woke up and looked at it through the window, "after all I cannot prevent the sun rising." At this thought she was very angry, and wakened her husband, and said, "Husband, go to the fish and tell him I must be lord of the sun and moon."

The fisherman was half asleep, but the thought frightened him so much that he started and fell out of bed. "Alas, wife!" said he, "cannot you be easy with being pope?"

"No," said she, "I am very uneasy as long as the sun and moon rise without my leave. Go to the fish at once!"

Then the man went shivering with fear; and as he was going down to the shore a dreadful storm arose, so that the trees and the very rocks shook. And all the heavens became black with stormy clouds, and the lightnings played, and the thunders rolled; and you might have seen in the sea great black waves, swelling up like mountains with crowns of white foam upon their heads. And the fisherman crept towards the sea, and cried out, as well as he could:

"O man of the sea!
Hearken to me!
My wife Ilsabill

Will have her own will,
And hath sent me to beg a boon of thee!"

"What does she want now?" said the fish.

"Ah!" said he, "she wants to be lord of the sun and moon."

"Go home," said the fish, "to your pigsty again."

And there they live to this very day.

The Willow Wren and the Bear

Once in summertime the bear and the wolf were walking in the forest, and the bear heard a bird singing so beautifully that he said, "Brother wolf, what bird is it that sings so well?"

"That is the King of birds," said the wolf, "before whom we must bow down." In reality the bird was the willow wren.

"IF that's the case," said the bear, "I should very much like to see his royal palace; come, take me thither."

"That is not done quite as you seem to think," said the wolf; "you must wait until the Queen comes." Soon afterwards, the Queen arrived with some food in her beak, and the lord King came too, and they began to feed their young ones. The bear would have liked to go at once, but the wolf held him back by the sleeve, and said: "No, you must wait until the lord and lady Queen have gone away again." So they took stock of the hole where the nest lay, and trotted away. The bear, however, could not rest until he had seen the royal palace, and when a short time had passed, went to it again.

The King and Queen had just flown out, so he peeped in and saw five or six young ones lying there. "Is that the royal palace?" cried the bear; "it is a wretched palace, and you are not King's children, you are disreputable children!"

When the young wrens heard that, they were frightfully angry, and screamed: "No, that we are not! Our parents are honest people! Bear, you will have to pay for that!"

The bear and the wolf grew uneasy, and turned back and went into their holes. The young willow wrens, however, continued to cry and scream, and when their parents again brought food they said: "We will not so much as touch one fly's leg, no, not if we were dying of hunger, until you have settled whether we are respectable children or not; the bear has been here and has insulted us!"

Then the old King said: "Be easy, he shall be punished," and he at once flew with the Queen to the bear's cave, and called in: "Old Growler, why have you insulted my children? You shall suffer for it—we will punish you by a bloody war." Thus war was announced to the bear, and all four-footed animals were summoned to take part in it, oxen, donkeys, cows, deer, and every other animal the earth contained. And the willow wren summoned everything which flew in the air, not only birds, large and small, but midges, and hornets, bees and flies had to come.

When the time came for the war to begin, the willow wren sent out spies to discover who was the enemy's commander in chief. The gnat, who was the most crafty, flew into the forest where the enemy was assembled, and hid herself beneath a leaf of the tree where the password was to be announced. There stood the bear, and he called the fox before him and said: "Fox, you are the most cunning of all animals, you shall be general and lead us."

"Good," said the fox, "but what signal shall we agree upon?" No one knew that, so the fox said: "I have a fine long bushy tail, which almost looks like a plume of red feathers. When I lift my tail up quite high, all is going well, and you must charge; but if I let it hang down, run away as fast as you can." When the gnat had heard that, she flew away again, and revealed everything, down to the minutest detail, to the willow wren. When day broke, and the battle was to begin, all the four-footed animals came running up with such a noise that the earth trembled. The willow wren with his army also came flying through the air with such a humming, and whirring, and swarming that everyone was uneasy and afraid, and on both sides they advanced against each other. But the willow wren sent down the hornet, with orders to settle beneath the fox's tail, and sting with all his might. When the fox felt the first string, he started so that he lifted one leg, from pain, but he bore it, and still kept his tail high in the air; at the second sting, he was forced to put it down for a moment; at the third, he could hold out no longer, screamed, and put his tail between his legs. When the animals saw that, they thought all was lost, and began to flee, each into his hole, and the birds had won the battle.

Then the King and Queen flew home to their children and cried: "Children, rejoice, eat and drink to your heart's content, we have won the battle!" But the young wrens said: "We will not eat yet, the bear must come to the nest, and beg for pardon and say that we are honourable children, before we will do that." Then the willow wren flew to the bear's hole and cried: "Growler, you are to come to the nest to my children, and beg their pardon, or else every rib of your body shall be broken." So the bear crept thither in the greatest fear, and begged their pardon. And now at last the young wrens were satisfied, and sat down together and ate and drank, and made merry till quite late into the night.

The Frog Prince

One fine evening a young princess put on her bonnet and clogs, and went out to take a walk by herself in a wood; and when she came to a cool spring of water, that rose in the midst of it, she sat herself down to rest awhile. Now she had a golden ball in her hand, which was her favourite plaything; and she was always tossing it up into the air, and catching it again as it fell. After a time she threw it up so high that she missed catching it as it fell; and the ball bounded away, and rolled along upon the ground, till at last it fell down into the spring. The princess looked into the spring after her ball, but it was very deep, so deep that she could not see the bottom of it. Then she began to bewail her loss, and said, "Alas! if I could only get my ball again, I would give all my fine clothes and jewels, and everything that I have in the world."

Whilst she was speaking, a frog put its head out of the water, and said, "Princess, why do you weep so bitterly?"

"Alas!" said she, "what can you do for me, you nasty frog? My golden ball has fallen into the spring."

The frog said, "I want not your pearls, and jewels, and fine clothes;

but if you will love me, and let me live with you and eat from off your golden plate, and sleep upon your bed, I will bring you your ball again."

"What nonsense," thought the princess, "this silly frog is talking! He can never even get out of the spring to visit me, though he may be able to get my ball for me, and therefore I will tell him he shall have what he asks." So she said to the frog, "Well, if you will bring me my ball, I will do all you ask."

Then the frog put his head down, and dived deep under the water; and after a little while he came up again, with the ball in his mouth, and threw it on the edge of the spring. As soon as the young princess saw her ball, she ran to pick it up; and she was so overjoyed to have it in her hand again, that she never thought of the frog, but ran home with it as fast as she could. The frog called after her, "Stay, princess, and take me with you as you said." But she did not stop to hear a word.

The next day, just as the princess had sat down to dinner, she heard a strange noise—tap, tap, plash, plash—as if something was coming up the marble staircase: and soon afterwards there was a gentle knock at the door, and a little voice cried out and said:

"Open the door, my princess dear,
Open the door to thy true love here!
And mind the words that thou and I said
By the fountain cool, in the greenwood shade."

Then the princess ran to the door and opened it, and there she saw the frog, whom she had quite forgotten. At this sight she was sadly frightened, and shutting the door as fast as she could came back to her seat. The king, her father, seeing that something had frightened her, asked her what was the matter. "There is a nasty frog," said she, "at the door, that lifted my ball for me out of the spring this morning: I told him that he should live with me here, thinking that he could never get out of the spring; but there he is at the door, and he wants to come in."

While she was speaking the frog knocked again at the door, and said:

"Open the door, my princess dear,
Open the door to thy true love here!
And mind the words that thou and I said
By the fountain cool, in the greenwood shade."

Then the king said to the young princess, "As you have given your word you must keep it; so go and let him in." She did so, and the frog hopped into the room, and then straight on—tap, tap, plash, plash—from the bottom of the room to the top, till he came up close to the table where the princess sat.

"Pray lift me upon a chair," said he to the princess, "and let me sit next to you." As soon as she had done this, the frog said, "Put your plate nearer to me, that I may eat out of it." This she did, and when he had eaten as much as he could, he said, "Now I am tired; carry me upstairs, and put me into your bed." And the princess, though very unwilling, took him up in her hand, and put him upon the pillow of her own bed, where he slept all night long. As soon as it was light he jumped up, hopped downstairs, and went out of the house. "Now, then," thought the princess, "at last he is gone, and I shall be troubled with him no more."

But she was mistaken; for when night came again she heard the same tapping at the door; and the frog came once more, and said:

"Open the door, my princess dear,
Open the door to thy true love here!
And mind the words that thou and I said
By the fountain cool, in the greenwood shade."

And when the princess opened the door the frog came in, and slept upon her pillow as before, till the morning broke. And the third night he did the same. But when the princess awoke on the following morning she was astonished to see, instead of the frog, a handsome prince, gazing on her with the most beautiful eyes she had ever seen, and standing at the head of her bed.

He told her that he had been enchanted by a spiteful fairy, who had changed him into a frog; and that he had been fated so to abide till some princess should take him out of the spring, and let him eat from her plate, and sleep upon her bed for three nights. "You," said the prince, "have broken his cruel charm, and now I have nothing to wish for but that you should go with me into my father's kingdom, where I will marry you, and love you as long as you live."

The young princess, you may be sure, was not long in saying "Yes" to all this; and as they spoke a gay coach drove up, with eight beautiful horses, decked with plumes of feathers and a golden harness; and behind the coach rode the prince's servant, faithful Heinrich, who had bewailed the misfortunes of his dear master during his enchantment so long and so bitterly, that his heart had well-nigh burst.

They then took leave of the king, and got into the coach with eight horses, and all set out, full of joy and merriment, for the prince's kingdom, which they reached safely; and there they lived happily a great many years.

Cat and Mouse in Partnership

A certain cat had made the acquaintance of a mouse, and had said so much to her about the great love and friendship she felt for her, that at length the mouse agreed that they should live and keep house together. "But we must make a provision for winter, or else we shall suffer from hunger," said the cat; "and you, little mouse, cannot venture everywhere, or you will be caught in a trap some day." The good advice was followed, and a pot of fat was bought, but they did not know where to put it. At length, after much consideration, the cat said: "I know no place where it will be better stored up than in the church, for no one dares take anything away from there. We will set it beneath the altar, and not touch it until we are really in need of it." So the pot was placed in safety, but it was not long before the cat had a great yearning for it, and said to the mouse: "I want to tell you something, little mouse; my cousin has brought a little son into the world, and has asked me to be godmother; he is white with brown spots, and I am to hold him over the font at the christening. Let me go out today, and you look after the house by yourself."

"Yes, yes," answered the mouse, "by all means go, and if you get anything very good to eat, think of me. I should like a drop of sweet red christening wine myself." All this, however, was untrue; the cat had no cousin, and had not been asked to be godmother. She went straight to the church, stole to the pot of fat, began to lick at it, and licked the top of the fat off. Then she took a walk upon the roofs of the town, looked out for opportunities, and then stretched herself in the sun, and licked her lips whenever she thought of the pot of fat, and not until it was evening did she return home.

"Well, here you are again," said the mouse, "no doubt you have had a merry day."

"All went off well," answered the cat.

"What name did they give the child?"

"Top-off!" said the cat quite coolly.

"Top-off!" cried the mouse, "that is a very odd and uncommon name, is it a usual one in your family?"

"What does that matter," said the cat, "it is no worse than Crumb-stealer, as your godchildren are called."

Before long the cat was seized by another fit of yearning. She said to the mouse: "You must do me a favour, and once more manage the house for a day alone. I am again asked to be godmother, and, as the child has a white ring round its neck, I cannot refuse." The good mouse consented, but the cat crept behind the town walls to the church, and devoured half the pot of fat. "Nothing ever seems so good as what one keeps to oneself," said she, and was quite satisfied with her day's work. When she went home the mouse inquired: "And what was the child christened?"

"Half-done," answered the cat.

"Half-done! What are you saying? I never heard the name in my life, I'll wager anything it is not in the calendar!"

The cat's mouth soon began to water for some more licking. "All good things go in threes," said she, "I am asked to stand godmother again. The child is quite black, only it has white paws, but with that exception, it has not a single white hair on its whole body; this only happens once every few years, you will let me go, won't you?"

"Top-off! Half-done!" answered the mouse, "they are such odd names, they make me very thoughtful."

"You sit at home," said the cat, "in your dark grey fur coat and long tail, and are filled with fancies, that's because you do not go out in the daytime."

During the cat's absence the mouse cleaned the house, and put it in order, but the greedy cat entirely emptied the pot of fat. "When everything is eaten up one has some peace," said she to herself, and well filled and fat she did not return home till night. The mouse at once asked what name had been given to the third child. "It will not please you more than the others," said the cat. "He is called All-gone."

"All-gone," cried the mouse "that is the most suspicious name of all! I have never seen it in print. All-gone; what can that mean?" and she shook her head, curled herself up, and lay down to sleep.

From this time forth no one invited the cat to be godmother, but when the winter had come and there was no longer anything to be found outside, the mouse thought of their provision, and said: "Come, cat, we will go to our pot of fat which we have stored up for ourselves—we shall enjoy that."

"Yes," answered the cat, "you will enjoy it as much as you would enjoy sticking that dainty tongue of yours out of the window."

They set out on their way, but when they arrived, the pot of fat certainly was still in its place, but it was empty.

"Alas!" said the mouse, "now I see what has happened, now it comes to light! You are a true friend! You have devoured all when you were standing godmother. First Top-off, then Half-done, then—"

"Will you hold your tongue," cried the cat, "one word more, and I will eat you too."

"All-gone" was already on the poor mouse's lips; scarcely had she spoken it before the cat sprang on her, seized her, and swallowed her down. Verily, that is the way of the world.

The Goose Girl

The king of a great land died, and left his queen to take care of their only child. This child was a daughter, who was very beautiful; and her mother loved her dearly, and was very kind to her. And there was a good fairy too, who was fond of the princess, and helped her mother to watch over her. When she grew up, she was betrothed to a prince who lived a great way off; and as the time drew near for her to be married, she got ready to set off on her journey to his country. Then the queen, her mother, packed up a great many costly things; jewels, and gold, and silver; trinkets, fine dresses, and in short everything that became a royal bride. And she gave her a waiting maid to ride with her, and give her into the bridegroom's hands; and each had a horse for the journey. Now the princess's horse was the fairy's gift, and it was called Falada, and could speak.

When the time came for them to set out, the fairy went into her bedchamber, and took a little knife, and cut off a lock of her hair, and gave it to the princess, and said, "Take care of it, dear child; for it is a charm that may be of use to you on the road." Then they all took a sorrowful leave of the princess; and she put the lock of hair into her bosom, got upon her horse, and set off on her journey to her bridegroom's kingdom.

One day, as they were riding along by a brook, the princess began to feel very thirsty: and she said to her maid, "Pray get down, and fetch me some water in my golden cup out of yonder brook, for I want to drink."

"Nay," said the maid, "if you are thirsty, get off yourself, and stoop down by the water and drink; I shall not be your waiting maid any longer."

Then she was so thirsty that she got down, and knelt over the little brook, and drank; for she was frightened, and dared not bring out her golden cup; and she wept and said, "Alas! what will become of me?" And the lock answered her, and said:

"Alas! alas! if thy mother knew it,
Sadly, sadly, would she rue it."

But the princess was very gentle and meek, so she said nothing to her maid's ill behaviour, but got upon her horse again.

Then all rode farther on their journey, till the day grew so warm, and the sun so scorching, that the bride began to feel very thirsty again; and at last, when they came to a river, she forgot her maid's rude speech, and said, "Pray get down, and fetch me some water to drink in my golden cup."

But the maid answered her, and even spoke more haughtily than before: "Drink if you will, but I shall not be your waiting maid."

Then the princess was so thirsty that she got off her horse, and lay down, and held her head over the running stream, and cried and said, "What will become of me?" And the lock of hair answered her again:

"Alas! alas! if thy mother knew it,
Sadly, sadly, would she rue it."

And as she leaned down to drink, the lock of hair fell from her bosom, and floated away with the water. Now she was so frightened that she did not see it; but her maid saw it, and was very glad, for she knew the charm; and she saw that the poor bride would be in her power, now that she had lost the hair. So when the bride had done drinking, and would have got upon Falada again, the maid said, "I shall ride upon Falada, and you may have my horse instead"; so she was forced to give up her horse, and soon afterwards to take off her royal clothes and put on her maid's shabby ones.

At last, as they drew near the end of their journey, this treacherous servant threatened to kill her mistress if she ever told anyone what had happened. But Falada saw it all, and marked it well.

Then the waiting maid got upon Falada, and the real bride rode upon the other horse, and they went on in this way till at last they came to the royal court. There was great joy at their coming, and the prince flew to meet them, and lifted the maid from her horse, thinking she was the one who was to be his wife; and she was led upstairs to the royal chamber; but the true princess was told to stay in the court below.

Now the old king happened just then to have nothing else to do; so he amused himself by sitting at his kitchen window, looking at what was going on; and he saw her in the courtyard. As she looked very pretty, and too delicate for a waiting maid, he went up into the royal chamber to ask the bride who it was she had brought with her, that was thus left standing in the court below. "I brought her with me for the sake of her company on the road," said she; "pray give the girl some work to do, that she may not be idle."

The old king could not for some time think of any work for her to do; but at last he said, "I have a lad who takes care of my geese; she may go and help him." Now the name of this lad, that the real bride was to help in watching the king's geese, was Curdken.

But the false bride said to the prince, "Dear husband, pray do me one piece of kindness."

"That I will," said the prince. "Then tell one of your slaughterers to cut off the head of the horse I rode upon, for it was very unruly, and plagued me sadly on the road"; but the truth was, she was very much afraid lest Falada should some day or other speak, and tell all she had done to the princess. She carried her point, and the faithful Falada was killed; but when the true princess heard of it, she wept, and begged the man to nail up Falada's head against a large dark gate of the city, through which she had to pass every morning and evening, that there she might still see him sometimes. Then the slaughterer said he would do as she wished; and cut off the head, and nailed it up under the dark gate.

Early the next morning, as she and Curdken went out through the gate, she said sorrowfully:

"Falada, Falada, there thou hangest!"

and the head answered:

"Bride, bride, there thou gangest!
Alas! alas! if thy mother knew it,
Sadly, sadly, would she rue it."

Then they went out of the city, and drove the geese on. And when she came to the meadow, she sat down upon a bank there, and let down her waving locks of hair, which were all of pure silver; and when Curdken saw it glitter in the sun, he ran up, and would have pulled some of the locks out, but she cried:

"Blow, breezes, blow!
Let Curdken's hat go!
Blow, breezes, blow!
Let him after it go!
O'er hills, dales, and rocks,
Away be it whirl'd
Till the silvery locks
Are all comb'd and curl'd!"

Then there came a wind, so strong that it blew off Curdken's hat; and away it flew over the hills: and he was forced to turn and run after it; till, by the time he came back, she had done combing and curling her hair, and had put it up again safe. Then he was very angry and sulky, and would not speak to her at all; but they watched the geese until it grew dark in the evening, and then drove them homewards.

The next morning, as they were going through the dark gate, the poor girl looked up at Falada's head, and cried:

"Falada, Falada, there thou hangest!"

and the head answered:

"Bride, bride, there thou gangest!
Alas! alas! if thy mother knew it,
Sadly, sadly, would she rue it."

Then she drove on the geese, and sat down again in the meadow, and began to comb out her hair as before; and Curdken ran up to her, and wanted to take hold of it; but she cried out quickly:

"Blow, breezes, blow!
Let Curdken's hat go!
Blow, breezes, blow!
Let him after it go!
O'er hills, dales, and rocks,
Away be it whirl'd
Till the silvery locks
Are all comb'd and curl'd!"

Then the wind came and blew away his hat; and off it flew a great way, over the hills and far away, so that he had to run after it; and when he came back she had bound up her hair again, and all was safe. So they watched the geese till it grew dark.

In the evening, after they came home, Curdken went to the old king,

GOOSE GIRL
O WIND, BLOW CONRADS HAT AWAY,
AND MAKE HIM FOLLOW AS IT FLIES,
WHILE I WITH MY GOLD HAIR WILL PLAY
AND BIND IT UP IN SEEMLY WISE!

and said, "I cannot have that strange girl to help me to keep the geese any longer."

"Why?" said the king.

"Because, instead of doing any good, she does nothing but tease me all day long." Then the king made him tell him what had happened.

And Curdken said, "When we go in the morning through the dark gate with our flock of geese, she cries and talks with the head of a horse that hangs upon the wall, and says:

"Falada, Falada, there thou hangest!"

and the head answers:

"Bride, bride, there thou gangest!
Alas! alas! if thy mother knew it,
Sadly, sadly, would she rue it."

And Curdken went on telling the king what had happened upon the meadow where the geese fed; how his hat was blown away; and how he was forced to run after it, and to leave his flock of geese to themselves. But the old king told the boy to go out again the next day: and when morning came, he placed himself behind the dark gate, and heard how she spoke to Falada, and how Falada answered. Then he went into the field, and hid himself in a bush by the meadow's side; and he soon saw with his own eyes how they drove the flock of geese; and how, after a little time, she let down her hair that glittered in the sun. And then he heard her say:

"Blow, breezes, blow!
Let Curdken's hat go!
Blow, breezes, blow!
Let him after it go!
O'er hills, dales, and rocks,

Away be it whirl'd
Till the silvery locks
Are all comb'd and curl'd!"

And soon came a gale of wind, and carried away Curdken's hat, and away went Curdken after it, while the girl went on combing and curling her hair. All this the old king saw: so he went home without being seen; and when the little goose girl came back in the evening he called her aside, and asked her why she did so: but she burst into tears, and said, "That I must not tell you or any man, or I shall lose my life."

But the old king begged so hard, that she had no peace till she had told him all the tale, from beginning to end, word for word. And it was very lucky for her that she did so, for when she had done the king ordered royal clothes to be put upon her, and gazed on her with wonder, she was so beautiful. Then he called his son and told him that he had only a false bride; for that she was merely a waiting maid, while the true bride stood by. And the young king rejoiced when he saw her beauty, and heard how meek and patient she had been; and without saying anything to the false bride, the king ordered a great feast to be got ready for all his court. The bridegroom sat at the top, with the false princess on one side, and the true one on the other; but nobody knew her again, for her beauty was quite dazzling to their eyes; and she did not seem at all like the little goose girl, now that she had her brilliant dress on.

When they had eaten and drank, and were very merry, the old king said he would tell them a tale. So he began, and told all the story of the princess, as if it was one that he had once heard; and he asked the true waiting maid what she thought ought to be done to anyone who would behave thus. "Nothing better," said this false bride, "than that she should be thrown into a cask stuck round with sharp nails, and that two white horses should be put to it, and should drag it from street to street till she was dead."

"Thou art she!" said the old king; "and as thou has judged thyself, so shall it be done to thee." And the young king was then married to his true wife, and they reigned over the kingdom in peace and happiness all their lives; and the good fairy came to see them, and restored the faithful Falada to life again.

The Adventures of Chanticleer and Partlet

"The nuts are quite ripe now," said Chanticleer to his wife Partlet, "suppose we go together to the mountains, and eat as many as we can, before the squirrel takes them all away."

"With all my heart," said Partlet, "let us go and make a holiday of it together."

So they went to the mountains; and as it was a lovely day, they stayed there till the evening. Now, whether it was that they had eaten so many nuts that they could not walk, or whether they were lazy and would not, I do not know: however, they took it into their heads that it did not become them to go home on foot. So Chanticleer began to build a little carriage of nutshells: and when it was finished, Partlet jumped into it and sat down, and bid Chanticleer harness himself to it and draw her home. "That's a good joke!" said Chanticleer; "no, that will never do; I had rather by half walk home; I'll sit on the box and be coachman, if you like, but I'll not draw." While this was passing, a duck came quacking up and cried out, "You thieving vagabonds, what business have you in my grounds? I'll give it you well for your insolence!" and upon that she fell upon Chanticleer most lustily. But Chanticleer was no coward, and returned the duck's blows with his sharp spurs so fiercely that she soon began to cry out for mercy; which was only granted her upon condition that she would draw the carriage home for them. This she agreed to do; and Chanticleer got upon the box, and drove, crying, "Now, duck, get on as fast as you can." And away they went at a pretty good pace.

After they had travelled along a little way, they met a needle and a pin walking together along the road: and the needle cried out, "Stop, stop!" and said it was so dark that they could hardly find their way, and such dirty walking they could not get on at all: he told them that he and his friend, the pin, had been at a public house a few miles off, and had sat drinking till they had forgotten how late it was; he begged therefore that the travellers would be so kind as to give them a lift in their carriage. Chanticleer observing that they were but thin fellows, and not likely to take up much room, told them they might ride, but made them promise not to dirty the wheels of the carriage in getting in, nor to tread on Partlet's toes.

Late at night they arrived at an inn; and as it was bad travelling in the dark, and the duck seemed much tired, and waddled about a good deal from one side to the other, they made up their minds to fix their quarters there: but the landlord at first was unwilling, and said his house was full, thinking they might not be very respectable company: however, they spoke civilly to him, and gave him the egg which Partlet had laid by the way, and said they would give him the duck, who was in the habit of laying one every day: so at last he let them come in, and they bespoke a handsome supper, and spent the evening very jollily.

Early in the morning, before it was quite light, and when nobody was stirring in the inn, Chanticleer awakened his wife, and, fetching the egg, they pecked a hole in it, ate it up, and threw the shells into the fireplace: they then went to the pin and needle, who were fast asleep, and seizing them by the heads, stuck one into the landlord's easy chair and the other into his handkerchief; and, having done this, they crept away as softly as possible. However, the duck, who slept in the open air in the yard, heard them coming, and jumping into the brook which ran close by the inn, soon swam out of their reach.

An hour or two afterwards the landlord got up, and took his handkerchief to wipe his face, but the pin ran into him and pricked him: then he walked into the kitchen to light his pipe at the fire, but when he stirred it up the eggshells flew into his eyes, and almost blinded him. "Bless me!" said he, "all the world seems to have a design against my head this morning": and so saying, he threw himself sulkily into his easy chair; but, oh dear! the needle ran into him; and this time the pain was not in his head. He now flew into a very great passion, and, suspecting the company who had come in the night before, he went to look after them, but they were all off; so he swore that he never again would take in such a troop of vagabonds, who ate a great deal, paid no reckoning, and gave him nothing for his trouble but their apish tricks.

Another day, Chanticleer and Partlet wished to ride out together; so Chanticleer built a handsome carriage with four red wheels, and harnessed six mice to it; and then he and Partlet got into the carriage, and away they drove. Soon afterwards a cat met them, and said, "Where are you going?" And Chanticleer replied,

"All on our way
A visit to pay
To Mr. Korbes, the fox, today."

Then the cat said, "Take me with you."

Chanticleer said, "With all my heart: get up behind, and be sure you do not fall off."

"Take care of this handsome coach of mine,
Nor dirty my pretty red wheels so fine!
Now, mice, be ready,
And, wheels, run steady!
For we are going a visit to pay
To Mr. Korbes, the fox, today."

Soon after came up a millstone, an egg, a duck, and a pin; and Chanticleer gave them all leave to get into the carriage and go with them.

When they arrived at Mr. Korbes's house, he was not at home; so the mice drew the carriage into the coach house, Chanticleer and Partlet flew upon a beam, the cat sat down in the fireplace, the duck got into the washing cistern, the pin stuck himself into the bed pillow, the millstone laid himself over the house door, and the egg rolled himself up in the towel.

When Mr. Korbes came home, he went to the fireplace to make a fire; but the cat threw all the ashes in his eyes: so he ran to the kitchen to wash himself; but there the duck splashed all the water in his face; and when he tried to wipe himself, the egg broke to pieces in the towel all over his face and eyes. Then he was very angry, and went without his supper to bed; but when he laid his head on the pillow, the pin ran into his cheek: at this he became quite furious, and, jumping up, would have run out of the house; but when he came to the door, the millstone fell down on his head, and killed him on the spot.

Another day Chanticleer and Partlet agreed to go again to the mountains to eat nuts; and it was settled that all the nuts which they found should be shared equally between them. Now Partlet found a very large nut; but she said nothing about it to Chanticleer, and kept it all to herself: however, it was so big that she could not swallow it, and it stuck in her throat. Then she was in a great fright, and cried out to Chanticleer, "Pray run as fast as you can, and fetch me some water, or I shall be choked."

Chanticleer ran as fast as he could to the river, and said, "River, give me some water, for Partlet lies in the mountain, and will be choked by a great nut."

The river said, "Run first to the bride, and ask her for a silken cord to draw up the water."

Chanticleer ran to the bride, and said, "Bride, you must give me a silken cord, for then the river will give me water, and the water I will carry to Partlet, who lies on the mountain, and will be choked by a great nut."

But the bride said, "Run first, and bring me my garland that is hanging on a willow in the garden." Then Chanticleer ran to the garden, and took the garland from the bough where it hung, and brought it to the bride; and then the bride gave him the silken cord, and he took the silken cord to the river, and the river gave him water, and he carried the water to Partlet; but in the meantime she was choked by the great nut, and lay quite dead, and never moved any more.

Then Chanticleer was very sorry, and cried bitterly; and all the beasts came and wept with him over poor Partlet. And six mice built a little hearse to carry her to her grave; and when it was ready they harnessed themselves before it, and Chanticleer drove them. On the way they met the fox. "Where are you going, Chanticleer?" said he.

"To bury my Partlet," said the other.

"May I go with you?" said the fox.

"Yes; but you must get up behind, or my horses will not be able to draw you." Then the fox got up behind; and presently the wolf, the bear, the goat, and all the beasts of the wood, came and climbed upon the hearse.

So on they went till they came to a rapid stream. "How shall we get over?" said Chanticleer.

Then said a straw, "I will lay myself across, and you may pass over upon me." But as the mice were going over, the straw slipped away and fell into the water, and the six mice all fell in and were drowned. What was to be done?

Then a large log of wood came and said, "I am big enough; I will lay myself across the stream, and you shall pass over upon me."

So he laid himself down; but they managed so clumsily, that the log of wood fell in and was carried away by the stream. Then a stone, who saw what had happened, came up and kindly offered to help poor Chanticleer by laying himself across the stream; and this time he got safely to the other side with the hearse, and managed to get Partlet out of it; but the fox and the other mourners, who were sitting behind, were too heavy, and fell back into the water and were all carried away by the stream and drowned.

Thus Chanticleer was left alone with his dead Partlet; and having dug a grave for her, he laid her in it, and made a little hillock over her. Then he sat down by the grave, and wept and mourned, till at last he died too; and so all were dead.

Rapunzel

There were once a man and a woman who had long in vain wished for a child. At length the woman hoped that God was about to grant her desire. These people had a little window at the back of their house from which a splendid garden could be seen, which was full of the most beautiful flowers and herbs. It was, however, surrounded by a high wall, and no one dared to go into it because it belonged to an enchantress, who had great power and was dreaded by all the world. One day the woman was standing by this window and looking down into the garden, when she saw a bed which was planted with the most beautiful rampion (Rapunzel), and it looked so fresh and green that she longed for it, she quite pined away, and began to look pale and miserable. Then her husband was alarmed, and asked: "What ails you, dear wife?"

"Ah," she replied, "if I can't eat some of the rampion, which is in the garden behind our house, I shall die."

The man, who loved her, thought: "Sooner than let your wife die, bring her some of the rampion yourself, let it cost what it will."

At twilight, he clambered down over the wall into the garden of the enchantress, hastily clutched a handful of rampion, and took it to his wife. She at once made herself a salad of it, and ate it greedily. It tasted so good to her—so very good, that the next day she longed for it three times as much as before. If he was to have any rest, her husband must once more descend into the garden. In the gloom of evening therefore, he let himself down again; but when he had clambered down the wall he was terribly afraid, for he saw the enchantress standing before him.

"How can you dare," said she with angry look, "descend into my garden and steal my rampion like a thief? You shall suffer for it!"

"Ah," answered he, "let mercy take the place of justice, I only made up my mind to do it out of necessity. My wife saw your rampion from the window, and felt such a longing for it that she would have died if she had not got some to eat."

Then the enchantress allowed her anger to be softened, and said to him: "If the case be as you say, I will allow you to take away with you as much rampion as you will, only I make one condition, you must give me the child which your wife will bring into the world; it shall be well treated, and I will care for it like a mother."

The man in his terror consented to everything, and when the woman was brought to bed, the enchantress appeared at once, gave the child the name of Rapunzel, and took it away with her.

Rapunzel grew into the most beautiful child under the sun. When she was twelve years old, the enchantress shut her into a tower, which lay in a forest, and had neither stairs nor door, but quite at the top was a little window. When the enchantress wanted to go in, she placed herself beneath it and cried:

"Rapunzel, Rapunzel,
Let down your hair to me."

Rapunzel had magnificent long hair, fine as spun gold, and when she heard the voice of the enchantress she unfastened her braided tresses, wound them round one of the hooks of the window above, and then the hair fell twenty ells down, and the enchantress climbed up by it.

RAPUNZEL
"O RAPUNZEL, RAPUNZEL!
LET DOWN THINE HAIR."

After a year or two, it came to pass that the king's son rode through the forest and passed by the tower. Then he heard a song, which was so charming that he stood still and listened. This was Rapunzel, who in her solitude passed her time in letting her sweet voice resound. The king's son wanted to climb up to her, and looked for the door of the tower, but none was to be found. He rode home, but the singing had so deeply touched his heart, that every day he went out into the forest and listened to it. Once when he was thus standing behind a tree, he saw that an enchantress came there, and he heard how she cried:

"Rapunzel, Rapunzel,
Let down your hair to me."

Then Rapunzel let down the braids of her hair, and the enchantress climbed up to her. "If that is the ladder by which one mounts, I too will try my fortune," said he, and the next day when it began to grow dark, he went to the tower and cried:

"Rapunzel, Rapunzel,
Let down your hair to me."

Immediately the hair fell down and the king's son climbed up.

At first Rapunzel was terribly frightened when a man, such as her eyes had never yet beheld, came to her; but the king's son began to talk to her quite like a friend, and told her that his heart had been so stirred that it had let him have no rest, and he had been forced to see her. Then Rapunzel lost her fear, and when he asked her if she would take him for her husband, and she saw that he was young and handsome, she thought: "He will love me more than old Dame Gothel does"; and she said yes, and laid her hand in his. She said: "I will willingly go away with you, but I do not know how to get down. Bring with you a skein of silk every time that you come, and I will weave a ladder with it, and when that is ready I will descend, and you will take me on your horse." They agreed that until that time he should come to her every evening, for the old woman came by day. The enchantress remarked nothing of this, until once Rapunzel said to her: "Tell me, Dame Gothel, how it happens that you are so much heavier for me to draw up than the young king's son—he is with me in a moment."

"Ah! you wicked child," cried the enchantress. "What do I hear you say! I thought I had separated you from all the world, and yet you have deceived me!" In her anger she clutched Rapunzel's beautiful tresses, wrapped them twice round her left hand, seized a pair of scissors with the right, and snip, snap, they were cut off, and the lovely braids lay on the ground. And she was so pitiless that she took poor Rapunzel into a desert where she had to live in great grief and misery.

On the same day that she cast out Rapunzel, however, the enchantress fastened the braids of hair, which she had cut off, to the hook of the window, and when the king's son came and cried:

"Rapunzel, Rapunzel,
Let down your hair to me."

She let the hair down. The king's son ascended, but instead of finding his dearest Rapunzel, he found the enchantress, who gazed at him with wicked and venomous looks. "Aha!" she cried mockingly, "you would fetch your dearest, but the beautiful bird sits no longer singing in the nest; the cat has got it, and will scratch out your eyes as well. Rapunzel is lost to you; you will never see her again."

The king's son was beside himself with pain, and in his despair he leapt down from the tower. He escaped with his life, but the thorns into which he fell pierced his eyes. Then he wandered quite blind about the forest, ate nothing but roots and berries, and did naught but lament and weep over the loss of his dearest wife. Thus he roamed about in misery for some years, and at length came to the desert where Rapunzel, with the twins to which she had given birth, a boy and a girl, lived in wretchedness. He heard a voice, and it seemed so familiar to him that he went towards it, and when he approached, Rapunzel knew him and fell on his neck and wept. Two of her tears wetted his eyes and they grew clear again, and he could see with them as before. He led her to his kingdom where he was joyfully received, and they lived for a long time afterwards, happy and contented.

Fundevogel

There was once a forester who went into the forest to hunt, and as he entered it he heard a sound of screaming as if a little child were there. He followed the sound, and at last came to a high tree, and at the top of this a little child was sitting, for the mother had fallen asleep under the tree with the child, and a bird of prey had seen it in her arms, had flown down, snatched it away, and set it on the high tree.

The forester climbed up, brought the child down, and thought to himself: "You will take him home with you, and bring him up with your Lina." He took it home, therefore, and the two children grew up together. And the one which he had found on a tree was called Fundevogel, because a bird had carried it away. Fundevogel and Lina loved each other so dearly that when they did not see each other they were sad.

Now the forester had an old cook, who one evening took two pails and began to fetch water, and did not go once only, but many times, out to the spring. Lina saw this and said, "Listen, old Sanna, why are you fetching so much water?"

"If you will never repeat it to anyone, I will tell you why." So Lina said, no, she would never repeat it to anyone, and then the cook said: "Early tomorrow morning, when the forester is out hunting, I will heat the water, and when it is boiling in the kettle, I will throw in Fundevogel, and will boil him in it."

Early next morning the forester got up and went out hunting, and when he was gone the children were still in bed.

Then Lina said to Fundevogel: "If you will never leave me, I too will never leave you."

Fundevogel said: "Neither now, nor ever will I leave you."

Then said Lina: "Then will I tell you. Last night, old Sanna carried so many buckets of water into the house that I asked her why she was doing that, and she said that if I would promise not to tell anyone, and she said that early tomorrow morning when father was out hunting, she would set the kettle full of water, throw you into it and boil you; but we will get up quickly, dress ourselves, and go away together."

The two children therefore got up, dressed themselves quickly, and went away. When the water in the kettle was boiling, the cook went into the bedroom to fetch Fundevogel and throw him into it. But when she came in, and went to the beds, both the children were gone. Then she was terribly alarmed, and she said to herself: "What shall I say now when the forester comes home and sees that the children are gone? They must be followed instantly to get them back again."

Then the cook sent three servants after them, who were to run and overtake the children. The children, however, were sitting outside the forest, and when they saw from afar the three servants running, Lina said to Fundevogel: "Never leave me, and I will never leave you."

Fundevogel said: "Neither now, nor ever."

Then said Lina: "Do you become a rose tree, and I the rose upon it." When the three servants came to the forest, nothing was there but a rose tree and one rose on it, but the children were nowhere. Then said they: "There is nothing to be done here," and they went home and told the cook that they had seen nothing in the forest but a little rosebush with one rose on it. Then the old cook scolded and said: "You simpletons, you should have cut the rosebush in two, and have broken off the rose and brought it home with you; go, and do it at once." They had therefore to go out and look for the second time. The children, however, saw them coming from a distance.

Then Lina said: "Fundevogel, never leave me, and I will never leave you."

Fundevogel said: "Neither now, nor ever."

Said Lina, "Then do you become a church, and I'll be the chandelier in it." So when the three servants came, nothing was there but a church, with a chandelier in it. They said therefore to each other: "What can we do here? Let us go home." When they got home, the cook asked if they had not found them; so they said no, they had found nothing but a church, and there was a chandelier in it. And the cook scolded them and said: "You fools! Why did you not pull the church to pieces, and bring the chandelier home with you?" And now the old cook herself got on her legs, and went with the three servants in pursuit of the children. The children, however, saw from afar that the three servants were coming, and the cook waddling after them.

Then said Lina: "Fundevogel, never leave me, and I will never leave you."

Then said Fundevogel: "Neither now, nor ever."

Said Lina: "Be a fishpond, and I will be the duck upon it."

The cook, however, came up to them, and when she saw the pond she lay down by it, and was about to drink it up. But the duck swam quickly to her, seized her head in its beak and drew her into the water, and there the old witch had to drown. Then the children went home together, and were heartily delighted, and if they have not died, they are living still.

The Valiant Little Tailor

One summer's morning a little tailor was sitting on his table by the window; he was in good spirits, and sewed with all his might. Then came a peasant woman down the street crying: "Good jams, cheap! Good jams, cheap!"

This rang pleasantly in the tailor's ears; he stretched his delicate head out of the window, and called: "Come up here, dear woman; here you will get rid of your goods." The woman came up the three steps to the tailor with her heavy basket, and he made her unpack all the pots for him. He inspected each one, lifted it up, put his nose to it, and at length said: "The jam seems to me to be good, so weigh me out four ounces, dear woman, and if it is a quarter of a pound that is of no consequence."

The woman who had hoped to find a good sale, gave him what he desired, but went away quite angry and grumbling. "Now, this jam shall be blessed by God," cried the little tailor, "and give me health and strength"; so he brought the bread out of the cupboard, cut himself a piece right across the loaf and spread the jam over it. "This won't taste bitter," said he, "but I will just finish the jacket before I take a bite." He laid the bread near him, sewed on, and in his joy, made bigger and bigger stitches. In the meantime the smell of the sweet jam rose to where the flies were sitting in great numbers, and they were attracted and descended on it in hosts. "Hi! who invited you?" said the little tailor, and drove the unbidden guests away. The flies, however, who understood no German, would not be turned away, but came back again in ever-increasing companies. The little tailor at last lost all patience, and drew a piece of cloth from the hole under his worktable, and saying: "Wait, and I will give it to you," struck it mercilessly on them. When he drew it away and counted, there lay before him no fewer than seven, dead and with legs stretched out. "Are you a fellow of that sort?" said he, and could not help admiring his own bravery. "The whole town shall know of this!" And the little tailor hastened to cut himself a girdle, stitched it, and embroidered on it in large letters: "Seven at one stroke!" "What, the town!" he continued, "the whole world shall hear of it!" and his heart wagged with joy like a lamb's tail.

The tailor put on the girdle, and resolved to go forth into the world, because he thought his workshop was too small for his valour. Before he went away, he sought about in the house to see if there was anything which he could take with him; however, he found nothing but an old cheese, and that he put in his pocket. In front of the door he observed a bird which had caught itself in the thicket. It had to go into his pocket with the cheese. Now he took to the road boldly, and as he was light and nimble, he felt no fatigue. The road led him up a mountain, and when he had reached the highest point of it, there sat a powerful giant looking peacefully about him. The little tailor went bravely up, spoke to him, and said: "Good day, comrade, so you are sitting there overlooking the widespread world! I am just on my way thither, and want to try my luck. Have you any inclination to go with me?"

The giant looked contemptuously at the tailor, and said: "You raga-muffin! You miserable creature!"

"Oh, indeed?" answered the little tailor, and unbuttoned his coat, and showed the giant the girdle, "there may you read what kind of a man I am!"

The giant read: "Seven at one stroke," and thought that they had been men whom the tailor had killed, and began to feel a little respect for the tiny fellow. Nevertheless, he wished to try him first, and took a stone in his hand and squeezed it together so that water dropped out of it. "Do that likewise," said the giant, "if you have strength."

"Is that all?" said the tailor, "that is child's play with us!" and put his hand into his pocket, brought out the soft cheese, and pressed it until the liquid ran out of it. "Faith," said he, "that was a little better, wasn't it?"

The giant did not know what to say, and could not believe it of the little man. Then the giant picked up a stone and threw it so high that the eye could scarcely follow it. "Now, little mite of a man, do that likewise,"

"Well thrown," said the tailor, "but after all the stone came down to earth again; I will throw you one which shall never come back at all," and he put his hand into his pocket, took out the bird, and threw it into the air. The bird, delighted with its liberty, rose, flew away and did not come back. "How does that shot please you, comrade?" asked the tailor.

"You can certainly throw," said the giant, "but now we will see if you are able to carry anything properly." He took the little tailor to a mighty oak tree which lay there felled on the ground, and said: "If you are strong enough, help me to carry the tree out of the forest."

"Readily," answered the little man; "take you the trunk on your shoulders, and I will raise up the branches and twigs; after all, they are the heaviest." The giant took the trunk on his shoulder, but the tailor seated himself on a branch, and the giant, who could not look round, had to carry away the whole tree, and the little tailor into the bargain: he behind, was quite merry and happy, and whistled the song: "Three tailors rode forth from the gate," as if carrying the tree were child's play. The giant, after he had dragged the heavy burden part of the way, could go no further, and cried: "Hark you, I shall have to let the tree fall!" The tailor sprang nimbly down, seized the tree with both arms as if he had been carrying it, and said to the giant: "You are such a great fellow, and yet cannot even carry the tree!"

They went on together, and as they passed a cherry tree, the giant laid hold of the top of the tree where the ripest fruit was hanging, bent it down, gave it into the tailor's hand, and bade him eat. But the little tailor was much too weak to hold the tree, and when the giant let it go, it sprang back again, and the tailor was tossed into the air with it. When he had fallen down again without injury, the giant said: "What is this? Have you not strength enough to hold the weak twig?"

"There is no lack of strength," answered the little tailor. "Do you think that could be anything to a man who has struck down seven at one blow? I leapt over the tree because the huntsmen are shooting down there in the thicket. Jump as I did, if you can do it." The giant made the attempt but he could not get over the tree, and remained hanging in the branches, so that in this also the tailor kept the upper hand.

The giant said: "If you are such a valiant fellow, come with me into our cavern and spend the night with us." The little tailor was willing, and followed him. When they went into the cave, other giants were sitting there by the fire, and each of them had a roasted sheep in his hand and was eating it. The little tailor looked round and thought: "It is much more spacious here than in my workshop." The giant showed him a bed, and said he was to lie down in it and sleep. The bed, however, was too big for the little tailor; he did not lie down in it, but crept into a corner. When it was midnight, and the giant thought that the little tailor was lying in a sound sleep, he got up, took a great iron bar, cut through the bed with one blow, and thought he had finished off the grasshopper for good. With the earliest dawn the giants went into the forest, and had quite forgotten the little tailor, when all at once he walked up to them quite merrily and boldly. The giants were terrified, they were afraid that he would strike them all dead, and ran away in a great hurry.

The little tailor went onwards, always following his own pointed nose. After he had walked for a long time, he came to the courtyard of a royal palace, and as he felt weary, he lay down on the grass and fell asleep. Whilst he lay there, the people came and inspected him on all sides, and read on his girdle: "Seven at one stroke."

"Ah!" said they, "what does the great warrior want here in the midst of peace? He must be a mighty lord." They went and announced him to the king, and gave it as their opinion that if war should break out, this would be a weighty and useful man who ought on no account to be allowed to depart. The counsel pleased the king, and he sent one of his courtiers to the little tailor to offer him military service when he awoke. The ambassador remained standing by the sleeper, waited until he stretched his limbs and opened his eyes, and then conveyed to him this proposal. "For this very reason have I come here," the tailor replied, "I am ready to enter the king's service." He was therefore honourably received, and a special dwelling was assigned him.

The soldiers, however, were set against the little tailor, and wished him a thousand miles away. "What is to be the end of this?" they said among themselves. "If we quarrel with him, and he strikes about him, seven of us will fall at every blow; not one of us can stand against him." They came therefore to a decision, betook themselves in a body to the king, and begged for their dismissal. "We are not prepared," said they, "to stay with a man who kills seven at one stroke." The king was sorry that for the sake of one he should lose all his faithful servants, wished that he had never set eyes on the tailor, and would willingly have been rid of him again. But he did not venture to give him his dismissal, for he dreaded lest he should strike him and all his people dead, and place himself on the royal throne. He thought about it for a long time, and at last found good counsel. He sent to the little tailor and caused him to be informed that as he was a great warrior, he had one request to make to him. In a forest of his country lived two giants, who caused great mischief with their robbing, murdering, ravaging, and burning, and no one could approach them without putting himself in danger of death. If the tailor conquered and killed these two giants, he would give him his only daughter to wife, and half of his kingdom as a dowry, likewise one hundred horsemen should go with him to assist him. "That would indeed be a fine thing for a man like me!" thought the little tailor. "One is not offered a beautiful princess and half a kingdom every day of one's life!"

"Oh, yes," he replied, "I will soon subdue the giants, and do not require the help of the hundred horsemen to do it; he who can hit seven with one blow has no need to be afraid of two."

The little tailor went forth, and the hundred horsemen followed him. When he came to the outskirts of the forest, he said to his followers: "Just stay waiting here, I alone will soon finish off the giants." Then he bounded into the forest and looked about right and left. After a while he perceived both giants. They lay sleeping under a tree, and snored so that the branches waved up and down. The little tailor, not idle, gathered two pocketsful of stones, and with these climbed up the tree. When he was halfway up, he slipped down by a branch, until he sat just above the sleepers, and then let one stone after another fall on the breast of one of the giants. For a long time the giant felt nothing, but at last he awoke, pushed his comrade, and said: "Why are you knocking me?"

"You must be dreaming," said the other, "I am not knocking you."

They laid themselves down to sleep again, and then the tailor threw a stone down on the second.

"What is the meaning of this?" cried the other. "Why are you pelting me?"

"I am not pelting you," answered the first, growling. They disputed about it for a time, but as they were weary they let the matter rest, and their eyes closed once more. The little tailor began his game again, picked out the biggest stone, and threw it with all his might on the breast of the first giant.

"That is too bad!" cried he, and sprang up like a madman, and pushed his companion against the tree until it shook. The other paid him back in the same coin, and they got into such a rage that they tore up trees and belaboured each other so long, that at last they both fell down dead on the ground at the same time. Then the little tailor leapt down. "It is a lucky thing," said he, "that they did not tear up the tree on which I was sitting, or I should have had to sprint on to another like a squirrel; but we tailors are nimble." He drew out his sword and gave each of them a couple of thrusts in the breast, and then went out to the horsemen and said: "The work is done; I have finished both of them off, but it was hard work! They tore up trees in their sore need, and defended themselves with them, but all that is to no purpose when a man like myself comes, who can kill seven at one blow."

"But are you not wounded?" asked the horsemen.

"You need not concern yourself about that," answered the tailor, "they have not bent one hair of mine." The horsemen would not believe him, and rode into the forest; there they found the giants swimming in their blood, and all round about lay the torn-up trees.

The little tailor demanded of the king the promised reward; he, however, repented of his promise, and again bethought himself how he could get rid of the hero.

"Before you receive my daughter, and the half of my kingdom," said he to him, "you must perform one more heroic deed. In the forest roams a unicorn which does great harm, and you must catch it first."

"I fear one unicorn still less than two giants. Seven at one blow is my kind of affair." He took a rope and an axe with him, went forth into the forest, and again bade those who were sent with him to wait outside. He had not long to seek. The unicorn soon came towards him, and rushed directly on the tailor, as if it would gore him with its horn without more ado. "Softly, softly; it can't be done as quickly as that," said he, and stood still and waited until the animal was quite close, and then sprang nimbly behind the tree. The unicorn ran against the tree with all its strength, and stuck its horn so fast in the trunk that it had not the strength enough to draw it out again, and thus it was caught. "Now, I have got the bird," said the tailor, and came out from behind the tree and put the rope round its neck, and then with his axe he hewed the horn out of the tree, and when all was ready he led the beast away and took it to the king.

The king still would not give him the promised reward, and made a third demand. Before the wedding the tailor was to catch him a wild boar that made great havoc in the forest, and the huntsmen should give him their help.

"Willingly," said the tailor, "that is child's play!" He did not take the huntsmen with him into the forest, and they were well pleased that he did not, for the wild boar had several times received them in such a manner that they had no inclination to lie in wait for him. When the boar perceived the tailor, it ran on him with foaming mouth and whetted tusks, and was about to throw him to the ground, but the hero fled and sprang into a chapel which was near and up to the window at once, and in one bound out again. The boar ran after him, but the tailor ran round outside and shut the door behind it, and then the raging beast, which was much too heavy and awkward to leap out of the window, was caught. The little tailor called the huntsmen thither that they might see the prisoner with their own eyes. The hero, however, went to the king, who was now, whether he liked it or not, obliged to keep his promise, and gave his daughter and the half of his kingdom. Had he known that it was no warlike hero, but a little tailor who was standing before him, it would have gone to his heart still more than it did. The wedding was held with great magnificence and small joy, and out of a tailor a king was made.

After some time the young queen heard her husband say in his dreams at night: "Boy, make me the doublet, and patch the pantaloons, or else I will rap the yard measure over your ears." Then she discovered in what state of life the young lord had been born, and next morning complained of her wrongs to her father, and begged him to help her to get rid of her husband, who was nothing else but a tailor. The king comforted her and said: "Leave your bedroom door open this night, and my servants shall stand outside, and when he has fallen asleep shall go in, bind him, and take him on board a ship which shall carry him into the wide world." The woman was satisfied with this; but the king's armour-bearer, who had heard all, was friendly with the young lord, and informed him of the whole plot. "I'll put a screw into that business," said the little tailor. At night he went to bed with his wife at the usual time, and when she thought that he had fallen asleep, she got up, opened the door, and then lay down again. The little tailor, who was only pretending to be asleep, began to cry out in a clear voice: "Boy, make me the doublet and patch me the pantaloons, or I will rap the yard measure over your ears. I smote seven at one blow. I killed two giants, I brought away one unicorn, and caught a wild boar, and am I to fear those who are standing outside the room?" When these men heard the tailor speaking thus, they were overcome by a great dread, and ran as if the wild huntsman were behind them, and none of them would venture anything further against him. So the little tailor was and remained a king to the end of his life.

Hansel and Gretel

Hard by a great forest dwelt a poor woodcutter with his wife and his two children. The boy was called Hansel and the girl Gretel. He had little to bite and to break, and once when great dearth fell on the land, he could no longer procure even daily bread. Now when he thought over this by night in his bed, and tossed about in his anxiety, he groaned and said to his wife: "What is to become of us? How are we to feed our poor children, when we no longer have anything even for ourselves?"

"I'll tell you what, husband," answered the woman, "early tomorrow morning we will take the children out into the forest to where it is the thickest; there we will light a fire for them, and give each of them one more piece of bread, and then we will go to our work and leave them alone. They will not find the way home again, and we shall be rid of them."

"No, wife," said the man, "I will not do that; how can I bear to leave my children alone in the forest? The wild animals would soon come and tear them to pieces."

"O, you fool!" said she, "then we must all four die of hunger, you may as well plane the planks for our coffins," and she left him no peace until he consented.

"But I feel very sorry for the poor children, all the same," said the man.

The two children had also not been able to sleep for hunger, and had heard what their stepmother had said to their father. Gretel wept bitter tears, and said to Hansel: "Now all is over with us."

"Be quiet, Gretel," said Hansel, "do not distress yourself, I will soon find a way to help us." And when the old folks had fallen asleep, he got up, put on his little coat, opened the door below, and crept outside. The moon shone brightly, and the white pebbles which lay in front of the house glittered like real silver pennies. Hansel stooped and stuffed the little pocket of his coat with as many as he could get in. Then he went back and said to Gretel: "Be comforted, dear little sister, and sleep in peace, God will not forsake us," and he lay down again in his bed. When day dawned, but before the sun had risen, the woman came and awoke the two children, saying: "Get up, you sluggards! we are going into the forest to fetch wood." She gave each a little piece of bread, and said: "There is something for your dinner, but do not eat it up before then, for you will get nothing else." Gretel took the bread under her apron, as Hansel had the pebbles in his pocket. Then they all set out together on the way to the forest. When they had walked a short time, Hansel stood still and peeped back at the house, and did so again and again. His father said: "Hansel, what are you looking at there and staying behind for? Pay attention, and do not forget how to use your legs."

"Ah, father," said Hansel, "I am looking at my little white cat, which is sitting up on the roof, and wants to say goodbye to me."

The wife said: "Fool, that is not your little cat, that is the morning sun which is shining on the chimneys." Hansel, however, had not been looking back at the cat, but had been constantly throwing one of the white pebble stones out of his pocket on the road.

When they had reached the middle of the forest, the father said: "Now, children, pile up some wood, and I will light a fire that you may not be cold."

Hansel and Gretel gathered brushwood together, as high as a little hill. The brushwood was lighted, and when the flames were burning very high, the woman said: "Now, children, lay yourselves down by the fire and rest, we will go into the forest and cut some wood. When we have done, we will come back and fetch you away."

Hansel and Gretel sat by the fire, and when noon came, each ate a little piece of bread, and as they heard the strokes of the wood axe they believed that their father was near. It was not the axe, however, but a branch which he had fastened to a withered tree which the wind was blowing backwards and forwards. And as they had been sitting such a long time, their eyes closed with fatigue, and they fell fast asleep. When at last they awoke, it was already dark night. Gretel began to cry and said: "How are we to get out of the forest now?"

But Hansel comforted her and said: "Just wait a little, until the moon has risen, and then we will soon find the way." And when the full moon had risen, Hansel took his little sister by the hand, and followed the pebbles which shone like newly coined silver pieces, and showed them the way.

They walked the whole night long, and by break of day came once more to their father's house. They knocked at the door, and when the woman opened it and saw that it was Hansel and Gretel, she said: "You naughty children, why have you slept so long in the forest? We thought you were never coming back at all!" The father, however, rejoiced, for it had cut him to the heart to leave them behind alone.

Not long afterwards, there was once more great dearth throughout the land, and the children heard their mother saying at night to their father: "Everything is eaten again, we have one half loaf left, and that is the end. The children must go, we will take them farther into the wood, so that they will not find their way out again; there is no other means of saving ourselves!" The man's heart was heavy, and he thought: "It would be better for you to share the last mouthful with your children." The woman, however, would listen to nothing that he had to say, but scolded and reproached him. He who says A must say B, likewise, and as he had yielded the first time, he had to do so a second time also.

The children, however, were still awake and had heard the

conversation. When the old folks were asleep, Hansel again got up, and wanted to go out and pick up pebbles as he had done before, but the woman had locked the door, and Hansel could not get out. Nevertheless he comforted his little sister, and said: "Do not cry, Gretel, go to sleep quietly, the good God will help us."

Early in the morning came the woman, and took the children out of their beds. Their piece of bread was given to them, but it was still smaller than the time before. On the way into the forest Hansel crumbled his in his pocket, and often stood still and threw a morsel on the ground. "Hansel, why do you stop and look round?" said the father, "go on."

"I am looking back at my little pigeon which is sitting on the roof, and wants to say goodbye to me," answered Hansel.

"Fool!" said the woman, "that is not your little pigeon, that is the morning sun that is shining on the chimney." Hansel, however, little by little, threw all the crumbs on the path.

The woman led the children still deeper into the forest, where they had never in their lives been before. Then a great fire was again made, and the mother said: "Just sit there, you children, and when you are tired you may sleep a little; we are going into the forest to cut wood, and in the evening when we are done, we will come and fetch you away."

When it was noon, Gretel shared her piece of bread with Hansel, who had scattered his by the way. Then they fell asleep and evening passed, but no one came to the poor children. They did not awake until it was dark night, and Hansel comforted his little sister and said: "Just wait, Gretel, until the moon rises, and then we shall see the crumbs of bread which I have strewn about, they will show us our way home again." When the moon came they set out, but they found no crumbs, for the many thousands of birds which fly about in the woods and fields had picked them all up. Hansel said to Gretel: "We shall soon find the way," but they did not find it. They walked the whole night and all the next day too from morning till evening, but they did not get out of the forest, and were very hungry, for they had nothing to eat but two or three berries, which grew on the ground. And as they were so weary that their legs would carry them no longer, they lay down beneath a tree and fell asleep.

It was now three mornings since they had left their father's house. They began to walk again, but they always came deeper into the forest, and if help did not come soon, they must die of hunger and weariness. When it was midday, they saw a beautiful snow white bird sitting on a bough, which sang so delightfully that they stood still and listened to it. And when its song was over, it spread its wings and flew away before them, and they followed it until they reached a little house, on the roof of which it alighted; and when they approached the little house they saw that it was built of bread and covered with cakes, but that the windows were of clear sugar.

"We will set to work on that," said Hansel, "and have a good meal. I will eat a bit of the roof, and you, Gretel, can eat some of the window, it will taste sweet."

Hansel reached up above, and broke off a little of the roof to try how it tasted, and Gretel leant against the window and nibbled at the panes. Then a soft voice cried from the parlour:

"Nibble, nibble, gnaw,
Who is nibbling at my little house?"

The children answered:

"The wind, the wind,
The heaven-born wind,"

and went on eating without disturbing themselves. Hansel, who liked the taste of the roof, tore down a great piece of it, and Gretel pushed out the whole of one round windowpane, sat down, and enjoyed herself with it. Suddenly the door opened, and a woman as old as the hills, who supported herself on crutches, came creeping out. Hansel and Gretel were so terribly frightened that they let fall what they had in their hands.

The old woman, however, nodded her head, and said: "Oh, you dear children, who has brought you here? do come in, and stay with me. No harm shall happen to you." She took them both by the hand, and led them into her little house. Then good food was set before them, milk and pancakes, with sugar, apples, and nuts. Afterwards two pretty little beds were covered with clean white linen, and Hansel and Gretel lay down in them, and thought they were in heaven.

The old woman had only pretended to be so kind; she was in reality a wicked witch, who lay in wait for children, and had only built the little house of bread in order to entice them there. When a child fell into her power, she killed it, cooked and ate it, and that was a feast day with her. Witches have red eyes, and cannot see far, but they have a keen scent like the beasts, and are aware when human beings draw near. When Hansel and Gretel came into her neighbourhood, she laughed with malice, and said mockingly: "I have them, they shall not escape me again!" Early in the morning before the children were awake, she was already up, and when she saw both of them sleeping and looking so pretty, with their plump and rosy cheeks, she muttered to herself: "That will be a dainty mouthful!" Then she seized Hansel with her shrivelled hand, carried him into a little stable, and locked him in behind a grated door. Scream as he might, it would not help him. Then she went to Gretel, shook her till she awoke, and cried: "Get up, lazy thing, fetch some water, and cook something good for your brother, he is in the stable outside, and is to be made fat. When he is fat, I will eat him." Gretel began to weep bitterly, but it was all in vain, for she was forced to do what the wicked witch commanded.

And now the best food was cooked for poor Hansel, but Gretel got nothing but crab shells. Every morning the woman crept to the little stable, and cried: "Hansel, stretch out your finger that I may feel if you will soon be fat." Hansel, however, stretched out a little bone to her, and the old woman, who had dim eyes, could not see it, and thought it was Hansel's finger, and was astonished that there was no way of fattening him. When four weeks had gone by, and Hansel still remained thin, she was seized with impatience and would not wait any longer. "Now, then, Gretel," she cried to the girl, "stir yourself, and bring some water. Let Hansel be fat or lean, tomorrow I will kill him, and cook him." Ah, how the poor little sister did lament when she had to fetch the water, and how her tears did flow down her cheeks!

"Dear God, do help us," she cried. "If the wild beasts in the forest had but devoured us, we should at any rate have died together."

"Just keep your noise to yourself," said the old woman, "it won't help you at all."

Early in the morning, Gretel had to go out and hang up the cauldron with the water, and light the fire. "We will bake first," said the old woman, "I have already heated the oven, and kneaded the dough." She pushed poor Gretel out to the oven, from which flames of fire were already darting. "Creep in," said the witch, "and see if it is properly heated, so that we can put the bread in." And once Gretel was inside, she intended to shut the oven and let her bake in it, and then she would eat her, too. But Gretel saw what she had in mind, and said: "I do not know how I am to do it; how do I get in?"

"Silly goose," said the old woman. "The door is big enough; just look, I can get in myself!" and she crept up and thrust her head into the oven. Then Gretel gave her a push that drove her far into it, and shut the iron door, and fastened the bolt. Oh! then she began to howl quite horribly, but Gretel ran away and the godless witch was miserably burnt to death.

Gretel, however, ran like lightning to Hansel, opened his little stable, and cried: "Hansel, we are saved! The old witch is dead!" Then Hansel sprang like a bird from its cage when the door is opened. How they did rejoice and embrace each other, and dance about and kiss each other! And as they had no longer any need to fear her, they went into the witch's house, and in every corner there stood chests full of pearls and jewels. "These are far better than pebbles!" said Hansel, and thrust into his pockets whatever could be got in, and Gretel said: "I, too, will take something home with me," and filled her pinafore full. "But now we must be off," said Hansel, "that we may get out of the witch's forest."

When they had walked for two hours, they came to a great stretch of water. "We cannot cross," said Hansel, "I see no foot plank, and no bridge."

"And there is also no ferry," answered Gretel, "but a white duck is swimming there: if I ask her, she will help us over." Then she cried:

"Little duck, little duck, dost thou see,
Hansel and Gretel are waiting for thee?
There's never a plank, or bridge in sight,
Take us across on thy back so white."

The duck came to them, and Hansel seated himself on its back, and told his sister to sit by him. "No," replied Gretel, "that will be too heavy for the little duck; she shall take us across, one after the other." The good little duck did so, and when they were once safely across and had walked for a short time, the forest seemed to be more and more familiar to them, and at length they saw from afar their father's house. Then they began to run, rushed into the parlour, and threw themselves round their father's neck. The man had not known one happy hour since he had left the children in the forest; the woman, however, was dead. Gretel emptied her pinafore until pearls and precious stones ran about the room, and Hansel threw one handful after another out of his pocket to add to them. Then all anxiety was at an end, and they lived together in perfect happiness. My tale is done, there runs a mouse; whosoever catches it may make himself a big fur cap out of it.

The Mouse, the Bird, and the Sausage

Once upon a time, a mouse, a bird, and a sausage entered into partnership and set up house together. For a long time all went well; they lived in great comfort, and prospered so far as to be able to add considerably to their stores. The bird's duty was to fly daily into the wood and bring in fuel; the mouse fetched the water, and the sausage saw to the cooking.

When people are too well-off they always begin to long for something new. And so it came to pass, that the bird, while out one day, met a fellow bird, to whom he boastfully expatiated on the excellence of his household arrangements. But the other bird sneered at him for being a poor simpleton, who did all the hard work, while the other two stayed at home and had a good time of it. For, when the mouse had made the fire and fetched in the water, she could retire into her little room and rest until it was time to set the table. The sausage had only to watch the pot to see that the food was properly cooked, and when it was near dinnertime, he just threw himself into the broth, or rolled in and out among the vegetables three or four times, and there they were, buttered, and salted, and ready to be served. Then, when the bird came home and had laid aside his burden, they sat down to table, and when they had finished their meal, they could sleep their fill till the following morning: and that was really a very delightful life.

Influenced by those remarks, the bird next morning refused to bring in the wood, telling the others that he had been their servant long enough, and had been a fool into the bargain, and that it was now time to make a change, and to try some other way of arranging the work. Beg and pray as the mouse and the sausage might, it was of no use; the bird remained master of the situation, and the venture had to be made. They therefore drew lots, and it fell to the sausage to bring in the wood, to the mouse to cook, and to the bird to fetch the water.

And now what happened? The sausage started in search of wood, the bird made the fire, and the mouse put on the pot, and then these two waited till the sausage returned with the fuel for the following day. But the sausage remained so long away, that they became uneasy, and the bird flew out to meet him. He had not flown far, however, when he came across a dog who, having met the sausage, had regarded him as his legitimate booty, and so seized and swallowed him. The bird complained to the dog of this barefaced robbery, but nothing he said was of any avail, for the dog answered that he found false credentials on the sausage, and that was the reason his life had been forfeited.

He picked up the wood, and flew sadly home, and told the mouse all he had seen and heard. They were both very unhappy, but agreed to make the best of things and to remain with one another.

So now the bird set the table, and the mouse looked after the food and, wishing to prepare it in the same way as the sausage, by rolling in and out among the vegetables to salt and butter them, she jumped into the pot; but she stopped short long before she reached the bottom, having already parted not only with her skin and hair, but also with life.

Presently the bird came in and wanted to serve up the dinner, but he could nowhere see the cook. In his alarm and flurry, he threw the wood here and there about the floor, called and searched, but no cook was to be found. Then some of the wood that had been carelessly thrown down caught fire and began to blaze. The bird hastened to fetch some water, but his pail fell into the well, and he after it, and as he was unable to recover himself, he was drowned.

Mother Hulda

Once upon a time there was a widow who had two daughters; one of them was beautiful and industrious, the other ugly and lazy. The mother, however, loved the ugly and lazy one best, because she was her own daughter, and so the other, who was only her stepdaughter, was made to do all the work of the house, and was quite the Cinderella of the family. Her stepmother sent her out every day to sit by the well in the high road, there to spin until she made her fingers bleed. Now it chanced one day that some blood fell on to the spindle, and as the girl stopped over the well to wash it off, the spindle suddenly sprang out of her hand and fell into the well. She ran home crying to tell of her misfortune, but her stepmother spoke harshly to her, and after giving her a violent scolding, said unkindly, "As you have let the spindle fall into the well you may go yourself and fetch it out."

The girl went back to the well not knowing what to do, and at last in her distress she jumped into the water after the spindle.

She remembered nothing more until she awoke and found herself in a beautiful meadow, full of sunshine, and with countless flowers blooming in every direction.

MOTHER HULDA
"THEN THE GIRL WENT BACK AGAIN TO THE WELL NOT KNOWING WHAT TO DO, AND IN THE DESPAIR OF HER HEART SHE JUMPED DOWN INTO THE WELL THE SAME WAY THE SPINDLE HAD GONE."
SWAIN SC

She walked over the meadow, and presently she came upon a baker's oven full of bread, and the loaves cried out to her, "Take us out, take us out, or alas! we shall be burnt to a cinder; we were baked through long ago." So she took the bread shovel and drew them all out.

She went on a little farther, till she came to a tree full of apples. "Shake me, shake me, I pray," cried the tree; "my apples, one and all, are ripe." So she shook the tree, and the apples came falling down upon her like rain; but she continued shaking until there was not a single apple left upon it. Then she carefully gathered the apples together in a heap and walked on again.

The next thing she came to was a little house, and there she saw an old woman looking out, with such large teeth, that she was terrified, and turned to run away. But the old woman called after her, "What are you afraid of, dear child? Stay with me, if you will do the work of my house properly for me, I will make you very happy. You must be very careful, however, to make my bed in the right way, for I wish you always to shake it thoroughly, so that the feathers fly about; then they say, down there in the world, that it is snowing; for I am Mother Hulda." The old woman spoke so kindly, that the girl summoned up courage and agreed to enter into her service.

She took care to do everything according to the old woman's bidding, and every time she made the bed she shook it with all her might, so that the feathers flew about like so many snowflakes. The old woman was as good as her word: she never spoke angrily to her, and gave her roast and boiled meats every day.

So she stayed on with Mother Hulda for some time, and then she began to grow unhappy. She could not at first tell why she felt sad, but she became conscious at last of great longing to go home; then she knew she was homesick, although she was a thousand times better off with Mother Hulda than with her mother and sister. After waiting awhile, she went to Mother Hulda and said, "I am so homesick, that I cannot stay with you any longer, for although I am so happy here, I must return to my own people."

Then Mother Hulda said, "I am pleased that you should want to go back to your own people, and as you have served me so well and faithfully, I will take you home myself."

Thereupon she led the girl by the hand up to a broad gateway. The gate was opened, and as the girl passed through, a shower of gold fell upon her, and the gold clung to her, so that she was covered with it from head to foot.

"That is a reward for your industry," said Mother Hulda, and as she spoke she handed her the spindle which she had dropped into the well.

The gate was then closed, and the girl found herself back in the old world close to her mother's house. As she entered the courtyard, the cock, who was perched on the well, called out:

"Cock-a-doodle-doo!
Your golden daughter's come back to you."

Then she went in to her mother and sister, and as she was so richly covered with gold, they gave her a warm welcome. She related to them all that had happened, and when the mother heard how she had come by her great riches, she thought she should like her ugly, lazy daughter to go and try her fortune. So she made the sister go and sit by the well and spin, and the girl pricked her finger and thrust her hand into a thornbush, so that she might drop some blood on to the spindle; then she threw it into the well, and jumped in herself.

Like her sister she awoke in the beautiful meadow, and walked over it till she came to the oven. "Take us out, take us out, or alas! we shall be burnt to a cinder; we were baked through long ago," cried the loaves as before. But the lazy girl answered, "Do you think I am going to dirty my hands for you?" and walked on.

Presently she came to the apple tree. "Shake me, shake me, I pray; my apples, one and all, are ripe," it cried. But she only answered, "A nice thing to ask me to do, one of the apples might fall on my head," and passed on.

At last she came to Mother Hulda's house, and as she had heard all about the large teeth from her sister, she was not afraid of them, and engaged herself without delay to the old woman.

The first day she was very obedient and industrious, and exerted herself to please Mother Hulda, for she thought of the gold she should get in return. The next day, however, she began to dawdle over her work, and the third day she was more idle still; then she began to lie in bed in the mornings and refused to get up. Worse still, she neglected to make the old woman's bed properly, and forgot to shake it so that the feathers might fly about. So Mother Hulda very soon got tired of her, and told her she might go. The lazy girl was delighted at this, and thought to herself, "The gold will soon be mine." Mother Hulda led her, as she had led her sister, to the broad gateway; but as she was passing through, instead of the shower of gold, a great bucketful of pitch came pouring over her.

"That is in return for your services," said the old woman, and she shut the gate.

So the lazy girl had to go home covered with pitch, and the cock on the well called out as he saw her:

"Cock-a-doodle-doo!
Your dirty daughter's come back to you."

But, try what she would, she could not get the pitch off and it stuck to her as long as she lived.

Little Red Riding Hood

Once upon a time there was a dear little girl who was loved by everyone who looked at her, but most of all by her grandmother, and there was nothing that she would not have given to the child. Once she gave her a little cap of red velvet, which suited her so well that she would never wear anything else; so she was always called "Little Red Riding Hood."

One day her mother said to her: "Come, Little Red Riding Hood, here is a piece of cake and a bottle of wine; take them to your grandmother, she is ill and weak, and they will do her good. Set out before it gets hot, and when you are going, walk nicely and quietly and do not run off the path, or you may fall and break the bottle, and then your grandmother will get nothing; and when you go into her room, don't forget to say, 'Good morning,' and don't peep into every corner before you do it."

"I will take great care," said Little Red Riding Hood to her mother, and gave her hand on it.

The grandmother lived out in the wood, half a league from the village, and just as Little Red Riding Hood entered the wood, a wolf met her. Little Red Riding Hood did not know what a wicked creature he was, and was not at all afraid of him.

"Good day, Little Red Riding Hood," said he.

"Thank you kindly, wolf."

"Whither away so early, Little Red Riding Hood?"

"To my grandmother's."

"What have you got in your apron?"

"Cake and wine; yesterday was baking day, so poor sick grandmother is to have something good, to make her stronger."

"Where does your grandmother live, Little Red Riding Hood?"

"A good quarter of a league farther on in the wood; her house stands under the three large oak trees, the nut trees are just below; you surely must know it," replied Little Red Riding Hood.

The wolf thought to himself: "What a tender young creature! what a nice plump mouthful—she will be better to eat than the old woman. I must act craftily, so as to catch both." So he walked for a short time by the side of Little Red Riding Hood, and then he said: "See, Little Red Riding Hood, how pretty the flowers are about here—why do you not look round? I believe, too, that you do not hear how sweetly the little birds are singing; you walk gravely along as if you were going to school, while everything else out here in the wood is merry."

Little Red Riding Hood raised her eyes, and when she saw the sunbeams dancing here and there through the trees, and pretty flowers growing everywhere, she thought: "Suppose I take grandmother a fresh nosegay; that would please her too. It is so early in the day that I shall still get there in good time"; and so she ran from the path into the wood to look for flowers. And whenever she had picked one, she fancied that she saw a still prettier one farther on, and ran after it, and so got deeper and deeper into the wood.

Meanwhile the wolf ran straight to the grandmother's house and knocked at the door.

"Who is there?"

"Little Red Riding Hood," replied the wolf. "She is bringing cake and wine; open the door."

"Lift the latch," called out the grandmother, "I am too weak, and cannot get up."

The wolf lifted the latch, the door sprang open, and without saying a word he went straight to the grandmother's bed, and devoured her. Then he put on her clothes, dressed himself in her cap, laid himself in bed, and drew the curtains.

Little Red Riding Hood, however, had been running about picking flowers, and when she had gathered so many that she could carry no more, she remembered her grandmother, and set out on the way to her.

She was surprised to find the cottage door standing open, and when she went into the room, she had such a strange feeling that she said to herself: "Oh dear! how uneasy I feel today, and at other times I like being with grandmother so much." She called out: "Good morning," but received no answer; so she went to the bed and drew back the curtains. There lay her grandmother with her cap pulled far over her face, and looking very strange.

"Oh! grandmother," she said, "what big ears you have!"

"The better to hear you with, my child," was the reply.

"But, grandmother, what big eyes you have!" she said.

"The better to see you with, my dear."

"But, grandmother, what large hands you have!"

"The better to hug you with."

"Oh! but, grandmother, what a terrible big mouth you have!"

"The better to eat you with!"

And scarcely had the wolf said this, than with one bound he was out of bed and swallowed up Little Red Riding Hood.

When the wolf had appeased his appetite, he lay down again in the bed, fell asleep and began to snore very loud. The huntsman was just passing the house, and thought to himself: "How the old woman is snoring! I must just see if she wants anything." So he went into the room, and when he came to the bed, he saw that the wolf was lying in it. "Do I find you here, you old sinner!" said he. "I have long sought you!" Then just as he was going to fire at him, it occurred to him that the wolf might have devoured the grandmother, and that she might still be saved, so he did not fire, but took a pair of scissors, and began to cut open the stomach of the sleeping wolf. When he had made two snips, he saw the little red cap shining, and then he made two snips more, and the little girl sprang out, crying: "Ah, how frightened I have been! How dark it was inside the wolf"; and after that the aged grandmother came out alive also, but scarcely able to breathe. Little Red Riding Hood, however, quickly fetched great stones with which they filled the wolf's belly, and when he awoke, he wanted to run away, but the stones were so heavy that he collapsed at once, and fell dead.

Then all three were delighted. The huntsman drew off the wolf's skin and went home with it; the grandmother ate the cake and drank the wine which Little Red Riding Hood had brought, and revived, but Little Red Riding Hood thought to herself: "As long as I live, I will never by myself leave the path, to run into the wood, when my mother has forbidden me to do so."

It is also related that once when Little Red Riding Hood was again taking cakes to the old grandmother, another wolf spoke to her, and tried to entice her from the path. Little Red Riding Hood, however, was on her guard, and went straight forward on her way, and told her grandmother that she had met the wolf, and that he had said "good morning" to her, but with such a wicked look in his eyes, that if they had not been on the public road she was certain he would have eaten her up. "Well," said the grandmother, "we will shut the door, that he may not come in." Soon afterwards the wolf knocked, and cried: "Open the door, grandmother, I am Little Red Riding Hood, and am bringing you some cakes." But they did not speak, or open the door, so the grey-beard stole twice or thrice round the house, and at last jumped on the roof, intending to wait until Little Red Riding Hood went home in the evening, and then to steal after her and devour her in the darkness. But the grandmother saw what was in his thoughts. In front of the house was a great stone trough, so she said to the child: "Take the pail, Little Red Riding Hood; I made some sausages yesterday, so carry the water in which I boiled them to the trough." Little Red Riding Hood carried until the great trough was quite full. Then the smell of the sausages reached the wolf, and he sniffed and peeped down, and at last stretched out his neck so far that he could no longer keep his footing and began to slip, and slipped down from the roof straight into the great trough, and was drowned. But Little Red Riding Hood went joyously home, and no one ever did anything to harm her again.

The Robber Bridegroom

There was once a miller who had one beautiful daughter, and as she was grown up, he was anxious that she should be well married and provided for. He said to himself, "I will give her to the first suitable man who comes and asks for her hand." Not long after a suitor appeared, and as he appeared to be very rich and the miller could see nothing in him with which to find fault, he betrothed his daughter to him. But the girl did not care for the man as a girl ought to care for her betrothed husband. She did not feel that she could trust him, and she could not look at him nor think of him without an inward shudder. One day he said to her, "You have not yet paid me a visit, although we have been betrothed for some time."

"I do not know where your house is," she answered.

"My house is out there in the dark forest," he said. She tried to excuse herself by saying that she would not be able to find the way thither.

Her betrothed only replied, "You must come and see me next Sunday; I have already invited guests for that day, and that you may not mistake the way, I will strew ashes along the path."

When Sunday came, and it was time for the girl to start, a feeling of dread came over her which she could not explain, and that she might be able to find her path again, she filled her pockets with peas and lentils to sprinkle on the ground as she went along. On reaching the entrance to the forest she found the path strewed with ashes, and these she followed, throwing down some peas on either side of her at every step she took. She walked the whole day until she came to the deepest, darkest part of the forest. There she saw a lonely house, looking so grim and mysterious, that it did not please her at all. She stepped inside, but not a soul was to be seen, and a great silence reigned throughout. Suddenly a voice cried:

"Turn back, turn back, young maiden fair,
Linger not in this murderers' lair."

The girl looked up and saw that the voice came from a bird hanging in a cage on the wall. Again it cried:

"Turn back, turn back, young maiden fair,
Linger not in this murderers' lair."

The girl passed on, going from room to room of the house, but they were all empty, and still she saw no one. At last she came to the cellar, and there sat a very, very old woman, who could not keep her head from shaking. "Can you tell me," asked the girl, "if my betrothed husband lives here?"

"Ah, you poor child," answered the old woman, "what a place for you to come to! This is a murderers' den. You think yourself a promised bride, and that your marriage will soon take place, but it is with death that you will keep your marriage feast. Look, do you see that large cauldron of water which I am obliged to keep on the fire! As soon as they have you in their power they will kill you without mercy, and cook and eat you, for they are eaters of men. If I did not take pity on you and save you, you would be lost."

THE
ROBBER
BRIDEGROOM

"TURN BACK, TURN BACK, THOU PRETTY BRIDE,
WITHIN THIS HOUSE THOU MUST NOT BIDE,
FOR HERE DO EVIL THINGS BETIDE."

Thereupon the old woman led her behind a large cask, which quite hid her from view. "Keep as still as a mouse," she said; "do not move or speak, or it will be all over with you. Tonight, when the robbers are all asleep, we will flee together. I have long been waiting for an opportunity to escape."

The words were hardly out of her mouth when the godless crew returned, dragging another young girl along with them. They were all drunk, and paid no heed to her cries and lamentations. They gave her wine to drink, three glasses full, one of white wine, one of red, and one of yellow, and with that her heart gave way and she died. Then they tore off her dainty clothing, laid her on a table, and cut her beautiful body into pieces, and sprinkled salt upon it.

The poor betrothed girl crouched trembling and shuddering behind the cask, for she saw what a terrible fate had been intended for her by the robbers. One of them now noticed a gold ring still remaining on the little finger of the murdered girl, and as he could not draw it off easily, he took a hatchet and cut off the finger; but the finger sprang into the air, and fell behind the cask into the lap of the girl who was hiding there. The robber took a light and began looking for it, but he could not find it. "Have you looked behind the large cask?" said one of the others. But the old woman called out, "Come and eat your suppers, and let the thing be till tomorrow; the finger won't run away."

"The old woman is right," said the robbers, and they ceased looking for the finger and sat down.

The old woman then mixed a sleeping draught with their wine, and before long they were all lying on the floor of the cellar, fast asleep and snoring. As soon as the girl was assured of this, she came from behind the cask. She was obliged to step over the bodies of the sleepers, who were lying close together, and every moment she was filled with renewed dread lest she should awaken them. But God helped her, so that she passed safely over them, and then she and the old woman went upstairs, opened the door, and hastened as fast as they could from the murderers' den. They found the ashes scattered by the wind, but the peas and lentils had sprouted, and grown sufficiently above the ground, to guide them in the moonlight along the path. All night long they walked, and it was morning before they reached the mill. Then the girl told her father all that had happened.

The day came that had been fixed for the marriage. The bridegroom arrived and also a large company of guests, for the miller had taken care to invite all his friends and relations. As they sat at the feast, each guest in turn was asked to tell a tale; the bride sat still and did not say a word.

"And you, my love," said the bridegroom, turning to her, "is there no tale you know? Tell us something."

"I will tell you a dream, then," said the bride. "I went alone through a forest and came at last to a house; not a soul could I find within, but a bird that was hanging in a cage on the wall cried:

"Turn back, turn back, young maiden fair,
Linger not in this murderers' lair."

And again a second time it said these words: "My darling, this is only a dream."

"I went on through the house from room to room, but they were all empty, and everything was so grim and mysterious. At last I went down to the cellar, and there sat a very, very old woman, who could not keep her head still. I asked her if my betrothed lived here, and she answered, 'Ah, you poor child, you are come to a murderers' den; your betrothed does indeed live here, but he will kill you without mercy and afterwards cook and eat you.'"

"My darling, this is only a dream."

"The old woman hid me behind a large cask, and scarcely had she done this when the robbers returned home, dragging a young girl along with them. They gave her three kinds of wine to drink, white, red, and yellow, and with that she died."

"My darling, this is only a dream."

"Then they tore off her dainty clothing, and cut her beautiful body into pieces and sprinkled salt upon it."

"My darling, this is only a dream."

"And one of the robbers saw that there was a gold ring still left on her finger, and as it was difficult to draw off, he took a hatchet and cut off her finger; but the finger sprang into the air and fell behind the great cask into my lap. And here is the finger with the ring." And with these words the bride drew forth the finger and shewed it to the assembled guests.

The bridegroom, who during this recital had grown deadly pale, up and tried to escape, but the guests seized him and held him fast. They delivered him up to justice, and he and all his murderous band were condemned to death for their wicked deeds.

Tom Thumb

A poor woodman sat in his cottage one night, smoking his pipe by the fireside, while his wife sat by his side spinning. "How lonely it is, wife," said he, as he puffed out a long curl of smoke, "for you and me to sit here by ourselves, without any children to play about and amuse us while other people seem so happy and merry with their children!"

"What you say is very true," said the wife, sighing, and turning round her wheel; "how happy should I be if I had but one child! If it were ever so small—nay, if it were no bigger than my thumb—I should be very happy, and love it dearly." Now—odd as you may think it—it came to pass that this good woman's wish was fulfilled, just in the very way she had wished it; for, not long afterwards, she had a little boy, who was quite healthy and strong, but was not much bigger than her thumb. So they said, "Well, we cannot say we have not got what we wished for, and, little as he is, we will love him dearly." And they called him Thomas Thumb.

They gave him plenty of food, yet for all they could do he never grew bigger, but kept just the same size as he had been when he was born. Still, his eyes were sharp and sparkling, and he soon showed himself to be a clever little fellow, who always knew well what he was about.

One day, as the woodman was getting ready to go into the wood to cut fuel, he said, "I wish I had someone to bring the cart after me, for I want to make haste."

"Oh, father," cried Tom, "I will take care of that; the cart shall be in the wood by the time you want it."

Then the woodman laughed, and said, "How can that be? you cannot reach up to the horse's bridle."

"Never mind that, father," said Tom; "if my mother will only harness the horse, I will get into his ear and tell him which way to go."

"Well," said the father, "we will try for once."

When the time came the mother harnessed the horse to the cart, and put Tom into his ear; and as he sat there the little man told the beast how to go, crying out, "Go on!" and "Stop!" as he wanted: and thus the horse went on just as well as if the woodman had driven it himself into the wood. It happened that as the horse was going a little too fast, and Tom was calling out, "Gently! gently!" two strangers came up.

"What an odd thing that is!" said one: "there is a cart going along, and I hear a carter talking to the horse, but yet I can see no one."

"That is queer, indeed," said the other; "let us follow the cart, and see where it goes." So they went on into the wood, till at last they came to the place where the woodman was.

Then Tom Thumb, seeing his father, cried out, "See, father, here I am with the cart, all right and safe! now take me down!" So his father took hold of the horse with one hand, and with the other took his son out of the horse's ear, and put him down upon a straw, where he sat as merry as you please.

The two strangers were all this time looking on, and did not know what to say for wonder. At last one took the other aside, and said, "That little urchin will make our fortune, if we can get him, and carry him about from town to town as a show; we must buy him." So they went up to the woodman, and asked him what he would take for the little man.

"He will be better off," said they, "with us than with you." "I won't sell him at all," said the father; "my own flesh and blood is dearer to me than all the silver and gold in the world." But Tom, hearing of the bargain they wanted to make, crept up his father's coat to his shoulder and whispered in his ear, "Take the money, father, and let them have me; I'll soon come back to you."

So the woodman at last said he would sell Tom to the strangers for a large piece of gold, and they paid the price. "Where would you like to sit?" said one of them.

"Oh, put me on the rim of your hat; that will be a nice gallery for me; I can walk about there and see the country as we go along." So they did as he wished; and when Tom had taken leave of his father they took him away with them.

They journeyed on till it began to be dusky, and then the little man said, "Let me get down, I'm tired." So the man took off his hat, and put him down on a clod of earth, in a ploughed field by the side of the road. But Tom ran about amongst the furrows, and at last slipped into an old mouse hole. "Good night, my masters!" said he, "I'm off! mind and look sharp after me the next time." Then they ran at once to the place, and poked the ends of their sticks into the mouse hole, but all in vain; Tom only crawled farther and farther in; and at last it became quite dark, so that they were forced to go their way without their prize, as sulky as could be.

When Tom found they were gone, he came out of his hiding place. "What dangerous walking it is," said he, "in this ploughed field! If I were to fall from one of these great clods, I should undoubtedly break my neck." At last, by good luck, he found a large empty snail shell. "This is lucky," said he, "I can sleep here very well"; and in he crept.

Just as he was falling asleep, he heard two men passing by, chatting together; and one said to the other, "How can we rob that rich parson's house of his silver and gold?"

"I'll tell you!" cried Tom.

"What noise was that?" said the thief, frightened; "I'm sure I heard someone speak."

They stood still listening, and Tom said, "Take me with you, and I'll soon show you how to get the parson's money."

"But where are you?" said they.

"Look about on the ground," answered he, "and listen where the sound comes from."

At last the thieves found him out, and lifted him up in their hands. "You little urchin!" they said, "what can you do for us?"

"Why, I can get between the iron window bars of the parson's house, and throw you out whatever you want."

"That's a good thought," said the thieves; "come along, we shall see what you can do."

When they came to the parson's house, Tom slipped through the window bars into the room, and then called out as loud as he could bawl, "Will you have all that is here?"

At this the thieves were frightened, and said, "Softly, softly! Speak low, that you may not awaken anybody."

But Tom seemed as if he did not understand them, and bawled out again, "How much will you have? Shall I throw it all out?"

Now the cook lay in the next room; and hearing a noise she raised herself up in her bed and listened. Meantime the thieves were frightened, and ran off a little way; but at last they plucked up their hearts, and said, "The little urchin is only trying to make fools of us." So they came back and whispered softly to him, saying, "Now let us have no more of your roguish jokes; but throw us out some of the money."

Then Tom called out as loud as he could, "Very well! hold your hands! here it comes."

The cook heard this quite plain, so she sprang out of bed, and ran to open the door. The thieves ran off as if a wolf was at their tails: and the maid, having groped about and found nothing, went away for a light. By the time she came back, Tom had slipped off into the barn; and when she had looked about and searched every hole and corner, and found nobody, she went to bed, thinking she must have been dreaming with her eyes open.

The little man crawled about in the hay loft, and at last found a snug place to finish his night's rest in; so he laid himself down, meaning to sleep till daylight, and then find his way home to his father and mother. But alas! how woefully he was undone! what crosses and sorrows happen to us all in this world! The cook got up early, before daybreak, to feed the cows; and going straight to the hay loft, carried away a large bundle of hay, with the little man in the middle of it, fast asleep. He still, however, slept on, and did not awake till he found himself in the mouth of the cow; for the cook had put the hay into the cow's rick, and the cow had taken Tom up in a mouthful of it.

"Good lack-a-day!" said he, "how came I to tumble into the mill?" But he soon found out where he really was, and was forced to have all his wits about him, that he might not get between the cow's teeth, and so be crushed to death. At last down he went into her stomach. "It is rather dark," said he; "they forgot to build windows in this room to let the sun in; a candle would be no bad thing."

Though he made the best of his bad luck, he did not like his quarters at all; and the worst of it was that more and more hay was always coming down, and the space left for him became smaller and smaller. At last he cried out as loud as he could, "Don't bring me any more hay! Don't bring me any more hay!"

The maid happened to be just then milking the cow; and hearing someone speak, but seeing nobody, and yet being quite sure it was the same voice that she had heard in the night, she was so frightened that she fell off her stool, and overset the milk pail. As soon as she could pick herself up out of the dirt, she ran off as fast as she could to her master the parson, and said, "Sir, sir, the cow is talking!" But the parson said, "Woman, thou art surely mad!" However, he went with her into the cow house, to try and see what was the matter.

Scarcely had they set foot on the threshold, when Tom called out, "Don't bring me any more hay!" Then the parson himself was frightened; and thinking the cow was surely bewitched, told his man to kill her on the spot. So the cow was killed, and cut up; and the stomach, in which Tom lay, was thrown out upon a dunghill.

Tom soon set himself to work to get out, which was not a very easy task; but at last, just as he had made room to get his head out, fresh ill luck befell him. A hungry wolf sprang out, and swallowed up the whole stomach, with Tom in it, at one gulp, and ran away.

Tom, however, was still not disheartened; and thinking the wolf would not dislike having some chat with him as he was going along, he called out, "My good friend, I can show you a famous treat."

"Where's that?" said the wolf.

"In such and such a house," said Tom, describing his own father's house. "You can crawl through the drain into the kitchen and then into the pantry, and there you will find cakes, ham, beef, cold chicken, roast pig, apple dumplings, and everything that your heart can wish."

The wolf did not want to be asked twice; so that very night he went to the house and crawled through the drain into the kitchen, and then into the pantry, and ate and drank there to his heart's content. As soon as he had had enough he wanted to get away; but he had eaten so much that he could not go out by the same way he came in.

This was just what Tom had reckoned upon; and now he began to set up a great shout, making all the noise he could. "Will you be easy?" said the wolf; "you'll awaken everybody in the house if you make such a clatter."

"What's that to me?" said the little man; "you have had your frolic, now I've a mind to be merry myself"; and he began, singing and shouting as loud as he could.

The woodman and his wife, being awakened by the noise, peeped through a crack in the door; but when they saw a wolf was there, you may well suppose that they were sadly frightened; and the woodman ran for his axe, and gave his wife a scythe. "Do you stay behind," said the woodman, "and when I have knocked him on the head you must rip him up with the scythe."

Tom heard all this, and cried out, "Father, father! I am here, the wolf has swallowed me."

And his father said, "Heaven be praised! we have found our dear child again"; and he told his wife not to use the scythe for fear she should hurt him. Then he aimed a great blow, and struck the wolf on the head, and killed him on the spot! And when he was dead they cut open his body, and set Tommy free.

"Ah!" said the father, "what fears we have had for you!"

"Yes, father," answered he; "I have travelled all over the world, I think, in one way or other, since we parted; and now I am very glad to come home and get fresh air again."

"Why, where have you been?" said his father. "I have been in a mouse hole, and in a snail shell, and down a cow's throat, and in the wolf's belly; and yet here I am again, safe and sound."

"Well," said they, "you are come back, and we will not sell you again for all the riches in the world."

Then they hugged and kissed their dear little son, and gave him plenty to eat and drink, for he was very hungry; and then they fetched new clothes for him, for his old ones had been quite spoiled on his journey. So Master Thumb stayed at home with his father and mother, in peace; for though he had been so great a traveller, and had done and seen so many fine things, and was fond enough of telling the whole story, he always agreed that, after all, there's no place like home!

Rumpelstiltskin

By the side of a wood, in a country a long way off, ran a fine stream of water; and upon the stream there stood a mill. The miller's house was close by, and the miller, you must know, had a very beautiful daughter. She was, moreover, very shrewd and clever; and the miller was so proud of her, that he one day told the king of the land, who used to come and hunt in the wood, that his daughter could spin gold out of straw. Now this king was very fond of money; and when he heard the miller's boast his greediness was raised, and he sent for the girl to be brought before him. Then he led her to a chamber in his palace where there was a great heap of straw, and gave her a spinning wheel, and said, "All this must be spun into gold before morning, as you love your life." It was in vain that the poor maiden said that it was only a silly boast of her father, for that she could do no such thing as spin straw into gold: the chamber door was locked, and she was left alone.

She sat down in one corner of the room, and began to bewail her hard fate; when on a sudden the door opened, and a droll-looking little man hobbled in, and said, "Good morrow to you, my good lass; what are you weeping for?"

"Alas!" said she, "I must spin this straw into gold, and I know not how."

"What will you give me," said the hobgoblin, "to do it for you?"

"My necklace," replied the maiden. He took her at her word, and sat himself down to the wheel, and whistled and sang:

"Round about, round about,
Lo and behold!
Reel away, reel away,
Straw into gold!"

And round about the wheel went merrily; the work was quickly done, and the straw was all spun into gold.

When the king came and saw this, he was greatly astonished and pleased; but his heart grew still more greedy of gain, and he shut up the poor miller's daughter again with a fresh task. Then she knew not what to do, and sat down once more to weep; but the dwarf soon opened the door, and said, "What will you give me to do your task?"

"The ring on my finger," said she. So her little friend took the ring, and began to work at the wheel again, and whistled and sang:

"Round about, round about,
Lo and behold!
Reel away, reel away,
Straw into gold!"

till, long before morning, all was done again.

The king was greatly delighted to see all this glittering treasure; but still he had not enough: so he took the miller's daughter to a yet larger heap, and said, "All this must be spun tonight; and if it is, you shall be my queen." As soon as she was alone that dwarf came in, and said, "What will you give me to spin gold for you this third time?"

"I have nothing left," said she.

"Then say you will give me," said the little man, "the first little child that you may have when you are queen."

"That may never be," thought the miller's daughter: and as she knew no other way to get her task done, she said she would do what he asked. Round went the wheel again to the old song, and the manikin once more spun the heap into gold. The king came in the morning, and, finding all he wanted, was forced to keep his word; so he married the miller's daughter, and she really became queen.

At the birth of her first little child she was very glad, and forgot the dwarf, and what she had said. But one day he came into her room, where she was sitting playing with her baby, and put her in mind of it. Then she grieved sorely at her misfortune, and said she would give him all the wealth of the kingdom if he would let her off, but in vain; till at last her tears softened him, and he said, "I will give you three days' grace, and if during that time you tell me my name, you shall keep your child."

Now the queen lay awake all night, thinking of all the odd names that she had ever heard; and she sent messengers all over the land to find out new ones. The next day the little man came, and she began with Timothy, Ichabod, Benjamin, Jeremiah, and all the names she could remember; but to all and each of them he said, "Madam, that is not my name."

The second day she began with all the comical names she could hear of, Bandy-Legs, Hatchback, Crookshanks, and so on; but the little gentleman still said to every one of them, "Madam, that is not my name."

The third day one of the messengers came back, and said, "I have travelled two days without hearing of any other names; but yesterday, as I was climbing a high hill, among the trees of the forest where the fox and the hare bid each other good night, I saw a little hut; and before the hut burnt a fire; and round about the fire a funny little dwarf was dancing upon one leg, and singing:

"Merrily the feast I'll make.
Today I'll brew, tomorrow bake;
Merrily I'll dance and sing,
For next day will a stranger bring.

Little does my lady dream
Rumpelstiltskin is my name!"

When the queen heard this she jumped for joy, and as soon as her little friend came she sat down upon her throne, and called all her court round to enjoy the fun; and the nurse stood by her side with the baby in her arms, as if it was quite ready to be given up. Then the little man began to chuckle at the thought of having the poor child, to take home with him to his hut in the woods; and he cried out, "Now, lady, what is my name?"

"Is it John?" asked she.

"No, madam!"

"Is it Tom?"

"No, madam!"

"Is it Jemmy?"

"It is not."

"Can your name be Rumpelstiltskin?" said the lady slyly.

"Some witch told you that! Some witch told you that!" cried the little man, and dashed his right foot in a rage so deep into the floor that he was forced to lay hold of it with both hands to pull it out.

Then he made the best of his way off, while the nurse laughed and the baby crowed; and all the court jeered at him for having had so much trouble for nothing, and said, "We wish you a very good morning, and a merry feast, Mr. Rumpelstiltskin!"

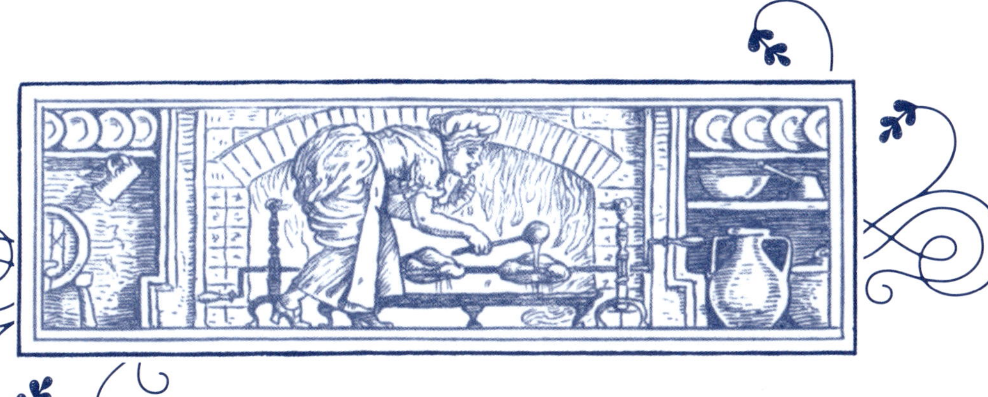

Clever Gretel

There was once a cook named Gretel, who wore shoes with red heels, and when she walked out with them on, she turned herself this way and that, was quite happy and thought: "You certainly are a pretty girl!" And when she came home she drank, in her gladness of heart, a draught of wine, and as wine excites a desire to eat, she tasted the best of whatever she was cooking until she was satisfied, and said: "The cook must know what the food is like."

It came to pass that the master one day said to her: "Gretel, there is a guest coming this evening; prepare me two fowls very daintily."

"I will see to it, master," answered Gretel. She killed two fowls, scalded them, plucked them, put them on the spit, and towards evening set them before the fire, that they might roast. The fowls began to turn brown, and were nearly ready, but the guest had not yet arrived. Then Gretel called out to her master: "If the guest does not come, I must take the fowls away from the fire, but it will be a sin and a shame if they are not eaten the moment they are at their juiciest."

The master said: "I will run myself, and fetch the guest." When the master had turned his back, Gretel laid the spit with the fowls on one side, and thought: "Standing so long by the fire there, makes one sweat and thirsty; who knows when they will come? Meanwhile, I will run into the cellar, and take a drink." She ran down, set a jug, said: "God bless it for you, Gretel," and took a good drink, and thought that wine should flow on, and should not be interrupted, and took yet another hearty draught.

Then she went and put the fowls down again to the fire, basted them, and drove the spit merrily round. But as the roast meat smelt so good, Gretel thought: "Something might be wrong, it ought to be tasted!" She touched it with her finger, and said: "Ah! how good fowls are! It certainly is a sin and a shame that they are not eaten at the right time!" She ran to the window, to see if the master was not coming with his guest, but she saw no one, and went back to the fowls and thought: "One of the wings is burning! I had better take it off and eat it." So she cut it off, ate it, and enjoyed it, and when she had done, she thought: "The other must go down too, or else master will observe that something is missing." When the two wings were eaten, she went and looked for her master, and did not see him. It suddenly occurred to her: "Who knows? They are perhaps not coming at all, and have turned in somewhere." Then she said: "Well, Gretel, enjoy yourself, one fowl has been cut into, take another drink, and eat it up entirely; when it is eaten you will have some peace, why should God's good gifts be spoilt?" So she ran into the cellar again, took an enormous drink and ate up the one chicken in great glee. When one of the chickens was swallowed down, and still her master did not come, Gretel looked at the other and said: "What one is, the other should be likewise, the two go together; what's right for the one is right for the other; I think if I were to take another draught it would do me no harm." So she took another hearty drink, and let the second chicken follow the first.

While she was making the most of it, her master came and cried: "Hurry up, Gretel, the guest is coming directly after me!"

"Yes, sir, I will soon serve up," answered Gretel. Meantime the master looked to see that the table was properly laid, and took the great knife, wherewith he was going to carve the chickens, and sharpened it on the steps. Presently the guest came, and knocked politely and courteously at the house door. Gretel ran, and looked to see who was there, and when she saw the guest, she put her finger to her lips and said: "Hush! hush! go away as quickly as you can, if my master catches you it will be the worse for you; he certainly did ask you to supper, but his intention is to cut off your two ears. Just listen how he is sharpening the knife for it!" The guest heard the sharpening, and hurried down the steps again as fast as he could. Gretel was not idle; she ran screaming to her master, and cried: "You have invited a fine guest!"

"Why, Gretel? What do you mean by that?"

"Yes," said she, "he has taken the chickens which I was just going to serve up, off the dish, and has run away with them!"

"That's a nice trick!" said her master, and lamented the fine chickens. "If he had but left me one, so that something remained for me to eat." He called to him to stop, but the guest pretended not to hear. Then he ran after him with the knife still in his hand, crying: "Just one, just one," meaning that the guest should leave him just one chicken, and not take both. The guest, however, thought no otherwise than that he was to give up one of his ears, and ran as if fire were burning under him, in order to take them both with him.

The Old Man and His Grandson

There was once a very old man, whose eyes had become dim, his ears dull of hearing, his knees trembled, and when he sat at table he could hardly hold the spoon, and spilt the broth upon the tablecloth or let it run out of his mouth. His son and his son's wife were disgusted at this, so the old grandfather at last had to sit in the corner behind the stove, and they gave him his food in an earthenware bowl, and not even enough of it. And he used to look towards the table with his eyes full of tears. Once, too, his trembling hands could not hold the bowl, and it fell to the ground and broke. The young wife scolded him, but he said nothing and only sighed. Then they brought him a wooden bowl for a few halfpence, out of which he had to eat.

They were once sitting thus when the little grandson of four years old began to gather together some bits of wood upon the ground. "What are you doing there?" asked the father.

"I am making a little trough," answered the child, "for father and mother to eat out of when I am big."

The man and his wife looked at each other for a while, and presently began to cry. Then they took the old grandfather to the table, and henceforth always let him eat with them, and likewise said nothing if he did spill a little of anything.

The Little Peasant

There was a certain village wherein no one lived but really rich peasants, and just one poor one, whom they called the little peasant. He had not even so much as a cow, and still less money to buy one, and yet he and his wife did so wish to have one. One day he said to her: "Listen, I have a good idea, there is our gossip the carpenter, he shall make us a wooden calf, and paint it brown, so that it looks like any other, and in time it will certainly get big and be a cow." The woman also liked the idea, and their gossip the carpenter cut and planed the calf, and painted it as it ought to be, and made it with its head hanging down as if it were eating.

Next morning when the cows were being driven out, the little peasant called the cowherd in and said: "Look, I have a little calf there, but it is still small and has to be carried."

The cowherd said: "All right," and took it in his arms and carried it to the pasture, and set it among the grass. The little calf always remained standing like one which was eating, and the cowherd said: "It will soon run by itself, just look how it eats already!" At night when he was going to drive the herd home again, he said to the calf: "If you can stand there and eat your fill, you can also go on your four legs; I don't care to drag you home again in my arms." But the little peasant stood at his door, and waited for his little calf, and when the cowherd drove the cows through the village, and the calf was missing, he inquired where it was. The cowherd answered: "It is still standing out there eating. It would not stop and come with us."

But the little peasant said: "Oh, but I must have my beast back again." Then they went back to the meadow together, but someone had stolen the calf, and it was gone.

The cowherd said: "It must have run away."

The peasant, however, said: "Don't tell me that," and led the cowherd before the mayor, who for his carelessness condemned him to give the peasant a cow for the calf which had run away.

And now the little peasant and his wife had the cow for which they had so long wished, and they were heartily glad, but they had no food for it, and could give it nothing to eat, so it soon had to be killed. They salted the flesh, and the peasant went into the town and wanted to sell the skin there, so that he might buy a new calf with the proceeds. On the way he passed by a mill, and there sat a raven with broken wings, and out of pity he took him and wrapped him in the skin. But as the weather grew so bad and there was a storm of rain and wind, he could go no farther, and turned back to the mill and begged for shelter. The miller's wife was alone in the house, and said to the peasant: "Lay yourself on the straw there," and gave him a slice of bread and cheese. The peasant ate it, and lay down with his skin beside him, and the woman thought: "He is tired and has gone to sleep." In the meantime came the parson; the miller's wife received him well, and said: "My husband is out, so we will have a feast." The peasant listened, and when he heard them talk about feasting he was vexed that he had been forced to make shift with a slice of bread and cheese. Then the woman served up four different things, roast meat, salad, cakes, and wine.

Just as they were about to sit down and eat, there was a knocking outside. The woman said: "Oh, heavens! It is my husband!" she quickly hid the roast meat inside the tiled stove, the wine under the pillow, the salad on the bed, the cakes under it, and the parson in the closet on the porch. Then she opened the door for her husband, and said: "Thank heaven, you are back again! There is such a storm, it looks as if the world were coming to an end."

The miller saw the peasant lying on the straw, and asked, "What is that fellow doing there?"

"Ah," said the wife, "the poor knave came in the storm and rain, and begged for shelter, so I gave him a bit of bread and cheese, and showed him where the straw was."

The man said: "I have no objection, but be quick and get me something to eat."

The woman said: "But I have nothing but bread and cheese."

"I am contented with anything," replied the husband, "so far as I am concerned, bread and cheese will do," and looked at the peasant and said: "Come and eat some more with me."

The peasant did not require to be invited twice, but got up and ate. After this the miller saw the skin in which the raven was, lying on the ground, and asked: "What have you there?" The peasant answered: "I have a soothsayer inside it."

"Can he foretell anything to me?" said the miller.

"Why not?" answered the peasant; "but he only says four things, and the fifth he keeps to himself."

The miller was curious, and said: "Let him foretell something for once." Then the peasant pinched the raven's head, so that he croaked and made a noise like krr, krr.

The miller said: "What did he say?"

The peasant answered: "In the first place, he says that there is some wine hidden under the pillow."

"Bless me!" cried the miller, and went there and found the wine. "Now go on," said he.

The peasant made the raven croak again, and said: "In the second place, he says that there is some roast meat in the tiled stove."

"Upon my word!" cried the miller, and went thither, and found the roast meat.

The peasant made the raven prophesy still more, and said: "Thirdly, he says that there is some salad on the bed."

"That would be a fine thing!" cried the miller, and went there and found the salad.

At last the peasant pinched the raven once more till he croaked, and said: "Fourthly, he says that there are some cakes under the bed."

"That would be a fine thing!" cried the miller, and looked there, and found the cakes.

And now the two sat down to the table together, but the miller's wife was frightened to death, and went to bed and took all the keys with her. The miller would have liked much to know the fifth, but the little peasant said: "First, we will quickly eat the four things, for the fifth is something bad." So they ate, and after that they bargained how much the miller was to give for the fifth prophecy, until they agreed on three hundred talers. Then the peasant once more pinched the raven's head till he croaked loudly.

The miller asked: "What did he say?"

The peasant replied: "He says that the Devil is hiding outside there in the closet on the porch."

The miller said: "The Devil must go out," and opened the house door; then the woman was forced to give up the keys, and the peasant unlocked the closet. The parson ran out as fast as he could, and the miller said: "It was true; I saw the black rascal with my own eyes." The peasant, however, made off next morning by daybreak with the three hundred talers.

At home the small peasant gradually launched out; he built a beautiful house, and the peasants said: "The small peasant has certainly been to the place where golden snow falls, and people carry the gold home in shovels." Then the small peasant was brought before the mayor, and bidden to say from whence his wealth came. He answered: "I sold my cow's skin in the town, for three hundred talers." When the peasants heard that, they too wished to enjoy this great profit, and ran home, killed all their cows, and stripped off their skins in order to sell them in the town to the greatest advantage. The mayor, however, said: "But my servant must go first." When she came to the merchant in the town, he did not give her more than two talers for a skin, and when the others came, he did not give them so much, and said: "What can I do with all these skins?"

Then the peasants were vexed that the small peasant should have thus outwitted them, wanted to take vengeance on him, and accused him of this treachery before the mayor. The innocent little peasant was unanimously sentenced to death, and was to be rolled into the water, in a barrel pierced full of holes. He was led forth, and a priest was brought who was to say a mass for his soul. The others were all obliged to retire to a distance, and when the peasant looked at the priest, he recognized the man who had been with the miller's wife. He said to him: "I set you free from the closet, set me free from the barrel." At this same moment up came, with a flock of sheep, the very shepherd whom the peasant knew had long been wishing to be mayor, so he cried with all his might: "No, I will not do it; if the whole world insists on it, I will not do it!"

The shepherd hearing that, came up to him, and asked: "What are you about? What is it that you will not do?"

The peasant said: "They want to make me mayor, if I will but put myself in the barrel, but I will not do it."

The shepherd said: "If nothing more than that is needful in order to be mayor, I would get into the barrel at once."

The peasant said: "If you will get in, you will be mayor." The shepherd was willing, and got in, and the peasant shut the top down on him; then he took the shepherd's flock for himself, and drove it away. The parson went to the crowd, and declared that the mass had been said. Then they came and rolled the barrel towards the water. When the barrel began to roll, the shepherd cried: "I am quite willing to be mayor." They believed no otherwise than that it was the peasant who was saying this, and answered: "That is what we intend, but first you shall look about you a little down below there," and they rolled the barrel down into the water.

After that the peasants went home, and as they were entering the village, the small peasant also came quietly in, driving a flock of sheep and looking quite contented. Then the peasants were astonished, and said: "Peasant, from whence do you come? Have you come out of the water?"

"Yes, truly," replied the peasant, "I sank deep, deep down, until at last I got to the bottom; I pushed the bottom out of the barrel, and crept out, and there were pretty meadows on which a number of lambs were feeding, and from thence I brought this flock away with me."

Said the peasants: "Are there any more there?"

"Oh, yes," said he, "more than I could want."

Then the peasants made up their minds that they too would fetch some sheep for themselves, a flock apiece, but the mayor said: "I come first." So they went to the water together, and just then there were some of the small fleecy clouds in the blue sky, which are called little lambs, and they were reflected in the water, whereupon the peasants cried: "We already see the sheep down below!"

The mayor pressed forward and said: "I will go down first, and look about me, and if things promise well I'll call you." So he jumped in; splash! went the water; it sounded as if he were calling them, and the whole crowd plunged in after him as one man. Then the entire village was dead, and the small peasant, as sole heir, became a rich man.

Frederick and Catherine

There was once a man called Frederick: he had a wife whose name was Catherine, and they had not long been married. One day Frederick said. "Kate! I am going to work in the fields; when I come back I shall be hungry so let me have something nice cooked, and a good draught of ale."

"Very well," said she, "it shall all be ready." When dinnertime drew nigh, Catherine took a nice steak, which was all the meat she had, and put it on the fire to fry. The steak soon began to look brown, and to crackle in the pan; and Catherine stood by with a fork and turned it: then she said to herself, "The steak is almost ready, I may as well go to the cellar for the ale." So she left the pan on the fire and took a large jug and went into the cellar and tapped the ale cask. The beer ran into the jug and Catherine stood looking on. At last it popped into her head, "The dog is not shut up—he may be running away with the steak; that's well thought of." So up she ran from the cellar; and sure enough the rascally cur had got the steak in his mouth, and was making off with it.

Away ran Catherine, and away ran the dog across the field: but he ran faster than she, and stuck close to the steak. "It's all gone, and what can't be cured must be endured," said Catherine. So she turned round; and as she had run a good way and was tired, she walked home leisurely to cool herself.

Now all this time the ale was running too, for Catherine had not turned the cock; and when the jug was full the liquor ran upon the floor till the cask was empty. When she got to the cellar stairs she saw what had happened. "My stars!" said she, "what shall I do to keep Frederick from seeing all this slopping about?" So she thought awhile; and at last remembered that there was a sack of fine meal bought at the last fair, and that if she sprinkled this over the floor it would suck up the ale nicely. "What a lucky thing," said she, "that we kept that meal! we have now a good use for it." So away she went for it: but she managed to set it down just upon the great jug full of beer, and upset it; and thus all the ale that had been saved was set swimming on the floor also. "Ah! well," said she, "when one goes another may as well follow." Then she strewed the meal all about the cellar, and was quite pleased with her cleverness, and said, "How very neat and clean it looks!"

At noon Frederick came home. "Now, wife," cried he, "what have you for dinner?" "O Frederick!" answered she, "I was cooking you a steak; but while I went down to draw the ale, the dog ran away with it; and while I ran after him, the ale ran out; and when I went to dry up the ale with the sack of meal that we got at the fair, I upset the jug: but the cellar is now quite dry, and looks so clean!"

"Kate, Kate," said he, "how could you do all this?" Why did you leave the steak to fry, and the ale to run, and then spoil all the meal?"

"Why, Frederick," said she, "I did not know I was doing wrong; you should have told me before."

The husband thought to himself, "If my wife manages matters thus, I must look sharp myself." Now he had a good deal of gold in the house: so he said to Catherine, "What pretty yellow buttons these are! I shall put them into a box and bury them in the garden; but take care that you never go near or meddle with them."

"No, Frederick," said she, "that I never will." As soon as he was gone, there came by some pedlars with earthenware plates and dishes, and they asked her whether she would buy. "Oh dear me, I should like to buy very much, but I have no money: if you had any use for yellow buttons, I might deal with you."

"Yellow buttons!" said they: "let us have a look at them."

"Go into the garden and dig where I tell you, and you will find the yellow buttons: I dare not go myself." So the rogues went: and when they found what these yellow buttons were, they took them all away, and left her plenty of plates and dishes. Then she set them all about the house for a show: and when Frederick came back, he cried out, "Kate, what have you been doing?"

"See," said she, "I have bought all these with your yellow buttons: but I did not touch them myself; the pedlars went themselves and dug them up."

"Wife, wife," said Frederick, "what a pretty piece of work you have made! those yellow buttons were all my money: how came you to do such a thing?"

"Why," answered she, "I did not know there was any harm in it; you should have told me."

Catherine stood musing for a while, and at last said to her husband, "Hark ye, Frederick, we will soon get the gold back: let us run after the thieves."

"Well, we will try," answered he; "but take some butter and cheese with you, that we may have something to eat by the way."

"Very well," said she; and they set out: and as Frederick walked the fastest, he left his wife some way behind. "It does not matter," thought she: "when we turn back, I shall be so much nearer home than he."

Presently she came to the top of a hill, down the side of which there was a road so narrow that the cart wheels always chafed the trees on each side as they passed. "Ah, see now," said she, "how they have bruised and wounded those poor trees; they will never get well." So she took pity on them, and made use of the butter to grease them all, so that the wheels might not hurt them so much. While she was doing this kind office one of her cheeses fell out of the basket, and rolled down the hill. Catherine looked, but could not see where it had gone; so she said, "Well, I suppose the other will go the same way and find you; he has younger legs than I have." Then she rolled the other cheese after it; and away it went, nobody knows where, down the hill. But she said she supposed that they knew the road, and would follow her, and she could not stay there all day waiting for them.

At last she overtook Frederick, who desired her to give him something to eat. Then she gave him the dry bread. "Where are the butter and cheese?" said he.

"Oh!" answered she, "I used the butter to grease those poor trees that the wheels chafed so: and one of the cheeses ran away so I sent the other after it to find it, and I suppose they are both on the road together somewhere."

"What a goose you are to do such silly things!" said the husband.

"How can you say so?" said she; "I am sure you never told me not."

They ate the dry bread together; and Frederick said, "Kate, I hope you locked the door safe when you came away."

"No," answered she, "you did not tell me."

"Then go home, and do it now before we go any farther," said Frederick, "and bring with you something to eat."

Catherine did as he told her, and thought to herself by the way, "Frederick wants something to eat; but I don't think he is very fond of butter and cheese: I'll bring him a bag of fine nuts, and the vinegar, for I have often seen him take some."

When she reached home, she bolted the back door, but the front door she took off the hinges, and said, "Frederick told me to lock the door, but surely it can nowhere be so safe if I take it with me." So she took her time by the way; and when she overtook her husband she cried out, "There, Frederick, there is the door itself, you may watch it as carefully as you please."

"Alas! alas!" said he, "what a clever wife I have! I sent you to make the house fast, and you take the door away, so that everybody may go in and out as they please—however, as you have brought the door, you shall carry it about with you for your pains."

"Very well," answered she, "I'll carry the door; but I'll not carry the nuts and vinegar bottle also—that would be too much of a load; so if you please, I'll fasten them to the door."

Frederick of course made no objection to that plan, and they set off into the wood to look for the thieves; but they could not find them: and when it grew dark, they climbed up into a tree to spend the night there. Scarcely were they up, than who should come by but the very rogues they were looking for. They were in truth great rascals, and belonged to that class of people who find things before they are lost; they were tired; so they sat down and made a fire under the very tree where Frederick and Catherine were. Frederick slipped down on the other side, and picked up some stones. Then he climbed up again, and tried to hit the thieves on the head with them: but they only said, "It must be near morning, for the wind shakes the fir apples down."

Catherine, who had the door on her shoulder, began to be very tired; but she thought it was the nuts upon it that were so heavy: so she said softly, "Frederick, I must let the nuts go."

"No," answered he, "not now, they will discover us."

"I can't help that: they must go."

"Well, then, make haste and throw them down, if you will." Then away rattled the nuts down among the boughs and one of the thieves cried, "Bless me, it is hailing."

A little while after, Catherine thought the door was still very heavy: so she whispered to Frederick, "I must throw the vinegar down."

"Pray don't," answered he, "it will discover us."

"I can't help that," said she, "go it must." So she poured all the vinegar down; and the thieves said, "What a heavy dew there is!"

At last it popped into Catherine's head that it was the door itself that was so heavy all the time: so she whispered, "Frederick, I must throw the door down soon." But he begged and prayed her not to do so, for he was sure it would betray them. "Here goes, however," said she: and down went the door with such a clatter upon the thieves, that they cried out "Murder!" and not knowing what was coming, ran away as fast as they could, and left all the gold. So when Frederick and Catherine came down, there they found all their money safe and sound.

Sweetheart Roland

There was once upon a time a woman who was a real witch and had two daughters, one ugly and wicked, and this one she loved because she was her own daughter, and one beautiful and good, and this one she hated, because she was her stepdaughter. The stepdaughter once had a pretty apron, which the other fancied so much that she became envious, and told her mother that she must and would have that apron. "Be quiet, my child," said the old woman, "and you shall have it. Your stepsister has long deserved death; tonight when she is asleep I will come and cut her head off. Only be careful that you are at the far side of the bed, and push her well to the front." It would have been all over with the poor girl if she had not just then been standing in a corner, and heard everything. All day long she dared not go out of doors, and when bedtime had come, the witch's daughter got into bed first, so as to lie at the far side, but when she was asleep, the other pushed her gently to the front, and took for herself the place at the back, close by the wall. In the night, the old woman came creeping in, she held an axe in her right hand, and felt with her left to see if anyone were lying at the outside, and then she grasped the axe with both hands, and cut her own child's head off.

When she had gone away, the girl got up and went to her sweetheart, who was called Roland, and knocked at his door. When he came out, she said to him: "Listen, dearest Roland, we must fly in all haste; my stepmother wanted to kill me, but has struck her own child. When daylight comes, and she sees what she has done, we shall be lost."

"But," said Roland, "I counsel you first to take away her magic wand, or we cannot escape if she pursues us." The maiden fetched the magic wand, and she took the dead girl's head and dropped three drops of blood on the ground, one in front of the bed, one in the kitchen, and one on the stairs. Then she hurried away with her lover.

When the old witch got up next morning, she called her daughter, and wanted to give her the apron, but she did not come. Then the witch cried: "Where are you?"

"Here, on the stairs, I am sweeping," answered the first drop of blood.

The old woman went out, but saw no one on the stairs, and cried again: "Where are you?"

"Here in the kitchen, I am warming myself," cried the second drop of blood. She went into the kitchen, but found no one. Then she cried again: "Where are you?"

"Ah, here in the bed, I am sleeping," cried the third drop of blood. She went into the room to the bed. What did she see there? Her own child, whose head she had cut off, bathed in her blood. The witch fell into a passion, sprang to the window, and as she could look forth quite far into the world, she perceived her stepdaughter hurrying away with her sweetheart Roland. "That shall not help you," cried she, "even if you have got a long way off, you shall still not escape me." She put on her many-league boots, in which she covered an hour's walk at every step, and it was not long before she overtook them. The girl, however, when she saw the old woman striding towards her, changed, with her magic wand, her sweetheart Roland into a lake, and herself into a duck swimming in the middle of it. The witch placed herself on the shore, threw breadcrumbs in, and went to endless trouble to entice the duck; but the duck did not let herself be enticed, and the old woman had to go home at night as she had come. At this the girl and her sweetheart Roland resumed their natural shapes again, and they walked on the whole night until daybreak. Then the maiden changed herself into a beautiful flower which stood in the midst of a briar hedge, and her sweetheart Roland into a fiddler. It was not long before the witch came striding up towards them, and said to the musician: "Dear musician, may I pluck that beautiful flower for myself?"

"Oh, yes," he replied, "I will play to you while you do it." As she was hastily creeping into the hedge and was just going to pluck the flower, knowing perfectly well who the flower was, he began to play, and whether she would or not, she was forced to dance, for it was a magical dance. The faster he played, the more violent springs was she forced to make, and the thorns tore her clothes from her body, and pricked her and wounded her till she bled, and as he did not stop, she had to dance till she lay dead on the ground.

As they were now set free, Roland said: "Now I will go to my father and arrange for the wedding."

"Then in the meantime I will stay here and wait for you," said the girl, "and that no one may recognize me, I will change myself into a red stone landmark."

Then Roland went away, and the girl stood like a red landmark in the field and waited for her beloved. But when Roland got home, he fell into the snares of another, who so fascinated him that he forgot the maiden. The poor girl remained there a long time, but at length, as he did not return at all, she was sad, and changed herself into a flower, and thought: "Someone will surely come this way, and trample me down."

It befell, however, that a shepherd kept his sheep in the field and saw the flower, and as it was so pretty, plucked it, took it with him, and laid it away in his chest. From that time forth, strange things happened in the shepherd's house. When he arose in the morning, all the work was already done, the room was swept, the table and benches cleaned, the fire in the hearth was lighted, and the water was fetched, and at noon, when he came home, the table was laid, and a good dinner served. He could not conceive how this came to pass, for he never saw a human being in his house, and no one could have concealed himself in it. He was certainly pleased with this good attendance, but still at last he was so afraid that he went to a wise woman and asked for her advice. The wise woman said: "There is some enchantment behind it, listen very early some morning if anything is moving in the room, and if you see anything, no matter what it is, throw a white cloth over it, and then the magic will be stopped."

The shepherd did as she bade him, and next morning just as day dawned, he saw the chest open, and the flower come out. Swiftly he sprang towards it, and threw a white cloth over it. Instantly the transformation came to an end, and a beautiful girl stood before him, who admitted to him that she had been the flower, and that up to this time she had attended to his housekeeping. She told him her story, and as she pleased him he asked her if she would marry him, but she answered: "No," for she wanted to remain faithful to her sweetheart Roland, although he had deserted her. Nevertheless, she promised not to go away, but to continue keeping house for the shepherd.

And now the time drew near when Roland's wedding was to be celebrated, and then, according to an old custom in the country, it was announced that all the girls were to be present at it, and sing in honour of the bridal pair. When the faithful maiden heard of this, she grew so sad that she thought her heart would break, and she would not go thither, but the other girls came and took her. When it came to her turn to sing, she stepped back, until at last she was the only one left, and then she could not refuse. But when she began her song, and it reached Roland's ears, he sprang up and cried: "I know the voice, that is the true bride, I will have no other!" Everything he had forgotten, and which had vanished from his mind, had suddenly come home again to his heart. Then the faithful maiden held her wedding with her sweetheart Roland, and grief came to an end and joy began.

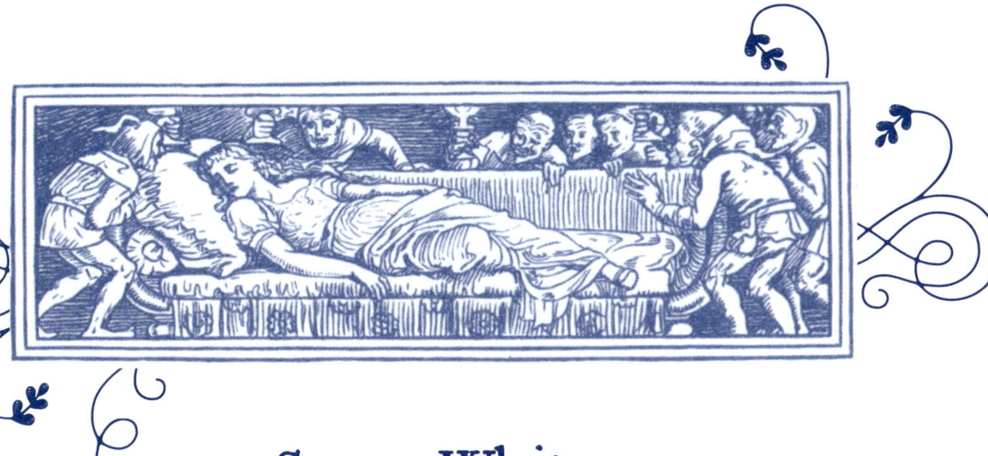

Snow White

It was the middle of winter, when the broad flakes of snow were falling around, that the queen of a country many thousand miles off sat working at her window. The frame of the window was made of fine black ebony, and as she sat looking out upon the snow, she pricked her finger, and three drops of blood fell upon it. Then she gazed thoughtfully upon the red drops that sprinkled the white snow, and said, "Would that my little daughter may be as white as that snow, as red as that blood, and as black as this ebony window frame!" And so the little girl really did grow up; her skin was as white as snow, her cheeks as rosy as the blood, and her hair as black as ebony; and she was called Snow White.

But this queen died; and the king soon married another wife, who became queen, and was very beautiful, but so vain that she could not bear to think that anyone could be handsomer than she was. She had a fairy looking glass, to which she used to go, and then she would gaze upon herself in it, and say:

"Tell me, glass, tell me true!

Of all the ladies in the land,
Who is fairest, tell me, who?"

And the glass had always answered:

"Thou, queen, art the fairest in all the land."

But Snow White grew more and more beautiful; and when she was seven years old she was as bright as the day, and fairer than the queen herself. Then the glass one day answered the queen, when she went to look in it as usual:

"Thou, queen, art fair, and beauteous to see,
But Snow White is lovelier far than thee!"

When she heard this she turned pale with rage and envy, and called to one of her servants, and said, "Take Snow White away into the wide wood, that I may never see her any more."

Then the servant led her away; but his heart melted when Snow White begged him to spare her life, and he said, "I will not hurt you, thou pretty child." So he left her by herself; and though he thought it most likely that the wild beasts would tear her in pieces, he felt as if a great weight were taken off his heart when he had made up his mind not to kill her but to leave her to her fate, with the chance of someone finding and saving her.

Then poor Snow White wandered along through the wood in great fear; and the wild beasts roared about her, but none did her any harm. In the evening she came to a cottage among the hills, and went in to rest, for her little feet would carry her no further. Everything was spruce and neat in the cottage: on the table was spread a white cloth, and there were seven little plates, seven little loaves, and seven little glasses with wine in them; and seven knives and forks laid in order; and by the wall stood seven little beds. As she was very hungry, she picked a little piece of each loaf and drank a very little wine out of each glass; and after that she thought she would lie down and rest. So she tried all the little beds; but one was too long, and another was too short, till at last the seventh suited her: and there she laid herself down and went to sleep.

By and by in came the masters of the cottage. Now they were seven little dwarfs, that lived among the mountains, and dug and searched for gold. They lighted up their seven lamps, and saw at once that all was not right. The first said, "Who has been sitting on my stool?"

The second, "Who has been eating off my plate?"

The third, "Who has been picking my bread?"

The fourth, "Who has been meddling with my spoon?"

The fifth, "Who has been handling my fork?"

The sixth, "Who has been cutting with my knife?"

The seventh, "Who has been drinking my wine?"

Then the first looked round and said, "Who has been lying on my bed?" And the rest came running to him, and everyone cried out that somebody had been upon his bed. But the seventh saw Snow White, and called all his brethren to come and see her; and they cried out with wonder and astonishment and brought their lamps to look at her, and said, "Good heavens! what a lovely child she is!" And they were very glad to see her, and took care not to wake her; and the seventh dwarf slept an hour with each of the other dwarfs in turn, till the night was gone.

In the morning Snow White told them all her story; and they pitied her, and said if she would keep all things in order, and cook and wash and knit and spin for them, she might stay where she was, and they would take good care of her. Then they went out all day long to their work, seeking for gold and silver in the mountains: but Snow White was left at home; and they warned her, and said, "The queen will soon find out where you are, so take care and let no one in."

But the queen, now that she thought Snow White was dead, believed that she must be the handsomest lady in the land; and she went to her glass and said:

"Tell me, glass, tell me true!
Of all the ladies in the land,
Who is fairest, tell me, who?"

And the glass answered:

"Thou, queen, art the fairest in all this land:
But over the hills, in the greenwood shade,
Where the seven dwarfs their dwelling have made,
There Snow White is hiding her head; and she
Is lovelier far, O queen! than thee."

Then the queen was very much frightened; for she knew that the glass always spoke the truth, and was sure that the servant had betrayed her. And she could not bear to think that anyone lived who was more beautiful than she was; so she dressed herself up as an old pedlar, and went her way over the hills, to the place where the dwarfs dwelt. Then she knocked at the door, and cried, "Fine wares to sell!"

Snow White looked out at the window, and said, "Good day, good woman! what have you to sell?"

"Good wares, fine wares," said she; "laces and bobbins of all colours."

"I will let the old lady in; she seems to be a very good sort of body," thought Snow White, as she ran down and unbolted the door.

"Bless me!" said the old woman, "how badly your stays are laced! Let me lace them up with one of my nice new laces."

Snow White did not dream of any mischief; so she stood before the old woman; but she set to work so nimbly, and pulled the lace so tight, that Snow White's breath was stopped, and she fell down as if she were dead.

"There's an end to all thy beauty," said the spiteful queen, and went away home.

In the evening the seven dwarfs came home; and I need not say how grieved they were to see their faithful Snow White stretched out upon the ground, as if she was quite dead. However, they lifted her up, and when they found what ailed her, they cut the lace; and in a little time she began to breathe, and very soon came to life again. Then they said, "The old woman was the queen herself; take care another time, and let no one in when we are away."

When the queen got home, she went straight to her glass, and spoke to it as before; but to her great grief it still said:

"Thou, queen, art the fairest in all this land:
But over the hills, in the greenwood shade,
Where the seven dwarfs their dwelling have made,
There Snow White is hiding her head; and she
Is lovelier far, O queen! than thee."

Then the blood ran cold in her heart with spite and malice, to see that Snow White still lived; and she dressed herself up again, but in quite another dress from the one she wore before, and took with her a poisoned comb. When she reached the dwarfs' cottage, she knocked at the door, and cried, "Fine wares to sell!"

But Snow White said, "I dare not let anyone in."

Then the queen said, "Only look at my beautiful combs!" and gave her the poisoned one. And it looked so pretty, that she took it up and put it into her hair to try it; but the moment it touched her head, the poison was so powerful that she fell down senseless. "There you may lie," said the queen, and went her way. But by good luck the dwarfs came in very early that evening; and when they saw Snow White lying on the ground, they thought what had happened, and soon found the poisoned comb. And when they took it away she got well, and told them all that had passed; and they warned her once more not to open the door to anyone.

Meantime the queen went home to her glass, and shook with rage when she read the very same answer as before; and she said, "Snow White shall die, if it cost me my life." So she went by herself into her chamber, and got ready a poisoned apple: the outside looked very rosy and tempting,

SNOW-WHITE
"QUEEN THOU ART OF BEAUTY RARE,
BUT SNOW-WHITE LIVING IN THE GLEN,
WITH THE SEVEN LITTLE MEN,
IS A THOUSAND TIMES MORE FAIR."
SWAIN SC

but whoever tasted it was sure to die. Then she dressed herself up as a peasant's wife, and travelled over the hills to the dwarfs' cottage, and knocked at the door; but Snow White put her head out of the window and said, "I dare not let anyone in, for the dwarfs have told me not."

"Do as you please," said the old woman, "but at any rate take this pretty apple; I will give it you."

"No," said Snow White, "I dare not take it."

"You silly girl!" answered the other, "what are you afraid of? Do you think it is poisoned? Come! do you eat one part, and I will eat the other."

Now the apple was so made up that one side was good, though the other side was poisoned. Then Snow White was much tempted to taste, for the apple looked so very nice; and when she saw the old woman eat, she could wait no longer. But she had scarcely put the piece into her mouth, when she fell down dead upon the ground. "This time nothing will save thee," said the queen; and she went home to her glass, and at last it said:

"Thou, queen, art the fairest of all the fair."

And then her wicked heart was glad, and as happy as such a heart could be.

When evening came, and the dwarfs had gone home, they found Snow White lying on the ground: no breath came from her lips, and they were afraid that she was quite dead. They lifted her up, and combed her hair, and washed her face with wine and water; but all was in vain, for the little girl seemed quite dead. So they laid her down upon a bier, and all seven watched and bewailed her three whole days; and then they thought they would bury her: but her cheeks were still rosy; and her face looked just as it did while she was alive; so they said, "We will never bury her in the cold ground." And they made a coffin of glass, so that they might still look at her, and wrote upon it in golden letters what her name was, and that she was a king's daughter. And the coffin was set among the hills, and one of the dwarfs always sat by it and watched. And the birds of the air came too, and bemoaned Snow White; and first of all came an owl, and then a raven, and at last a dove, and sat by her side.

And thus Snow White lay for a long, long time, and still only looked as though she was asleep; for she was even now as white as snow, and as red as blood, and as black as ebony. At last a prince came and called at the dwarfs' house; and he saw Snow White, and read what was written in golden letters. Then he offered the dwarfs money, and prayed and besought them to let him take her away; but they said, "We will not part with her for all the gold in the world."

At last, however, they had pity on him, and gave him the coffin; but the moment he lifted it up to carry it home with him, the piece of apple fell from between her lips, and Snow White awoke, and said, "Where am I?" And the prince said, "Thou art quite safe with me."

Then he told her all that had happened, and said, "I love you far better than all the world; so come with me to my father's palace, and you shall be my wife." And Snow White consented, and went home with the prince; and everything was got ready with great pomp and splendour for their wedding.

To the feast was asked, among the rest, Snow White's old enemy the queen; and as she was dressing herself in fine rich clothes, she looked in the glass and said:

"Tell me, glass, tell me true!
Of all the ladies in the land,
Who is fairest, tell me, who?"

And the glass answered:

"Thou, lady, art loveliest here, I ween;
But lovelier far is the new-made queen."

When she heard this she started with rage; but her envy and curiosity were so great, that she could not help setting out to see the bride. And when she got there, and saw that it was no other than Snow White, who, as she thought, had been dead a long while, she choked with rage, and fell down and died: but Snow White and the prince lived and reigned happily over that land many, many years; and sometimes they went up into the mountains, and paid a visit to the little dwarfs, who had been so kind to Snow White in her time of need.

The Pink

There was once upon a time a queen to whom God had given no children. Every morning she went into the garden and prayed to God in heaven to bestow on her a son or a daughter. Then an angel from heaven came to her and said: "Be at rest, you shall have a son with the power of wishing, so that whatsoever in the world he wishes for, that shall he have." Then she went to the king, and told him the joyful tidings, and when the time was come she gave birth to a son, and the king was filled with gladness.

Every morning she went with the child to the garden where the wild beasts were kept, and washed herself there in a clear stream. It happened once when the child was a little older, that it was lying in her arms and she fell asleep. Then came the old cook, who knew that the child had the power of wishing, and stole it away, and he took a hen, and cut it in pieces, and dropped some of its blood on the queen's apron and on her dress. Then he carried the child away to a secret place, where a nurse was obliged to suckle it, and he ran to the king and accused the queen of having allowed her child to be taken from her by the wild beasts. When the king saw the blood on her apron, he believed this, and fell into such a passion that he ordered a high tower to be built, in which neither sun nor moon could be seen and had his wife put into it, and walled up. Here she was to stay for seven years without meat or drink, and die of hunger. But

God sent two angels from heaven in the shape of white doves, which flew to her twice a day, and carried her food until the seven years were over.

The cook, however, thought to himself: "If the child has the power of wishing, and I am here, he might very easily get me into trouble." So he left the palace and went to the boy, who was already big enough to speak, and said to him: "Wish for a beautiful palace for yourself with a garden, and all else that pertains to it." Scarcely were the words out of the boy's mouth, when everything was there that he had wished for.

After a while the cook said to him: "It is not well for you to be so alone, wish for a pretty girl as a companion." Then the king's son wished for one, and she immediately stood before him, and was more beautiful than any painter could have painted her. The two played together, and loved each other with all their hearts, and the old cook went out hunting like a nobleman. The thought occurred to him, however, that the king's son might some day wish to be with his father, and thus bring him into great peril. So he went out and took the maiden aside, and said: "Tonight when the boy is asleep, go to his bed and plunge this knife into his heart, and bring me his heart and tongue, and if you do not do it, you shall lose your life."

Thereupon he went away, and when he returned next day she had not done it, and said: "Why should I shed the blood of an innocent boy who has never harmed anyone?"

The cook once more said: "If you do not do it, it shall cost you your own life." When he had gone away, she had a little hind brought to her, and ordered her to be killed, and took her heart and tongue, and laid them on a plate, and when she saw the old man coming, she said to the boy: "Lie down in your bed, and draw the clothes over you."

Then the wicked wretch came in and said: "Where are the boy's heart and tongue?" The girl reached the plate to him, but the king's son threw off the quilt, and said: "You old sinner, why did you want to kill me? Now will I pronounce thy sentence. You shall become a black poodle and have a gold collar round your neck, and shall eat burning coals, till the flames burst forth from your throat."

And when he had spoken these words, the old man was changed into a poodle dog, and had a gold collar round his neck, and the cooks were ordered to bring up some live coals, and these he ate, until the flames broke forth from his throat. The king's son remained there a short while longer, and he thought of his mother, and wondered if she were still alive. At length he said to the maiden: "I will go home to my own country; if you will go with me, I will provide for you."

"Ah," she replied, "the way is so long, and what shall I do in a strange land where I am unknown?" As she did not seem quite willing, and as they could not be parted from each other, he wished that she might be changed into a beautiful pink, and took her with him. Then he went away to his own country, and the poodle had to run after him. He went to the tower in which his mother was confined, and as it was so high, he wished for a ladder which would reach up to the very top. Then he mounted up and looked inside, and cried: "Beloved mother, Lady Queen, are you still alive, or are you dead?"

She answered: "I have just eaten, and am still satisfied," for she thought the angels were there.

Said he: "I am your dear son, whom the wild beasts were said to have torn from your arms; but I am alive still, and will soon set you free." Then he descended again, and went to his father, and caused himself to be announced as a strange huntsman, and asked if he could offer him service. The king said yes, if he was skillful and could get game for him, he should come to him, but that deer had never taken up their quarters in any part of the district or country. Then the huntsman promised to procure as much game for him as he could possibly use at the royal table. So he summoned all the huntsmen together, and bade them go out into the forest with him. And he went with them and made them form a great circle, open at one end where he stationed himself, and began to wish. Two hundred deer and more came running inside the circle at once, and the huntsmen shot them. Then they were all placed on sixty country carts, and driven home to the king, and for once he was able to deck his table with game, after having had none at all for years.

Now the king felt great joy at this, and commanded that his entire household should eat with him next day, and made a great feast. When they were all assembled together, he said to the huntsman: "As you are so clever, you shall sit by me."

He replied: "Lord King, your majesty must excuse me, I am a poor huntsman."

But the king insisted on it, and said: "You shall sit by me," until he did it.

Whilst he was sitting there, he thought of his dearest mother, and wished that one of the king's principal servants would begin to speak of her, and would ask how it was faring with the queen in the tower, and if she were alive still, or had perished. Hardly had he formed the wish than the marshal began, and said: "Your majesty, we live joyously here, but how is the queen living in the tower? Is she still alive, or has she died?"

But the king replied: "She let my dear son be torn to pieces by wild beasts; I will not have her named."

Then the huntsman arose and said: "Gracious lord father she is alive still, and I am her son, and I was not carried away by wild beasts, but by that wretch the old cook, who tore me from her arms when she was asleep, and sprinkled her apron with the blood of a chicken."

Thereupon he took the dog with the golden collar, and said: "That is the wretch!" and caused live coals to be brought, and these the dog was compelled to devour before the sight of all, until flames burst forth from its throat. On this the huntsman asked the king if he would like to see the dog in his true shape, and wished him back into the form of the cook, in which he stood immediately, with his white apron, and his knife by his side. When the king saw him he fell into a passion, and ordered him to be cast into the deepest dungeon. Then the huntsman spoke further and said: "Father, will you see the maiden who brought me up so tenderly and who was afterwards to murder me, but did not do it, though her own life depended on it?"

The king replied: "Yes, I would like to see her."

The son said: "Most gracious father, I will show her to you in the form of a beautiful flower," and he thrust his hand into his pocket and brought forth the pink, and placed it on the royal table, and it was so beautiful that the king had never seen one to equal it. Then the son said: "Now will I show her to you in her own form," and wished that she might become a maiden, and she stood there looking so beautiful that no painter could have made her look more so.

And the king sent two waiting maids and two attendants into the tower, to fetch the queen and bring her to the royal table. But when she was led in she ate nothing, and said: "The gracious and merciful God who has supported me in the tower, will soon set me free." She lived three days more, and then died happily, and when she was buried, the two white doves which had brought her food to the tower, and were angels of heaven, followed her body and seated themselves on her grave. The aged king ordered the cook to be torn in four pieces, but grief consumed the king's own heart, and he soon died. His son married the beautiful maiden whom he had brought with him as a flower in his pocket, and whether they are still alive or not is known to God.

Clever Elsie

There was once a man who had a daughter who was called Clever Elsie. And when she had grown up her father said: "We will get her married."

"Yes," said the mother, "if only someone would come who would have her." At length a man came from a distance and wooed her, who was called Hans; but he stipulated that Clever Elsie should be really smart.

"Oh," said the father, "she has plenty of good sense"; and the mother said: "Oh, she can see the wind coming up the street, and hear the flies coughing."

"Well," said Hans, "if she is not really smart, I won't have her."

When they were sitting at dinner and had eaten, the mother said: "Elsie, go into the cellar and fetch some beer." Then Clever Elsie took the pitcher from the wall, went into the cellar, and tapped the lid briskly as she went, so that the time might not appear long. When she was below she fetched herself a chair, and set it before the barrel so that she had no need to stoop, and did not hurt her back or do herself any unexpected injury. Then she placed the can before her, and turned the tap, and while the beer was running she would not let her eyes be idle, but looked up at the wall, and after much peering here and there, saw a pickaxe exactly above her, which the masons had accidentally left there.

Then Clever Elsie began to weep and said: "If I get Hans, and we have a child, and he grows big, and we send him into the cellar here to draw beer, then the pickaxe will fall on his head and kill him." Then she sat and wept and screamed with all the strength of her body, over the misfortune which lay before her. Those upstairs waited for the drink, but Clever Elsie still did not come.

Then the woman said to the servant: "Just go down into the cellar and see where Elsie is." The maid went and found her sitting in front of the barrel, screaming loudly. "Elsie why do you weep?" asked the maid.

"Ah," she answered, "have I not reason to weep? If I get Hans, and we have a child, and he grows big, and has to draw beer here, the pickaxe will perhaps fall on his head, and kill him."

Then said the maid: "What a clever Elsie we have!" and sat down beside her and began loudly to weep over the misfortune. After a while, as the maid did not come back, and those upstairs were thirsty for the beer, the man said to the boy: "Just go down into the cellar and see where Elsie and the girl are."

The boy went down, and there sat Clever Elsie and the girl both weeping together. Then he asked: "Why are you weeping?"

"Ah," said Elsie, "have I not reason to weep? If I get Hans, and we have a child, and he grows big, and has to draw beer here, the pickaxe will fall on his head and kill him."

Then said the boy: "What a clever Elsie we have!" and sat down by her, and likewise began to howl loudly. Upstairs they waited for the boy, but as he still did not return, the man said to the woman: "Just go down into the cellar and see where Elsie is!"

The woman went down, and found all three in the midst of their lamentations, and inquired what was the cause; then Elsie told her also that her future child was to be killed by the pickaxe, when it grew big and had to draw beer, and the pickaxe fell down. Then said the mother likewise: "What a clever Elsie we have!" and sat down and wept with them.

The man upstairs waited a short time, but as his wife did not come back and his thirst grew ever greater, he said: "I must go into the cellar myself and see where Elsie is." But when he got into the cellar, and they were all sitting together crying, and he heard the reason, and that Elsie's child was the cause, and the Elsie might perhaps bring one into the world some day, and that he might be killed by the pickaxe, if he should happen to be sitting beneath it, drawing beer just at the very time when it fell down, he cried: "Oh, what a clever Elsie!" and sat down, and likewise wept with them.

The bridegroom stayed upstairs alone for a long time; then as no one would come back he thought: "They must be waiting for me below: I too must go there and see what they are about." When he got down, the five of them were sitting screaming and lamenting quite piteously, each outdoing the other. "What misfortune has happened then?" asked he.

"Ah, dear Hans," said Elsie, "if we marry each other and have a child, and he is big, and we perhaps send him here to draw something to drink, then the pickaxe which has been left up there might dash his brains out if it were to fall down, so have we not reason to weep?"

"Come," said Hans, "more understanding than that is not needed for my household, as you are such a clever Elsie, I will have you," and seized her hand, took her upstairs with him, and married her.

After Hans had had her some time, he said: "Wife, I am going out to work and earn some money for us; go into the field and cut the corn that we may have some bread."

"Yes, dear Hans, I will do that." After Hans had gone away, she cooked herself some good broth and took it into the field with her. When she came to the field she said to herself: "What shall I do; shall I cut first, or shall I eat first? Oh, I will eat first." Then she drank her cup of broth and when she was fully satisfied, she once more said: "What shall I do? Shall I cut first, or shall I sleep first? I will sleep first." Then she lay down among the corn and fell asleep.

Hans had been at home for a long time, but Elsie did not come; then said he. "What a clever Elsie I have; she is so industrious that she does not even come home to eat." But when evening came and she still stayed away, Hans went out to see what she had cut, but nothing was cut, and she was lying among the corn asleep. Then Hans hastened home and brought a fowler's net with little bells and hung it round about her, and she still went on sleeping. Then he ran home, shut the house door, and sat down in his chair and worked. At length, when it was quite dark, Clever Elsie awoke and when she got up there was a jingling all round about her, and the bells rang at each step which she took. Then she was alarmed, and became uncertain whether she really was Clever Elsie or not, and said: "Is it I, or is it not I?" But she knew not what answer to make to this, and stood for a time in doubt; at length she thought: "I will go home and ask if it be I, or if it be not I, they will be sure to know." She ran to the door of her own house, but it was shut; then she knocked at the window and cried: "Hans, is Elsie within?"

"Yes," answered Hans, "she is within." Hereupon she was terrified, and said: "Ah, heavens! Then it is not I," and went to another door; but when the people heard the jingling of the bells they would not open it, and she could get in nowhere. Then she ran out of the village, and no one has seen her since.

The Miser in the Bush

A farmer had a faithful and diligent servant, who had worked hard for him three years, without having been paid any wages. At last it came into the man's head that he would not go on thus without pay any longer; so he went to his master, and said, "I have worked hard for you a long time, I will trust to you to give me what I deserve to have for my trouble." The farmer was a sad miser, and knew that his man was very simplehearted; so he took out threepence, and gave him for every year's service a penny. The poor fellow thought it was a great deal of money to have, and said to himself, "Why should I work hard, and live here on bad fare any longer? I can now travel into the wide world, and make myself merry." With that he put his money into his purse, and set out, roaming over hill and valley.

As he jogged along over the fields, singing and dancing, a little dwarf met him, and asked him what made him so merry. "Why, what should make me downhearted?" said he; "I am sound in health and rich in purse, what should I care for? I have saved up my three years' earnings and have it all safe in my pocket."

"How much may it come to?" said the little man.

"Full threepence," replied the countryman.

"I wish you would give them to me," said the other; "I am very poor."

Then the man pitied him, and gave him all he had; and the little dwarf said in return, "As you have such a kind, honest heart, I will grant you three wishes—one for every penny; so choose whatever you like."

Then the countryman rejoiced at his good luck, and said, "I like many things better than money: first, I will have a bow that will bring down everything I shoot at; secondly, a fiddle that will set everyone dancing that hears me play upon it; and thirdly, I should like that everyone should grant what I ask." The dwarf said he should have his three wishes; so he gave him the bow and fiddle, and went his way.

Our honest friend journeyed on his way too; and if he was merry before, he was now ten times more so. He had not gone far before he met an old miser: close by them stood a tree, and on the topmost twig sat a thrush singing away most joyfully. "Oh, what a pretty bird!" said the miser; "I would give a great deal of money to have such a one."

"If that's all," said the countryman, "I will soon bring it down." Then he took up his bow, and down fell the thrush into the bushes at the foot of the tree. The miser crept into the bush to find it; but directly he had got into the middle, his companion took up his fiddle and played away, and the miser began to dance and spring about, capering higher and higher in the air. The thorns soon began to tear his clothes till they all hung in rags about him, and he himself was all scratched and wounded, so that the blood ran down. "Oh, for heaven's sake!" cried the miser, "Master! master! pray let the fiddle alone. What have I done to deserve this?"

"Thou hast shaved many a poor soul close enough," said the other; "thou art only meeting thy reward": so he played up another tune. Then the miser began to beg and promise, and offered money for his liberty; but he did not come up to the musician's price for some time, and he danced him along brisker and brisker, and the miser bid higher and higher, till at last he offered a round hundred of florins that he had in his purse, and had just gained by cheating some poor fellow.

When the countryman saw so much money, he said, "I will agree to your proposal." So he took the purse, put up his fiddle, and travelled on very pleased with his bargain.

Meanwhile the miser crept out of the bush half naked and in a piteous plight, and began to ponder how he should take his revenge, and serve his late companion some trick. At last he went to the judge, and complained that a rascal had robbed him of his money, and beaten him into the bargain; and that the fellow who did it carried a bow at his back and a fiddle hung round his neck. Then the judge sent out his officers to bring up the accused wherever they should find him; and he was soon caught and brought up to be tried.

The miser began to tell his tale, and said he had been robbed of his money. "No, you gave it me for playing a tune to you," said the countryman; but the judge told him that was not likely, and cut the matter short by ordering him off to the gallows.

So away he was taken; but as he stood on the steps he said, "My Lord Judge, grant me one last request."

"Anything but thy life," replied the other.

"No," said he, "I do not ask my life; only to let me play upon my fiddle for the last time."

The miser cried out, "Oh, no! no! for heaven's sake don't listen to him! don't listen to him!"

But the judge said, "It is only this once, he will soon have done." The fact was, he could not refuse the request, on account of the dwarf's third gift.

Then the miser said, "Bind me fast, bind me fast, for pity's sake." But the countryman seized his fiddle, and struck up a tune, and at the first note judge, clerks, and jailer were in motion; all began capering, and no one could hold the miser. At the second note the hangman let his prisoner go, and danced also, and by the time he had played the first bar of the tune, all were dancing together—judge, court, and miser, and all the people who had followed to look on. At first the thing was merry and pleasant enough; but when it had gone on a while, and there seemed to be no end of playing or dancing, they began to cry out, and beg him to leave off; but he stopped not a whit the more for their entreaties, till the judge not only gave him his life, but promised to return him the hundred florins.

Then he called to the miser, and said, "Tell us now, you vagabond, where you got that gold, or I shall play on for your amusement only."

"I stole it," said the miser in the presence of all the people; "I acknowledge that I stole it, and that you earned it fairly." Then the countryman stopped his fiddle, and left the miser to take his place at the gallows.

Cinderella

The wife of a rich man fell sick; and when she felt that her end drew nigh, she called her only daughter to her bedside, and said, "Always be a good girl, and I will look down from heaven and watch over you." Soon afterwards she shut her eyes and died, and was buried in the garden; and the little girl went every day to her grave and wept, and was always good and kind to all about her. And the snow fell and spread a beautiful white covering over the grave; but by the time the spring came, and the sun had melted it away again, her father had married another wife. This new wife had two daughters of her own, that she brought home with her; they were fair in face but foul at heart, and it was now a sorry time for the poor little girl.

"What does the good-for-nothing want in the parlour?" said they; "they who would eat bread should first earn it; away with the kitchen maid!" Then they took away her fine clothes, and gave her an old grey frock to put on, and laughed at her, and turned her into the kitchen.

There she was forced to do hard work; to rise early before daylight, to bring the water, to make the fire, to cook and to wash. Besides that, the sisters plagued her in all sorts of ways, and laughed at her. In the evening when she was tired, she had no bed to lie down on, but was made to lie by the hearth among the ashes; and as this, of course, made her always dusty and dirty, they called her Cinderella.

It happened once that the father was going to the fair, and asked his wife's daughters what he should bring them.

"Fine clothes," said the first.

"Pearls and diamonds," cried the second.

"Now, child," said he to his own daughter, "what will you have?"

"The first twig, dear father, that brushes against your hat when you turn your face to come homewards," said she.

Then he bought for the first two the fine clothes and pearls and diamonds they had asked for: and on his way home, as he rode through a green copse, a hazel twig brushed against him, and almost pushed off his hat: so he broke it off and brought it away; and when he got home he gave it to his daughter. Then she took it, and went to her mother's grave and planted it there; and cried so much that it was watered with her tears; and there it grew and became a fine tree. Three times every day she went to it and cried; and soon a little bird came and built its nest upon the tree, and talked with her, and watched over her, and brought her whatever she wished for.

Now it happened that the king of that land held a feast, which was to last three days; and out of those who came to it his son was to choose a bride for himself. Cinderella's two sisters were asked to come; so they called her up, and said, "Now, comb our hair, brush our shoes, and tie our sashes for us, for we are going to dance at the king's feast." Then she did as she was told; but when all was done she could not help crying, for she thought to herself, she should so have liked to have gone with them to the ball; and at last she begged her mother very hard to let her go.

"You, Cinderella!" said she; "you who have nothing to wear, no clothes at all, and who cannot even dance—you want to go to the ball? And when she kept on begging, she said at last, to get rid of her, "I will throw this dishful of peas into the ash heap, and if in two hours' time you have picked them all out, you shall go to the feast too."

Then she threw the peas down among the ashes, but the little maiden ran out at the back door into the garden, and cried out:

"Hither, hither, through the sky,
Turtledoves and linnets, fly!
Blackbird, thrush, and chaffinch gay,
Hither, hither, haste away!
One and all come help me, quick!
Haste ye, haste ye! Pick, pick, pick!"

Then first came two white doves, flying in at the kitchen window; next came two turtledoves; and after them came all the little birds under heaven, chirping and fluttering in: and they flew down into the ashes. And the little doves stooped their heads down and set to work, pick, pick, pick; and then the others began to pick, pick, pick: and among them all they soon picked out all the good grain, and put it into a dish but left the ashes. Long before the end of the hour the work was quite done, and all flew out again at the windows.

Then Cinderella brought the dish to her mother, overjoyed at the thought that now she should go to the ball. But the mother said, "No, no, you have no clothes, and cannot dance; you shall not go." And when Cinderella begged very hard to go, she said, "If you can in one hour's time pick two of those dishes of peas out of the ashes, you shall go too." And thus she thought she should at least get rid of her. So she shook two dishes of peas into the ashes.

But the little maiden went out into the garden at the back of the house, and cried out as before:

"Hither, hither, through the sky,
Turtledoves and linnets, fly!

Blackbird, thrush, and chaffinch gay,
Hither, hither, haste away!
One and all come help me, quick!
Haste ye, haste ye! Pick, pick, pick!"

Then first came two white doves in at the kitchen window; next came two turtledoves; and after them came all the little birds under heaven, chirping and hopping about. And they flew down into the ashes; and the little doves put their heads down and set to work, pick, pick, pick; and then the others began, pick, pick, pick; and they put all the good grain into the dishes, and left all the ashes. Before half an hour's time all was done, and out they flew again. And then Cinderella took the dishes to her mother, rejoicing to think that she should now go to the ball. But her mother said, "It is all of no use, you cannot go; you have no clothes, and cannot dance, and you would only put us to shame": and off she went with her two daughters to the ball.

Now when all were gone, and nobody left at home, Cinderella went sorrowfully and sat down under the hazel tree, and cried out:

"Shake, shake, hazel tree,
Gold and silver over me!"

Then her friend the bird flew out of the tree, and brought a gold and silver dress for her, and slippers of spangled silk; and she put them on, and followed her sisters to the feast. But they did not know her, and thought it must be some strange princess, she looked so fine and beautiful in her rich clothes; and they never once thought of Cinderella, taking it for granted that she was safe at home in the dirt.

The king's son soon came up to her, and took her by the hand and danced with her, and no one else: and he never left her hand; but when anyone else came to ask her to dance, he said, "This lady is dancing with me."

Thus they danced till a late hour of the night; and then she wanted to go home: and the king's son said, "I shall go and take care of you to your home"; for he wanted to see where the beautiful maiden lived. But she slipped away from him, unawares, and ran off towards home; and as the prince followed her, she jumped up into the pigeon house and shut the door. Then he waited till her father came home, and told him that the unknown maiden, who had been at the feast, had hid herself in the pigeon house. But when they had broken open the door they found no one within; and as they came back into the house, Cinderella was lying, as she always did, in her dirty frock by the ashes, and her dim little lamp was burning in the chimney. For she had run as quickly as she could through the pigeon house and on to the hazel tree, and had there taken off her beautiful clothes, and put them beneath the tree, that the bird might carry them away, and had lain down again amid the ashes in her little grey frock.

The next day when the feast was again held, and her father, mother, and sisters were gone, Cinderella went to the hazel tree, and said:

"Shake, shake, hazel tree,
Gold and silver over me!"

And the bird came and brought a still finer dress than the one she had worn the day before. And when she came in it to the ball, everyone wondered at her beauty: but the king's son, who was waiting for her, took her by the hand, and danced with her; and when anyone asked her to dance, he said as before, "This lady is dancing with me."

When night came she wanted to go home; and the king's son followed here as before, that he might see into what house she went: but she sprang away from him all at once into the garden behind her father's house. In this garden stood a fine large pear tree full of ripe fruit; and Cinderella, not knowing where to hide herself, jumped up into it without being seen. Then the king's son lost sight of her, and could not find out where she was gone, but waited till her father came home, and said to him, "The unknown lady who danced with me has slipped away, and I think she must have sprung into the pear tree."

The father thought to himself, "Can it be Cinderella?" So he had an axe brought; and they cut down the tree, but found no one upon it. And when they came back into the kitchen, there lay Cinderella among the ashes; for she had slipped down on the other side of the tree, and carried her beautiful clothes back to the bird at the hazel tree, and then put on her little grey frock.

The third day, when her father and mother and sisters were gone, she went again into the garden, and said:

"Shake, shake, hazel tree,
Gold and silver over me!"

Then her kind friend the bird brought a dress still finer than the former one, and slippers which were all of gold: so that when she came to the feast no one knew what to say, for wonder at her beauty: and the king's son danced with nobody but her; and when anyone else asked her to dance, he said, "This lady is my partner, sir."

When night came she wanted to go home; and the king's son would go with her, and said to himself, "I will not lose her this time"; but, however, she again slipped away from him, though in such a hurry that she dropped her left golden slipper upon the stairs.

The prince took the shoe, and went the next day to the king his father, and said, "I will take for my wife the lady that this golden slipper fits." Then both the sisters were overjoyed to hear it; for they had beautiful feet, and had no doubt that they could wear the golden slipper. The eldest went first into the room where the slipper was, and wanted to try it on, and the mother stood by. But her great toe could not go into it, and the shoe was altogether much too small for her. Then the mother gave her a knife, and said, "Never mind, cut it off; when you are queen you will not care about toes; you will not want to walk." So the silly girl cut off her great toe, and thus squeezed on the shoe, and went to the king's son. Then he took her for his bride, and set her beside him on his horse, and rode away with her homewards.

But on their way home they had to pass by the hazel tree that Cinderella had planted; and on the branch sat a little dove singing:

"Back again! back again! look to the shoe!
The shoe is too small, and not made for you!
Prince! prince! look again for thy bride,
For she's not the true one that sits by thy side."

Then the prince got down and looked at her foot; and he saw, by the blood that streamed from it, what a trick she had played him. So he turned his horse round, and brought the false bride back to her home, and said, "This is not the right bride; let the other sister try and put on the slipper." Then she went into the room and got her foot into the shoe, all but the heel, which was too large. But her mother squeezed it in till the blood came, and took her to the king's son: and he set her as his bride by his side on his horse, and rode away with her.

But when they came to the hazel tree the little dove sat there still, and sang:

"Back again! back again! look to the shoe!
The shoe is too small, and not made for you!
Prince! prince! look again for thy bride,
For she's not the true one that sits by thy side."

Then he looked down, and saw that the blood streamed so much from the shoe, that her white stockings were quite red. So he turned his horse and brought her also back again. "This is not the true bride," said he to the father; "have you no other daughters?"

"No," said he; "there is only a little dirty Cinderella here, the child of my first wife; I am sure she cannot be the bride." The prince told him to send her. But the mother said, "No, no, she is much too dirty; she will not dare to show herself." However, the prince would have her come; and she first washed her face and hands, and then went in and curtsied to him, and he reached her the golden slipper. Then she took her clumsy shoe off her left foot, and put on the golden slipper; and it fitted her as if it had been made for her. And when he drew near and looked at her face he knew her, and said, "This is the right bride." But the mother and both the sisters were frightened, and turned pale with anger as he took Cinderella on his horse, and rode away with her. And when they came to the hazel tree, the white dove sang:

"Home! home! look at the shoe!
Princess! the shoe was made for you!
Prince! prince! take home thy bride,
For she is the true one that sits by thy side!"

And when the dove had done its song, it came flying, and perched upon her right shoulder, and so went home with her.

The White Snake

A long time ago there lived a king who was famed for his wisdom through all the land. Nothing was hidden from him, and it seemed as if news of the most secret things was brought to him through the air. But he had a strange custom; every day after dinner, when the table was cleared, and no one else was present, a trusty servant had to bring him one more dish. It was covered, however, and even the servant did not know what was in it, neither did anyone know, for the king never took off the cover to eat of it until he was quite alone.

This had gone on for a long time, when one day the servant, who took away the dish, was overcome with such curiosity that he could not help carrying the dish into his room. When he had carefully locked the door, he lifted up the cover, and saw a white snake lying on the dish. But when he saw it he could not deny himself the pleasure of tasting it, so he cut of a little bit and put it into his mouth. No sooner had it touched his tongue than he heard a strange whispering of little voices outside his window. He went and listened, and then noticed that it was the sparrows who were chattering together, and telling one another of all kinds of things which they had seen in the fields and woods. Eating the snake had given him power of understanding the language of animals.

Now it so happened that on this very day the queen lost her most beautiful ring, and suspicion of having stolen it fell upon this trusty servant, who was allowed to go everywhere. The king ordered the man to be brought before him, and threatened with angry words that unless he could before the morrow point out the thief, he himself should be looked upon as guilty and executed. In vain he declared his innocence; he was dismissed with no better answer.

In his trouble and fear he went down into the courtyard and took thought how to help himself out of his trouble. Now some ducks were sitting together quietly by a brook and taking their rest; and, whilst they were making their feathers smooth with their bills, they were having a confidential conversation together. The servant stood by and listened. They were telling one another of all the places where they had been waddling about all the morning, and what good food they had found; and one said in a pitiful tone: "Something lies heavy on my stomach; as I was eating in haste I swallowed a ring which lay under the queen's window."

The servant at once seized her by the neck, carried her to the kitchen, and said to the cook: "Here is a fine duck; pray, kill her."

"Yes," said the cook, and weighed her in his hand; "she has spared no trouble to fatten herself, and has been waiting to be roasted long enough." So he cut off her head, and as she was being dressed for the spit, the queen's ring was found inside her.

The servant could now easily prove his innocence; and the king, to make amends for the wrong, allowed him to ask a favour, and promised him the best place in the court that he could wish for. The servant refused everything, and only asked for a horse and some money for travelling, as he had a mind to see the world and go about a little. When his request was granted he set out on his way, and one day came to a pond, where he saw three fishes caught in the reeds and gasping for water. Now, though it is said that fishes are dumb, he heard them lamenting that they must perish so miserably, and, as he had a kind heart, he got off his horse and put the three prisoners back into the water. They leapt with delight, put out their heads, and cried to him: "We will remember you and repay you for saving us!"

He rode on, and after a while it seemed to him that he heard a voice in the sand at his feet. He listened, and heard an ant king complain: "Why cannot folks, with their clumsy beasts, keep off our bodies? That stupid horse, with his heavy hoofs, has been treading down my people without mercy!" So he turned on to a side path and the ant king cried out to him: "We will remember you—one good turn deserves another!"

The path led him into a wood, and there he saw two old ravens standing by their nest, and throwing out their young ones. "Out with you, you idle, good-for-nothing creatures!" cried they; "we cannot find food for you any longer; you are big enough, and can provide for yourselves."

But the poor young ravens lay upon the ground, flapping their wings, and crying: "Oh, what helpless chicks we are! We must shift for ourselves, and yet we cannot fly! What can we do, but lie here and starve?" So the good young fellow alighted and killed his horse with his sword, and gave it to them for food. Then they came hopping up to it, satisfied their hunger, and cried: "We will remember you—one good turn deserves another!"

And now he had to use his own legs, and when he had walked a long way, he came to a large city. There was a great noise and crowd in the streets, and a man rode up on horseback, crying aloud: "The king's daughter wants a husband; but whoever seeks her hand must perform a hard task, and if he does not succeed he will forfeit his life." Many had already made the attempt, but in vain; nevertheless when the youth saw the king's daughter he was so overcome by her great beauty that he forgot all danger, went before the king, and declared himself a suitor.

So he was led out to the sea, and a gold ring was thrown into it, before his eyes; then the king ordered him to fetch this ring up from the bottom of the sea, and added: "If you come up again without it you will be thrown in again and again until you perish amid the waves." All the people grieved for the handsome youth; then they went away, leaving him alone by the sea.

He stood on the shore and considered what he should do, when suddenly he saw three fishes come swimming towards him, and they were the very fishes whose lives he had saved. The one in the middle held a mussel in its mouth, which it laid on the shore at the youth's feet, and when he had taken it up and opened it, there lay the gold ring in the shell. Full of joy he took it to the king and expected that he would grant him the promised reward.

But when the proud princess perceived that he was not her equal in birth, she scorned him, and required him first to perform another task. She went down into the garden and strewed with her own hands ten sacksful of millet seed on the grass; then she said: "Tomorrow morning before sunrise these must be picked up, and not a single grain be wanting."

The youth sat down in the garden and considered how it might be possible to perform this task, but he could think of nothing, and there he sat sorrowfully awaiting the break of day, when he should be led to death. But as soon as the first rays of the sun shone into the garden he saw all the ten sacks standing side by side, quite full, and not a single grain was missing. The ant king had come in the night with thousands and thousands of ants, and the grateful creatures had by great industry picked up all the millet seed and gathered them into the sacks.

Presently the king's daughter herself came down into the garden, and was amazed to see that the young man had done the task she had given him. But she could not yet conquer her proud heart, and said: "Although he has performed both the tasks, he shall not be my husband until he had brought me an apple from the Tree of Life." The youth did not know where the Tree of Life stood, but he set out, and would have gone on forever, as long as his legs would carry him, though he had no hope of finding it. After he had wandered through three kingdoms, he came one evening to a wood, and lay down under a tree to sleep. But he heard a rustling in the branches, and a golden apple fell into his hand. At the same time three ravens flew down to him, perched themselves upon his knee, and said: "We are the three young ravens whom you saved from starving; when we had grown big, and heard that you were seeking the Golden Apple, we flew over the sea to the end of the world, where the Tree of Life stands, and have brought you the apple." The youth, full of joy, set out homewards, and took the Golden Apple to the king's beautiful daughter, who had now no more excuses left to make. They cut the Apple of Life in two and ate it together; and then her heart became full of love for him, and they lived in undisturbed happiness to a great age.

The Wolf and the Seven Little Kids

There was once upon a time an old goat who had seven little kids, and loved them with all the love of a mother for her children. One day she wanted to go into the forest and fetch some food. So she called all seven to her and said: "Dear children, I have to go into the forest, be on your guard against the wolf; if he comes in, he will devour you all—skin, hair, and everything. The wretch often disguises himself, but you will know him at once by his rough voice and his black feet."

The kids said: "Dear mother, we will take good care of ourselves; you may go away without any anxiety." Then the old one bleated, and went on her way with an easy mind.

It was not long before someone knocked at the house door and called: "Open the door, dear children; your mother is here, and has brought something back with her for each of you."

But the little kids knew that it was the wolf, by the rough voice. "We will not open the door," cried they, "you are not our mother. She has a soft, pleasant voice, but your voice is rough; you are the wolf!" Then the wolf went away to a shopkeeper and bought himself a great lump of chalk, ate this, and made his voice soft with it. Then he came back, knocked at the door of the house, and called: "Open the door, dear children, your mother is here and has brought something back with her for each of you." But the wolf had laid his black paws against the window, and the children saw them and cried: "We will not open the door, our mother has not black feet like you: you are the wolf!"

Then the wolf ran to a baker and said: "I have hurt my feet, rub some dough over them for me." And when the baker had rubbed his feet over, he ran to the miller and said: "Strew some white meal over my feet for me." The miller thought to himself: "The wolf wants to deceive someone," and refused; but the wolf said: "If you will not do it, I will devour you." Then the miller was afraid, and made his paws white for him. Truly, this is the way of mankind.

So now the wretch went for the third time to the house door, knocked at it and said: "Open the door for me, children, your dear little mother has come home, and has brought every one of you something back from the forest with her." The little kids cried: "First show us your paws that we may know if you are our dear little mother." Then he put his paws in through the window and when the kids saw that they were white, they believed that all he said was true, and opened the door. But who should come in but the wolf! They were terrified and wanted to hide themselves. One sprang under the table, the second into the bed, the third into the stove, the fourth into the kitchen, the fifth into the cupboard, the sixth under the washing bowl, and the seventh into the clock case. But the wolf found them all, and used no great ceremony; one after the other he swallowed them down his throat. The youngest, who was in the clock case, was the only one he did not find. When the wolf had satisfied his appetite he took himself off, laid himself down under a tree in the green meadow outside, and began to sleep. Soon afterwards the old goat came home again from the forest. Ah! what a sight she saw there! The house door stood wide open. The table, chairs, and benches were thrown down, the washing bowl lay broken to pieces, and the quilts and pillows were pulled off the bed. She sought her children, but they were nowhere to be found. She called them one after another by name, but no one answered.

At last, when she came to the youngest, a soft voice cried: "Dear mother, I am in the clock case." She took the kid out, and it told her that the wolf had come and had eaten all the others. Then you may imagine how she wept over her poor children.

At length in her grief she went out, and the youngest kid ran with her. When they came to the meadow, there lay the wolf by the tree and snored so loud that the branches shook. She looked at him on every side and saw that something was moving and struggling in his gorged belly. "Ah, heavens," she said, "is it possible that my poor children, whom he has swallowed down for his supper, can be still alive?" Then the kid had to run home and fetch scissors, and a needle and thread, and the goat cut open the monster's stomach, and hardly had she made one cut, than one little kid thrust its head out, and when she had cut farther, all six sprang out one after another, and were all still alive, and had suffered no injury whatever, for in his greediness the monster had swallowed them down whole. What rejoicing there was! They embraced their dear mother, and jumped like a tailor at his wedding. The mother, however, said: "Now go and look for some big stones, and we will fill the wicked beast's stomach with them while he is still asleep." Then the seven kids dragged the stones thither with all speed, and put as many of them into this stomach as they could get in; and the mother sewed him up again in the greatest haste, so that he was not aware of anything and never once stirred.

When the wolf at length had had his fill of sleep, he got on his legs, and as the stones in his stomach made him very thirsty, he wanted to go to a well to drink. But when he began to walk and to move about, the stones in his stomach knocked against each other and rattled. Then cried he:

"What rumbles and tumbles
Against my poor bones?
I thought 'twas six kids,
But it feels like big stones."

And when he got to the well and stooped over the water to drink, the heavy stones made him fall in, and he drowned miserably. When the seven kids saw that, they came running to the spot and cried aloud: "The wolf is dead! The wolf is dead!" and danced for joy round about the well with their mother.

The Queen Bee

Two kings' sons once upon a time went into the world to seek their fortunes; but they soon fell into a wasteful foolish way of living, so that they could not return home again. Then their brother, who was a little insignificant dwarf, went out to seek for his brothers: but when he had found them they only laughed at him, to think that he, who was so young and simple, should try to travel through the world, when they, who were so much wiser, had been unable to get on. However, they all set out on their journey together, and came at last to an anthill. The two elder brothers would have pulled it down, in order to see how the poor ants in their fright would run about and carry off their eggs. But the little dwarf said, "Let the poor things enjoy themselves, I will not suffer you to trouble them."

So on they went, and came to a lake where many, many ducks were swimming about. The two brothers wanted to catch two, and roast them. But the dwarf said, "Let the poor things enjoy themselves, you shall not kill them." Next they came to a bees' nest in a hollow tree, and there was so much honey that it ran down the trunk; and the two brothers wanted to light a fire under the tree and kill the bees, so as to get their honey.

But the dwarf held them back, and said, "Let the pretty insects enjoy themselves, I cannot let you burn them."

At length the three brothers came to a castle: and as they passed by the stables they saw fine horses standing there, but all were of marble, and no man was to be seen. Then they went through all the rooms, till they came to a door on which were three locks: but in the middle of the door was a wicket, so that they could look into the next room. There they saw a little grey old man sitting at a table; and they called to him once or twice, but he did not hear: however, they called a third time, and then he rose and came out to them.

He said nothing, but took hold of them and led them to a beautiful table covered with all sorts of good things: and when they had eaten and drunk, he showed each of them to a bed chamber.

The next morning he came to the eldest and took him to a marble table, where there were three tablets, containing an account of the means by which the castle might be disenchanted. The first tablet said: "In the wood, under the moss, lie the thousand pearls belonging to the king's daughter; they must all be found: and if one be missing by set of sun, he who seeks them will be turned into marble."

The eldest brother set out, and sought for the pearls the whole day: but the evening came, and he had not found the first hundred: so he was turned into stone as the tablet had foretold.

The next day the second brother undertook the task; but he succeeded no better than the first; for he could only find the second hundred of the pearls; and therefore he too was turned into stone.

At last came the little dwarf's turn; and he looked in the moss; but it was so hard to find the pearls, and the job was so tiresome! So he sat down upon a stone and cried. And as he sat there, the king of the ants (whose life he had saved) came to help him, with five thousand ants; and it was not long before they had found all the pearls and laid them in a heap.

The second tablet said: "The key of the princess's bed chamber must be fished up out of the lake." And as the dwarf came to the brink of it, he saw the two ducks whose lives he had saved swimming about; and they dived down and soon brought in the key from the bottom.

The third task was the hardest. It was to choose out the youngest and the best of the king's three daughters. Now they were all beautiful, and all exactly alike: but he was told that the eldest had eaten a piece of sugar, the next some sweet syrup, and the youngest a spoonful of honey; so he was to guess which it was that had eaten the honey.

Then came the queen of the bees, who had been saved by the little dwarf from the fire, and she tried the lips of all three; but at last she sat upon the lips of the one that had eaten the honey: and so the dwarf knew which was the youngest. Thus the spell was broken, and all who had been turned into stones awoke, and took their proper forms. And the dwarf married the youngest and the best of the princesses, and was king after her father's death; but his two brothers married the other two sisters.

The Elves and the Shoemaker

There was once a shoemaker, who worked very hard and was very honest: but still he could not earn enough to live upon; and at last all he had in the world was gone, save just leather enough to make one pair of shoes.

Then he cut his leather out, all ready to make up the next day, meaning to rise early in the morning to his work. His conscience was clear and his heart light amidst all his troubles; so he went peaceably to bed, left all his cares to heaven, and soon fell asleep. In the morning after he had said his prayers, he sat himself down to his work; when, to his great wonder, there stood the shoes all ready made, upon the table. The good man knew not what to say or think at such an odd thing happening. He looked at the workmanship; there was not one false stitch in the whole job; all was so neat and true, that it was quite a masterpiece.

The same day a customer came in, and the shoes suited him so well that he willingly paid a price higher than usual for them; and the poor shoemaker, with the money, bought leather enough to make two pairs more. In the evening he cut out the work, and went to bed early, that he might get up and begin betimes next day; but he was saved all the trouble, for when he got up in the morning the work was done ready to his hand. Soon in came buyers, who paid him handsomely for his goods, so that he bought leather enough for four pair more. He cut out the work again overnight and found it done in the morning, as before; and so it went on for some time: what was got ready in the evening was always done by daybreak, and the good man soon became thriving and well-off again.

One evening, about Christmastime, as he and his wife were sitting over the fire chatting together, he said to her, "I should like to sit up and watch tonight, that we may see who it is that comes and does my work for me." The wife liked the thought; so they left a light burning, and hid themselves in a corner of the room, behind a curtain that was hung up there, and watched what would happen.

As soon as it was midnight, there came in two little naked dwarfs; and they sat themselves upon the shoemaker's bench, took up all the work that was cut out, and began to ply with their little fingers, stitching and rapping and tapping away at such a rate, that the shoemaker was all wonder, and could not take his eyes off them. And on they went, till the job was quite done, and the shoes stood ready for use upon the table. This was long before daybreak; and then they bustled away as quick as lightning.

The next day the wife said to the shoemaker. "These little wights have made us rich, and we ought to be thankful to them, and do them a good turn if we can. I am quite sorry to see them run about as they do; and indeed it is not very decent, for they have nothing upon their backs to keep off the cold. I'll tell you what, I will make each of them a shirt, and a coat and waistcoat, and a pair of pantaloons into the bargain; and do you make each of them a little pair of shoes."

The thought pleased the good cobbler very much; and one evening, when all the things were ready, they laid them on the table, instead of the work that they used to cut out, and then went and hid themselves, to watch what the little elves would do.

About midnight in they came, dancing and skipping, hopped round the room, and then went to sit down to their work as usual; but when they saw the clothes lying for them, they laughed and chuckled, and seemed mightily delighted.

Then they dressed themselves in the twinkling of an eye, and danced and capered and sprang about, as merry as could be; till at last they danced out at the door, and away over the green.

The good couple saw them no more; but everything went well with them from that time forward, as long as they lived.

The Almond Tree

Long, long ago, some two thousand years or so, there lived a rich man with a good and beautiful wife. They loved each other dearly, but sorrowed much that they had no children. So greatly did they desire to have one, that the wife prayed for it day and night, but still they remained childless.

In front of the house there was a court, in which grew an almond tree. One winter's day the wife stood under the tree to peel some apples, and as she was peeling them, she cut her finger, and the blood fell on the snow.

"Ah," sighed the woman heavily, "if I had but a child, as red as blood and as white as snow," and as she spoke the words, her heart grew light within her, and it seemed to her that her wish was granted, and she returned to the house feeling glad and comforted. A month passed, and the snow had all disappeared; then another month went by, and all the earth was green. So the months followed one another, and first the trees budded in the woods, and soon the green branches grew thickly intertwined, and then the blossoms began to fall. Once again the wife stood under the almond tree, and it was so full of sweet scent that her heart leaped for joy, and she was so overcome with her happiness, that she fell on her knees. Presently the fruit became round and firm, and she was glad and at peace; but when they were fully ripe she picked the berries and ate eagerly of them, and then she grew sad and ill. A little while later she called her husband, and said to him, weeping. "If I die, bury me under the almond tree." Then she felt comforted and happy again, and before another month had passed she had a little child, and when she saw that it was as white as snow and as red as blood, her joy was so great that she died.

Her husband buried her under the almond tree, and wept bitterly for her. By degrees, however, his sorrow grew less, and although at times he still grieved over his loss, he was able to go about as usual, and later on he married again.

He now had a little daughter born to him; the child of his first wife was a boy, who was as red as blood and as white as snow. The mother loved her daughter very much, and when she looked at her and then looked at the boy, it pierced her heart to think that he would always stand in the way of her own child, and she was continually thinking how she could get the whole of the property for her. This evil thought took possession of her more and more, and made her behave very unkindly to the boy. She drove him from place to place with cuffings and buffetings, so that the poor child went about in fear, and had no peace from the time he left school to the time he went back.

One day the little daughter came running to her mother in the store-room, and said, "Mother, give me an apple."

"Yes, my child," said the wife, and she gave her a beautiful apple out of the chest; the chest had a very heavy lid and a large iron lock.

"Mother," said the little daughter again, "may not brother have one too?"

The mother was angry at this, but she answered, "Yes, when he comes out of school."

Just then she looked out of the window and saw him coming, and it seemed as if an evil spirit entered into her, for she snatched the apple out of her little daughter's hand, and said, "You shall not have one before your brother." She threw the apple into the chest and shut it to. The little boy now came in, and the evil spirit in the wife made her say kindly to him, "My son, will you have an apple?" but she gave him a wicked look.

"Mother," said the boy, "how dreadful you look! Yes, give me an apple." The thought came to her that she would kill him.

"Come with me," she said, and she lifted up the lid of the chest; "take one out for yourself." And as he bent over to do so, the evil spirit urged her, and crash! down went the lid, and off went the little boy's head. Then she was overwhelmed with fear at the thought of what she had done. "If only I can prevent anyone knowing that I did it," she thought. So she went upstairs to her room, and took a white handkerchief out of her top drawer; then she set the boy's head again on his shoulders, and bound it with the handkerchief so that nothing could be seen, and placed him on a chair by the door with an apple in his hand.

Soon after this, little Marleen came up to her mother who was stirring a pot of boiling water over the fire, and said, "Mother, brother is sitting by the door with an apple in his hand, and he looks so pale; and when I asked him to give me the apple, he did not answer, and that frightened me."

"Go to him again," said her mother, "and if he does not answer, give him a box on the ear." So little Marleen went, and said, "Brother, give me that apple," but he did not say a word; then she gave him a box on the ear, and his head rolled off. She was so terrified at this, that she ran crying and screaming to her mother. "Oh!" she said, "I have knocked off brother's head," and then she wept and wept, and nothing would stop her.

"What have you done!" said her mother, "but no one must know about it, so you must keep silence; what is done can't be undone; we will make him into puddings." And she took the little boy and cut him up, made him into puddings, and put him in the pot. But Marleen stood looking on, and wept and wept, and her tears fell into the pot, so that there was no need of salt.

Presently the father came home and sat down to his dinner; he asked, "Where is my son?" The mother said nothing, but gave him a large dish of black pudding, and Marleen still wept without ceasing.

The father again asked, "Where is my son?"

"Oh," answered the wife, "he is gone into the country to his mother's great uncle; he is going to stay there some time."

"What has he gone there for, and he never even said goodbye to me!"

"Well, he likes being there, and he told me he should be away quite six weeks; he is well looked after there."

"I feel very unhappy about it," said the husband, "in case it should not be all right, and he ought to have said goodbye to me."

With this he went on with his dinner, and said, "Little Marleen, why do you weep? Brother will soon be back." Then he asked his wife for more pudding, and as he ate, he threw the bones under the table.

Little Marleen went upstairs and took her best silk handkerchief out of her bottom drawer, and in it she wrapped all the bones from under the table and carried them outside, and all the time she did nothing but weep. Then she laid them in the green grass under the almond tree, and she had no sooner done so, than all her sadness seemed to leave her, and she wept no more. And now the almond tree began to move, and the branches waved backwards and forwards, first away from one another, and then together again, as it might be someone clapping their hands for joy. After this a mist came round the tree, and in the midst of it there was a burning as of fire, and out of the fire there flew a beautiful bird, that rose high into the air, singing magnificently, and when it could no more be seen, the almond tree stood there as before, and the silk handkerchief and the bones were gone.

Little Marleen now felt as lighthearted and happy as if her brother were still alive, and she went back to the house and sat down cheerfully to the table and ate.

The bird flew away and alighted on the house of a goldsmith and began to sing:

"My mother killed her little son;
My father grieved when I was gone;
My sister loved me best of all;

THE
ALMOND TREE
"KYWITT, KYWITT, KYWITT, I CRY,
OH WHAT A BEAUTIFUL BIRD AM I!"
SWAIN SC

She laid her kerchief over me,
And took my bones that they might lie
Underneath the almond tree
Kywitt, Kywitt, what a beautiful bird am I!"

The goldsmith was in his workshop making a gold chain, when he heard the song of the bird on his roof. He thought it so beautiful that he got up and ran out, and as he crossed the threshold he lost one of his slippers. But he ran on into the middle of the street, with a slipper on one foot and a sock on the other; he still had on his apron, and still held the gold chain and the pincers in his hands, and so he stood gazing up at the bird, while the sun came shining brightly down on the street.

"Bird," he said, "how beautifully you sing! Sing me that song again."

"Nay," said the bird, "I do not sing twice for nothing. Give that gold chain, and I will sing it to you again."

"Here is the chain, take it," said the goldsmith. "Only sing me that again."

The bird flew down and took the gold chain in his right claw, and then he alighted again in front of the goldsmith and sang:

"My mother killed her little son;
My father grieved when I was gone;
My sister loved me best of all;
She laid her kerchief over me,
And took my bones that they might lie
Underneath the almond tree
Kywitt, Kywitt, what a beautiful bird am I!"

Then he flew away, and settled on the roof of a shoemaker's house and sang:

"My mother killed her little son;
My father grieved when I was gone;

My sister loved me best of all;
She laid her kerchief over me,
And took my bones that they might lie
Underneath the almond tree
Kywitt, Kywitt, what a beautiful bird am I!"

The shoemaker heard him, and he jumped up and ran out in his shirt sleeves, and stood looking up at the bird on the roof with his hand over his eyes to keep himself from being blinded by the sun.

"Bird," he said, "how beautifully you sing!" Then he called through the door to his wife: "Wife, come out; here is a bird, come and look at it and hear how beautifully it sings." Then he called his daughter and the children, then the apprentices, girls and boys, and they all ran up the street to look at the bird, and saw how splendid it was with its red and green feathers, and its neck like burnished gold, and eyes like two bright stars in its head.

"Bird," said the shoemaker, "sing me that song again."

"Nay," answered the bird, "I do not sing twice for nothing; you must give me something."

"Wife," said the man, "go into the garret; on the upper shelf you will see a pair of red shoes; bring them to me." The wife went in and fetched the shoes.

"There, bird," said the shoemaker, "now sing me that song again."

The bird flew down and took the red shoes in his left claw, and then he went back to the roof and sang:

"My mother killed her little son;
My father grieved when I was gone;
My sister loved me best of all;
She laid her kerchief over me,
And took my bones that they might lie
Underneath the almond tree
Kywitt, Kywitt, what a beautiful bird am I!"

When he had finished, he flew away. He had the chain in his right claw and the shoes in his left, and he flew right away to a mill, and the mill went "Click clack, click clack, click clack." Inside the mill were twenty of the miller's men hewing a stone, and as they went "Hick hack, hick hack, hick hack," the mill went "Click clack, click clack, click clack."

The bird settled on a lime tree in front of the mill and sang:

"My mother killed her little son;"

then one of the men left off,

"My father grieved when I was gone;"

two more men left off and listened,

"My sister loved me best of all;"

then four more left off,

"She laid her kerchief over me,
And took my bones that they might lie"

Now there were only eight at work,

"Underneath,"

and now only five,

"the almond tree."

and now only one,

"Kywitt, Kywitt, what a beautiful bird am I!"

then he looked up and the last one had left off work.

"Bird," he said, "what a beautiful song that is you sing! Let me hear it too; sing it again."

"Nay," answered the bird, "I do not sing twice for nothing; give me that millstone, and I will sing it again."

"If it belonged to me alone," said the man, "you should have it."

"Yes, yes," said the others: "if he will sing again, he can have it."

The bird came down, and all the twenty millers set to and lifted up the stone with a beam; then the bird put his head through the hole and took the stone round his neck like a collar, and flew back with it to the tree and sang,

"My mother killed her little son;
My father grieved when I was gone;
My sister loved me best of all;
She laid her kerchief over me,
And took my bones that they might lie
Underneath the almond tree
Kywitt, Kywitt, what a beautiful bird am I!"

And when he had finished his song, he spread his wings, and with the chain in his right claw, the shoes in his left, and the millstone round his neck, he flew right away to his father's house.

The father, the mother, and little Marleen were having their dinner.

"How lighthearted I feel," said the father, "so pleased and cheerful."

"And I," said the mother, "I feel so uneasy, as if a heavy thunderstorm were coming."

But little Marleen sat and wept and wept.

Then the bird came flying towards the house and settled on the roof.

"I do feel so happy," said the father, "and how beautifully the sun shines; I feel just as if I were going to see an old friend again."

"Ah!" said the wife, "and I am so full of distress and uneasiness that my teeth chatter, and I feel as if there were a fire in my veins," and she tore open her dress; and all the while little Marleen sat in the corner and wept, and the plate on her knees was wet with her tears.

The bird now flew to the almond tree and began singing,

"My mother killed her little son;

the mother shut her eyes and her ears, that she might see and hear nothing, but there was a roaring sound in her ears like that of a violent storm, and in her eyes a burning and flashing like lightning:

"My father grieved when I was gone;"

"Look, mother," said the man, "at the beautiful bird that is singing so magnificently; and how warm and bright the sun is, and what a delicious scent of spice in the air!"

"My sister loved me best of all;"

then little Marleen laid her head down on her knees and sobbed.

"I must go outside and see the bird nearer," said the man.

"Ah, do not go!" cried the wife. "I feel as if the whole house were in flames!"

But the man went out and looked at the bird.

"She laid her kerchief over me,
And took my bones that they might lie
Underneath the almond tree
Kywitt, Kywitt, what a beautiful bird am I!"

With that the bird let fall the gold chain, and it fell just round the man's neck, so that it fitted him exactly.

He went inside, and said, "See, what a splendid bird that is; he has given me this beautiful gold chain, and looks so beautiful himself."

But the wife was in such fear and trouble, that she fell on the floor, and her cap fell from her head.

Then the bird began again:

"My mother killed her little son;

"Ah me!" cried the wife, "if I were but a thousand feet beneath the earth, that I might not hear that song."

"My father grieved when I was gone;"

then the woman fell down again as if dead.

"My sister loved me best of all;"

"Well," said little Marleen, "I will go out too and see if the bird will give me anything."

So she went out.

"She laid her kerchief over me,
And took my bones that they might lie"

and he threw down the shoes to her,

"Underneath the almond tree
Kywitt, Kywitt, what a beautiful bird am I!"

And she now felt quite happy and lighthearted; she put on the shoes and danced and jumped about in them. "I was so miserable," she said, "when I came out, but that has all passed away; that is indeed a splendid bird, and he has given me a pair of red shoes."

The wife sprang up, with her hair standing out from her head like flames of fire. "Then I will go out too," she said, "and see if it will lighten my misery, for I feel as if the world were coming to an end."

But as she crossed the threshold, crash! the bird threw the millstone down on her head, and she was crushed to death.

The father and little Marleen heard the sound and ran out, but they only saw mist and flame and fire rising from the spot, and when these had passed, there stood the little brother, and he took the father and little Marleen by the hand; then they all three rejoiced, and went inside together and sat down to their dinners and ate.

The Turnip

There were two brothers who were both soldiers; the one was rich and the other poor. The poor man thought he would try to better himself; so, pulling off his red coat, he became a gardener, and dug his ground well, and sowed turnips.

When the seed came up, there was one plant bigger than all the rest; and it kept getting larger and larger, and seemed as if it would never cease growing; so that it might have been called the prince of turnips, for there never was such a one seen before, and never will again. At last it was so big that it filled a cart, and two oxen could hardly draw it; and the gardener knew not what in the world to do with it, nor whether it would be a blessing or a curse to him. One day he said to himself, "What shall I do with it? if I sell it, it will bring no more than another; and for eating, the little turnips are better than this; the best thing perhaps is to carry it and give it to the king as a mark of respect."

Then he yoked his oxen, and drew the turnip to the court, and gave it to the king. "What a wonderful thing!" said the king; "I have seen many strange things, but such a monster as this I never saw. Where did you get the seed? or is it only your good luck? If so, you are a true child of fortune."

"Ah, no!" answered the gardener, "I am no child of fortune; I am a poor soldier, who never could get enough to live upon; so I laid aside my

red coat, and set to work, tilling the ground. I have a brother, who is rich, and your majesty knows him well, and all the world knows him; but because I am poor, everybody forgets me."

The king then took pity on him, and said, "You shall be poor no longer. I will give you so much that you shall be even richer than your brother." Then he gave him gold and lands and flocks, and made him so rich that his brother's fortune could not at all be compared with his.

When the brother heard of all this, and how a turnip had made the gardener so rich, he envied him sorely, and bethought himself how he could contrive to get the same good fortune for himself. However, he determined to manage more cleverly than his brother, and got together a rich present of gold and fine horses for the king; and thought he must have a much larger gift in return; for if his brother had received so much for only a turnip, what must his present be worth?

The king took the gift very graciously, and said he knew not what to give in return more valuable and wonderful than the great turnip; so the soldier was forced to put it into a cart, and drag it home with him. When he reached home, he knew not upon whom to vent his rage and spite; and at length wicked thoughts came into his head, and he resolved to kill his brother.

So he hired some villains to murder him; and having shown them where to lie in ambush, he went to his brother, and said, "Dear brother, I have found a hidden treasure; let us go and dig it up, and share it between us." The other had no suspicions of his roguery: so they went out together, and as they were travelling along, the murderers rushed out upon him, bound him, and were going to hang him on a tree.

But whilst they were getting all ready, they heard the trampling of a horse at a distance, which so frightened them that they pushed their prisoner neck and shoulders together into a sack, and swung him up by a cord to the tree, where they left him dangling, and ran away. Meantime he worked and worked away, till he made a hole large enough to put out his head.

When the horseman came up, he proved to be a student, a merry fellow, who was journeying along on his nag, and singing as he went. As soon as the man in the sack saw him passing under the tree, he cried out, "Good morning! good morning to thee, my friend!" The student looked about everywhere; and seeing no one, and not knowing where the voice came from, cried out, "Who calls me?"

Then the man in the tree answered, "Lift up thine eyes, for behold here I sit in the sack of wisdom; here have I, in a short time, learned great and wondrous things. Compared to this seat, all the learning of the schools is as empty air. A little longer, and I shall know all that man can know, and shall come forth wiser than the wisest of mankind. Here I discern the signs and motions of the heavens and the stars; the laws that control the winds; the number of the sands on the seashore; the healing of the sick; the virtues of all simples, of birds, and of precious stones. Wert thou but once here, my friend, though wouldst feel and own the power of knowledge.

The student listened to all this and wondered much; at last he said, "Blessed be the day and hour when I found you; cannot you contrive to let me into the sack for a little while?" Then the other answered, as if very unwillingly, "A little space I may allow thee to sit here, if thou wilt reward me well and entreat me kindly; but thou must tarry yet an hour below, till I have learnt some little matters that are yet unknown to me."

So the student sat himself down and waited awhile; but the time hung heavy upon him, and he begged earnestly that he might ascend forthwith, for his thirst for knowledge was great. Then the other pretended to give way, and said, "Thou must let the sack of wisdom descend, by untying yonder cord, and then thou shalt enter."

So the student let him down, opened the sack, and set him free. "Now then," cried he, "let me ascend quickly."

As he began to put himself into the sack heels first, "Wait awhile," said the gardener, "that is not the way." Then he pushed him in head first, tied up the sack, and soon swung up the searcher after wisdom dangling in the air. "How is it with thee, friend?" said he, "dost thou not feel that wisdom comes unto thee? Rest there in peace, till thou art a wiser man than thou wert."

So saying, he trotted off on the student's nag, and left the poor fellow to gather wisdom till somebody should come and let him down.

The Three Languages

An aged count once lived in Switzerland, who had an only son, but he was stupid, and could learn nothing. Then said the father: "Hark you, my son, try as I will I can get nothing into your head. You must go from hence, I will give you into the care of a celebrated master, who shall see what he can do with you." The youth was sent into a strange town, and remained a whole year with the master.

At the end of this time, he came home again, and his father asked: "Now, my son, what have you learnt?"

"Father, I have learnt what the dogs say when they bark."

"Lord have mercy on us!" cried the father; "is that all you have learnt? I will send you into another town, to another master."

The youth was taken thither, and stayed a year with this master likewise. When he came back the father again asked: "My son, what have you learnt?"

He answered: "Father, I have learnt what the birds say."

Then the father fell into a rage and said: "Oh, you lost man, you have spent the precious time and learnt nothing; are you not ashamed to appear before my eyes? I will send you to a third master, but if you learn nothing this time also, I will no longer be your father."

The youth remained a whole year with the third master also, and when he came home again, and his father inquired: "My son, what have you learnt?" he answered: "Dear father, I have this year learnt what the frogs croak." Then the father fell into the most furious anger, sprang up, called his people thither, and said: "This man is no longer my son, I drive him forth, and command you to take him out into the forest, and kill him."

They took him forth, but when they should have killed him, they could not do it for pity, and let him go, and they cut the eyes and tongue out of a deer that they might carry them to the old man as a token.

The youth wandered on, and after some time came to a fortress where he begged for a night's lodging. "Yes," said the lord of the castle, "if you will pass the night down there in the old tower, go thither; but I warn you, it is at the peril of your life, for it is full of wild dogs, which bark and howl without stopping, and at certain hours a man has to be given to them, whom they at once devour." The whole district was in sorrow and dismay because of them, and yet no one could do anything to stop this. The youth, however, was without fear, and said: "Just let me go down to the barking dogs, and give me something that I can throw to them; they will do nothing to harm me." As he himself would have it so, they gave him some food for the wild animals, and led him down to the tower. When he went inside, the dogs did not bark at him, but wagged their tails quite amicably around him, ate what he set before them, and did not hurt one hair of his head. Next morning, to the astonishment of everyone, he came out again safe and unharmed, and said to the lord of the castle: "The dogs have revealed to me, in their own language, why they dwell there, and bring evil on the land. They are bewitched, and are obliged to watch over a great treasure which is below in the tower, and they can have no rest until it is taken away, and I have likewise learnt, from their discourse, how that is to be done." Then all who heard this rejoiced, and the lord of the castle said he would adopt him as a son if he accomplished it successfully. He went down again, and as he knew what he had to do, he did it thoroughly, and brought a chest full of gold out with him. The howling of the wild dogs was henceforth heard no more; they had disappeared, and the country was freed from the trouble.

After some time he took it in his head that he would travel to Rome. On the way he passed by a marsh, in which a number of frogs were sitting croaking. He listened to them, and when he became aware of what they were saying, he grew very thoughtful and sad. At last he arrived in Rome, where the Pope had just died, and there was great doubt among the cardinals as to whom they should appoint as his successor. They at length agreed that the person should be chosen as pope who should be distinguished by some divine and miraculous token. And just as that was decided on, the young count entered into the church, and suddenly two snow white doves flew on his shoulders and remained sitting there. The ecclesiastics recognized therein the token from above, and asked him on the spot if he would be pope. He was undecided, and knew not if he were worthy of this, but the doves counselled him to do it, and at length he said yes. Then was he anointed and consecrated, and thus was fulfilled what he had heard from the frogs on his way, which had so affected him, that he was to be his Holiness the Pope. Then he had to sing a mass, and did not know one word of it, but the two doves sat continually on his shoulders, and said it all in his ear.

Faithful John

Once upon a time there lived an old King, who fell very sick, and thought he was lying upon his deathbed; so he said, "Let faithful John come to me." This faithful John was his affectionate servant, and was so called because he had been true to him all his lifetime.

As soon as John came to the bedside, the King said, "My faithful John, I feel that my end approaches, and I have no other care than about my son, who is still so young that he cannot always guide himself aright. If you do not promise to instruct him in everything he ought to know, and to be his guardian, I cannot close my eyes in peace."

Then John answered, "I will never leave him; I will always serve him truly, even if it costs me my life."

So the old King was comforted, and said, "Now I can die in peace. After my death you must show him all the chambers, halls, and vaults in the castle, and all the treasures which are in them; but the last room in the long corridor you must not show him, for in it hangs the portrait of the daughter of the King of the Golden Palace; if he sees her picture, he will conceive a great love for her, and will fall down in a swoon, and on her account undergo great perils, therefore you must keep him away."

The faithful John pressed his master's hand again in token of assent, and soon after the King laid his head upon the pillow and expired.

After the old King had been borne to his grave, the faithful John related to the young King all that his father had said upon his deathbed, and declared, "All this I will certainly fulfil; I will be as true to you as I was to him, if it costs me my life." When the time of mourning was passed, John said to the young King, "It is now time for you to see your inheritance; I will show you your paternal castle." So he led the King all over it, upstairs and downstairs, and showed him all the riches, and all the splendid chambers; only one room he did not open, containing the perilous portrait, which was so placed that one saw it directly the door was opened, and, moreover, it was so beautifully painted that one thought it breathed and moved; nothing in all the world could be more lifelike or more beautiful. The young King remarked, however, that the faithful John always passed by one door, so he asked, "Why do you not open that one?"

"There is something in it," he replied, "which will frighten you."

But the King said, "I have seen all the rest of the castle, and I will know what is in there," and he went and tried to open the door by force. The faithful John pulled him back, and said, "I promised your father before he died that you should not see the contents of that room; it would bring great misfortunes both upon you and me."

"Oh, no," replied the young King, "if I do not go in it will be my certain ruin; I should have no peace night nor day until I had seen it with my own eyes. Now I will not stir from the place till you unlock the door."

Then the faithful John saw that it was of no use talking; so, with a heavy heart and many sighs, he picked the key out of the great bunch. When he had opened the door, he went in first, and thought he would cover up the picture, that the King should not see it; but it was of no use, for the King stepped upon tiptoes and looked over his shoulder; and as soon as he saw the portrait of the maiden, which was so beautiful and glittered with precious stones, he fell down on the ground insensible. The faithful John lifted him up and carried him to his bed, and thought with great concern, "Mercy on us! the misfortune has happened; what will come of it?" and he gave the young King wine until he came to himself. The first words he spoke were, "Who does that beautiful picture represent?" "That is the daughter of the King of the Golden Palace," was the reply.

"Then," said the King, "my love for her is so great that if all the leaves on the trees had tongues, they should not gainsay it; my life is set upon the search for her. You are my faithful John, you must accompany me."

The trusty servant deliberated for a long while how to set about this business, for it was very difficult to get into the presence of the King's daughter. At last he bethought himself of a way, and said to the King, "Everything which she has around her is of gold—chairs, tables, dishes, bowls, and all the household utensils. Among your treasures are five tons of gold; let one of the goldsmiths of your kingdom manufacture vessels and utensils of all kinds therefrom—all kinds of birds, and wild and wonderful beasts, such as will please her, then we will travel with these, and try our luck." Then the King summoned all his goldsmiths, who worked day and night until many very beautiful things were ready. When all had been placed on board a ship, the faithful John put on merchant's clothes, and the King likewise, so that they might travel quite unknown. Then they sailed over the wide sea, and sailed away until they came to the city where dwelt the daughter of the King of the Golden Palace.

The faithful John told the King to remain in the ship, and wait for him. "Perhaps," said he, "I shall bring the King's daughter with me; therefore take care that all is in order, and set out the golden vessels and adorn the whole ship." Thereupon John placed in a napkin some of the golden cups, stepped upon land, and went straight to the King's palace. When he came into the castle yard, a beautiful maid stood by the brook, who had two golden pails in her hand, drawing water; and when she had filled them and had turned round, she saw a strange man, and asked who he was. Then John answered, "I am a merchant"; and opening his napkin he showed her its contents. Then she exclaimed, "Oh, what beautiful golden things!" and, setting the pails down, she looked at the cups one after another, and said, "The King's daughter must see these; she is so pleased with anything made of gold that she will buy all these." And taking him by the hand, she led him in; for she was the lady's maid.

When the King's daughter saw the golden cups, she was much pleased, and said, "They are so finely worked that I will purchase them all." But the faithful John replied, "I am only the servant of a rich merchant; what I have here is nothing in comparison to those which my master has in his ship, than which nothing more delicate or costly has ever been worked in gold." Then the King's daughter wished to have them all brought; but he said, "It would take many days, and so great is the quantity that your palace has not halls enough in it to place them around." Then her curiosity and desire were still more excited, and at last she said, "Take me to the ship; I will go myself and look at your master's treasure."

The faithful John conducted her to the ship with great joy, and the King, when he beheld her, saw that her beauty was still greater than the picture had represented, and thought nothing else but that his heart would jump out of his mouth. Presently she stepped on board, and the King conducted her below; but the faithful John remained on deck by the steersman, and told him to unmoor the ship and put on all the sail he could, that it might fly as a bird through the air. Meanwhile the King showed the Princess all the golden treasures—the dishes, cups, bowls, the birds, the wild and wonderful beasts. Many hours passed away while she looked at everything, and in her joy she did not remark that the ship sailed on and on. As soon as she had looked at the last, and thanked the merchant, she wished to depart. But when she came on deck, she perceived that they were upon the high sea, far from the shore, and were hastening on with all sail. "Ah," she exclaimed in affright, "I am betrayed; I am carried off and taken away in the power of a strange merchant. I would rather die!"

But the King, taking her by the hand, said, "I am not a merchant, but a king, thine equal in birth. It is true that I have carried thee off; but that is because of my overwhelming love for thee. Dost thou know

FAITHFUL·JOHN
"IT HAPPENED, AS THEY WERE STILL
JOURNEYING ON THE OPEN SEA, THAT
FAITHFUL IOHN, AS HE SAT IN THE FORE
PART OF THE SHIP, & MADE MUSIC, CAUGHT
SIGHT OF THREE RAVENS FLYING OVER-
HEAD. THEN HE STOPPED PLAYING &
LISTENED TO WHAT THEY SAID TO ONE ANOTHER"

that when I first saw the portrait of thy beauteous face I fell down in a swoon before it?"

When the King's daughter heard these words, she was reassured, and her heart was inclined toward him, so that she willingly became his bride. While they thus went on their voyage on the high sea, it happened that the faithful John, as he sat on the deck of the ship, playing music, saw three crows in the air, who came flying toward them. He stopped playing, and listened to what they were saying to each other, for he understood them perfectly.

The first one exclaimed, "There he is, carrying home the daughter of the King of the Golden Palace."

"But he is not home yet," replied the second.

"But he has her," said the third; "she is sitting by him in the ship."

Then the first began again, and exclaimed, "What matters that? When they go on shore a fox- coloured horse will spring toward them, on which he will mount; and as soon as he is on it, it will jump up with him into the air, so that he will never again see his bride."

The second one asked, "Is there no escape?"

"Oh, yes, if another mounts behind quickly, and takes out the fire-arms which are in the holster, and with them shoots the horse dead, then the young King will be saved. But who knows that? And if anyone does know it, and tells him, such a one will be turned to stone from the toe to the knee."

Then the second spoke again, "I know still more: if the horse should be killed, the young King will not then retain his bride; for when they come into the castle a beautiful bridal shirt will lie there upon a dish, and seem to be woven of gold and silver, but it is nothing but sulphur and pitch, and if he puts it on it will burn him to his marrow and bones."

Then the third Crow asked, "Is there no escape?"

"Oh, yes," answered the second, "if someone takes up the shirt with his glove on, and throws it into the fire, so that it is burnt, the young King will be saved. But what does that signify? Whoever knows it, and tells him, will be turned to stone from his knee to his heart."

Then the third Crow spoke: "I know still more: even if the bridal shirt be consumed, still the young King will not retain his bride. For if, after the wedding, a dance is held, while the young Queen dances she will suddenly turn pale, and fall down as if dead; and if someone does not raise her up, and take three drops of blood from her right breast and throw them away, she will die. But whoever knows that, and tells it, will have his whole body turned to stone, from the crown of his head to the toes of his feet."

After the crows had thus talked with one another, they flew away, and the trusty John, who had perfectly understood all they had said, was from that time very quiet and sad; for if he concealed from his master what he had heard, misfortune would happen to him, and if he told him all he must give up his own life. But at last he thought, "I will save my master, even if I destroy myself."

As soon as they came on shore, it happened just as the Crow had foretold, and an immense fox-red horse sprang up. "Capital!" said the King, "this shall carry me to my castle," and he tried to mount; but the faithful John came straight up, and swinging himself quickly on, drew the firearms out of the holster and shot the horse dead. Then the other servants of the King, who were not on good terms with the faithful John, exclaimed, "How shameful to kill the beautiful creature, which might have borne the King to the castle!"

But the King replied, "Be silent, and let him go; he is my very faithful John—who knows the good he may have done?" Now they went into the castle, and there stood a dish in the hall, and the splendid bridal shirt lay in it, and seemed nothing else than gold and silver. The young King went up to it and wished to take it up, but the faithful John pushed him away, and taking it up with his gloves on, bore it quickly to the fire and let it burn. The other servants thereupon began to murmur, saying, "See, now he is burning the King's bridal shirt!" But the young King replied, "Who knows what good he has done? Let him alone—he is my faithful John."

Soon after, the wedding was celebrated, and a grand ball was given, and the bride began to dance. So the faithful John paid great attention, and watched her countenance; all at once she grew pale, and fell as if dead to the ground. Then he sprang up hastily, raised her up and bore her to a chamber, where he laid her down, kneeled beside her, and drawing the three drops of blood out of her right breast, threw them away. As soon as she breathed again, she raised herself up; but the young King had witnessed everything, and not knowing why the faithful John had done this was very angry, and called out, "Throw him into prison!"

The next morning the trusty John was brought up for trial, and led to the gallows; and as he stood upon them, and was about to be executed, he said, "Everyone condemned to die may once before his death speak. Shall I also have that privilege?"

"Yes," answered the King, "it shall be granted you."

Then the faithful John replied, "I have been unrighteously judged, and have always been true to you"; and he narrated the conversation of the crows which he heard at sea; and how, in order to save his master, he was obliged to do all he had done.

Then the King cried out, "Oh, my most trusty John, pardon, pardon; lead him away!" But the trusty John had fallen down at the last word and was turned into stone.

At this event both the King and the Queen were in great grief, and the King thought, "Ah, how wickedly have I rewarded his great fidelity!" and he had the stone statue raised up and placed in his sleeping chamber, near his bed; and as often as he looked at it, he wept and said, "Ah, could I bring you back to life again, my faithful John!"

After some time had passed, the Queen bore twins, two little sons, who were her great joy. Once, when the Queen was in church, and the two children at home playing by their father's side, he looked up at the stone statue full of sorrow, and exclaimed with a sigh, "Ah, could I restore you to life, my faithful John!"

At these words the statue began to speak, saying, "Yes, you can make me alive again, if you will bestow on me that which is dearest to you."

The King replied, "All that I have in the world I will give up for you."

The statue spake again: "If you, with your own hand, cut off the heads of both your children, and sprinkle me with their blood, I shall be brought to life again."

The King was terrified when he heard that he must himself kill his two dear children; but he remembered his servant's great fidelity, and how the faithful John had died for him, and drawing his sword he cut off the heads of both his children with his own hand. And as soon as he had sprinkled the statue with blood, life came back to it, and the trusty John stood again alive and well before him, and said, "Your faith shall not go unrewarded"; and taking the heads of the two children he set them on again, and anointed their wounds with their blood, and thereupon they healed again in a moment, and the children sprang away and played as if nothing had happened.

Now the King was full of happiness, and as soon as he saw the Queen coming, he hid the faithful John and both the children in a great closet. As soon as she came in he said to her, "Have you prayed in the church?"

"Yes," she answered; "but I thought continually of the faithful John, who has come to such misfortune through us."

Then he replied, "My dear wife, we can restore his life again to him, but it will cost us both our little sons, whom we must sacrifice."

The Queen became pale and was terrified at heart, but she said, "We are guilty of his life on account of his great fidelity."

Then he was very glad that she thought as he did, and going up to the closet, he unlocked it, brought out the children and the faithful John, saying, "God be praised! he is saved, and we have still our little sons"; and then he told her all that happened. Afterward they lived happily together to the end of their days.

The Fox and the Cat

It happened that the cat met the fox in a forest, and as she thought to herself: "He is clever and full of experience, and much esteemed in the world," she spoke to him in a friendly way. "Good day, dear Mr. Fox, how are you? How is all with you? How are you getting on in these hard times?"

The fox, full of all kinds of arrogance, looked at the cat from head to foot, and for a long time did not know whether he would give any answer or not. At last he said: "Oh, you wretched beard cleaner, you piebald fool, you hungry mouse hunter, what can you be thinking of? Have you the cheek to ask how I am getting on? What have you learnt? How many arts do you understand?"

"I understand but one," replied the cat, modestly.

"What art is that?" asked the fox.

"When the hounds are following me, I can spring into a tree and save myself."

"Is that all?" said the fox. "I am master of a hundred arts, and have into the bargain a sackful of cunning. You make me sorry for you; come with me, I will teach you how people get away from the hounds." Just then came a hunter with four dogs. The cat sprang nimbly up a tree, and sat down at the top of it, where the branches and foliage quite concealed her.

"Open your sack, Mr. Fox, open your sack," cried the cat to him, but the dogs had already seized him, and were holding him fast.

"Ah, Mr. Fox," cried the cat. "You with your hundred arts are left in the lurch! Had you been able to climb like me, you would not have lost your life."

The Raven

There was once a queen who had a little daughter, still too young to run alone. One day the child was very troublesome, and the mother could not quiet it, do what she would. She grew impatient, and seeing the ravens flying round the castle, she opened the window, and said: "I wish you were a raven and would fly away, then I should have a little peace." Scarcely were the words out of her mouth, when the child in her arms was turned into a raven, and flew away from her through the open window. The bird took its flight to a dark wood and remained there for a long time, and meanwhile the parents could hear nothing of their child.

Long after this, a man was making his way through the wood when he heard a raven calling, and he followed the sound of the voice. As he drew near, the raven said, "I am by birth a king's daughter, but am now under the spell of some enchantment; you can, however, set me free."

"What am I to do?" he asked.

She replied, "Go farther into the wood until you come to a house, wherein lives an old woman; she will offer you food and drink, but you must not take of either; if you do, you will fall into a deep sleep, and will not be able to help me. In the garden behind the house is a large tan heap, and on that you must stand and watch for me. I shall drive there in my carriage at two o'clock in the afternoon for three successive days; the first day it will be drawn by four white, the second by four chestnut, and the last by four black horses; but if you fail to keep awake and I find you sleeping, I shall not be set free."

The man promised to do all that she wished, but the raven said, "Alas! I know even now that you will take something from the woman and be unable to save me." The man assured her again that he would on no account touch a thing to eat or drink.

When he came to the house and went inside, the old woman met him, and said, "Poor man! how tired you are! Come in and rest and let me give you something to eat and drink."

"No," answered the man, "I will neither eat nor drink."

But she would not leave him alone, and urged him, saying, "If you will not eat anything, at least you might take a draught of wine; one drink counts for nothing," and at last he allowed himself to be persuaded, and drank.

As it drew towards the appointed hour, he went outside into the garden and mounted the tan heap to await the raven. Suddenly a feeling of fatigue came over him, and unable to resist it, he lay down for a little while, fully determined, however, to keep awake; but in another minute his eyes closed of their own accord, and he fell into such a deep sleep, that all the noises in the world would not have awakened him. At two o'clock the raven came driving along, drawn by her four white horses; but even before she reached the spot, she said to herself, sighing, "I know he has fallen asleep." When she entered the garden, there she found him as she had feared, lying on the tan heap, fast asleep. She got out of her carriage and went to him; she called him and shook him, but it was all in vain, he still continued sleeping.

The next day at noon, the old woman came to him again with food and drink which he at first refused. At last, overcome by her persistent entreaties that he would take something, he lifted the glass and drank again.

Towards two o'clock he went into the garden and on to the tan heap to watch for the raven. He had not been there long before he began to feel so tired that his limbs seemed hardly able to support him, and he could not stand upright any longer; so again he lay down and fell fast asleep. As the raven drove along her four chestnut horses, she said sorrowfully to herself, "I know he has fallen asleep." She went as before to look for him, but he slept, and it was impossible to awaken him.

The following day the old woman said to him, "What is this? You are not eating or drinking anything, do you want to kill yourself?"

He answered, "I may not and will not either eat or drink."

But she put down the dish of food and the glass of wine in front of him, and when he smelt the wine, he was unable to resist the temptation, and took a deep draught.

When the hour came round again he went as usual on to the tan-heap in the garden to await the king's daughter, but he felt even more overcome with weariness than on the two previous days, and throwing himself down, he slept like a log. At two o'clock the raven could be seen approaching, and this time her coachman and everything about her, as well as her horses, were black.

She was sadder than ever as she drove along, and said mournfully, "I know he has fallen asleep, and will not be able to set me free." She found him sleeping heavily, and all her efforts to awaken him were of no avail. Then she placed beside him a loaf, and some meat, and a flask of wine, of such a kind, that however much he took of them, they would never grow less. After that she drew a gold ring, on which her name was engraved, off her finger, and put it upon one of his. Finally, she laid a letter near him, in which, after giving him particulars of the food and drink she had left for him, she finished with the following words: "I see that as long as you remain here you will never be able to set me free; if, however, you still wish to do so, come to the golden castle of Stromberg; this is well within your power to accomplish." She then returned to her carriage and drove to the golden castle of Stromberg.

When the man awoke and found that he had been sleeping, he was grieved at heart, and said, "She has no doubt been here and driven away again, and it is now too late for me to save her." Then his eyes fell on the things which were lying beside him; he read the letter, and knew from it all that had happened. He rose up without delay, eager to start on his way and to reach the castle of Stromberg, but he had no idea in which direction he ought to go. He travelled about a long time in search of it and came at last to a dark forest, through which he went on walking for fourteen days and still could not find a way out. Once more the night came on, and worn out he lay down under a bush and fell asleep. Again the next day he pursued his way through the forest, and that evening, thinking to rest again, he lay down as before, but he heard such a howling and wailing that he found it impossible to sleep. He waited till it was darker and people had begun to light up their houses, and then seeing a little glimmer ahead of him, he went towards it.

He found that the light came from a house which looked smaller than it really was, from the contrast of its height with that of an immense giant who stood in front of it. He thought to himself, "If the giant sees me going in, my life will not be worth much."

However, after a while he summoned up courage and went forward. When the giant saw him, he called out, "It is lucky for that you have come, for I have not had anything to eat for a long time. I can have you now for my supper."

"I would rather you let that alone," said the man, "for I do not willingly give myself up to be eaten; if you are wanting food I have enough to satisfy your hunger."

"If that is so," replied the giant, "I will leave you in peace; I only thought of eating you because I had nothing else."

So they went indoors together and sat down, and the man brought out the bread, meat, and wine, which although he had eaten and drunk of them, were still unconsumed. The giant was pleased with the good cheer, and ate and drank to his heart's content. When he had finished his supper the man asked him if he could direct him to the castle of Stromberg. The giant said, "I will look on my map; on it are marked all the towns, villages, and houses." So he fetched his map, and looked for the castle, but could not find it. "Never mind," he said, "I have larger maps upstairs in the cupboard, we will look on those," but they searched in vain, for the castle was not marked even on these. The man now thought he should like to continue his journey, but the giant begged him to remain for a day or two longer until the return of his brother, who was away in search of provisions. When the brother came home, they asked him about the castle of Stromberg, and he told them he would look on his own maps as soon as he had eaten and appeased his hunger. Accordingly, when he had finished his supper, they all went up together to his room and looked through his maps, but the castle was not to be found. Then he fetched other older maps, and they went on looking for the castle until at last they found it, but it was many thousand miles away.

"How shall I be able to get there?" asked the man.

"I have two hours to spare," said the giant, "and I will carry you into the neighbourhood of the castle; I must then return to look after the child who is in our care."

The giant, thereupon, carried the man to within about a hundred leagues of the castle, where he left him, saying, "You will be able to walk the remainder of the way yourself." The man journeyed on day and night till he reached the golden castle of Stromberg. He found it situated, however, on a glass mountain, and looking up from the foot he saw the enchanted maiden drive round her castle and then go inside. He was overjoyed to see her, and longed to get to the top of the mountain, but the sides were so slippery that every time he attempted to climb he fell back again. When he saw that it was impossible to reach her, he was greatly grieved, and said to himself, "I will remain here and wait for her," so he built himself a little hut, and there he sat and watched for a whole year, and every day he saw the king's daughter driving round her castle, but still was unable to get nearer to her.

Looking out from his hut one day he saw three robbers fighting and he called out to them, "God be with you." They stopped when they heard the call, but looking round and seeing nobody, they went on again with their fighting, which now became more furious. "God be with you," he cried again, and again they paused and looked about, but seeing no one went back to their fighting. A third time he called out, "God be with you," and then thinking he should like to know the cause of dispute between the three men, he went out and asked them why they were fighting so angrily with one another. One of them said that he had found a stick, and that he had but to strike it against any door through which he wished to pass, and it immediately flew open. Another told him that he had found a cloak which rendered its wearer invisible; and the third had caught a horse which would carry its rider over any obstacle, and even up the glass mountain. They had been unable to decide whether they would keep together and have the things in common, or whether they would separate. On hearing this, the man said, "I will give you something in exchange for those three things; not money, for that I have not got, but something that is of far more value. I must first, however, prove whether all you have told me about your three things is true." The robbers, therefore, made him get on the horse, and handed him the stick and the cloak, and when he had put this round him he was no longer visible. Then he fell upon them with the stick and beat them one after another, crying, "There, you idle vagabonds, you have got what you deserve; are you satisfied now!"

After this he rode up the glass mountain. When he reached the gate of the castle, he found it closed, but he gave it a blow with his stick, and it flew wide open at once and he passed through. He mounted the steps and entered the room where the maiden was sitting, with a golden goblet full of wine in front of her. She could not see him, for he still wore his cloak. He took the ring which she had given him off his finger, and threw it into the goblet, so that it rang as it touched the bottom. "That is my own ring," she exclaimed, "and if that is so the man must also be here who is coming to set me free."

She sought for him about the castle, but could find him nowhere. Meanwhile he had gone outside again and mounted his horse and thrown off the cloak. When therefore she came to the castle gate she saw him, and cried aloud for joy. Then he dismounted and took her in his arms; and she kissed him, and said, "Now you have indeed set me free, and tomorrow we will celebrate our marriage."

The Four Clever Brothers

"Dear children," said a poor man to his four sons, "I have nothing to give you; you must go out into the wide world and try your luck. Begin by learning some craft or another, and see how you can get on." So the four brothers took their walking sticks in their hands, and their little bundles on their shoulders, and after bidding their father goodbye, went all out at the gate together. When they had got on some way they came to four crossways, each leading to a different country. Then the eldest said, "Here we must part; but this day in four years we will come back to this spot, and in the meantime each must try what he can do for himself."

So each brother went his way; and as the eldest was hastening on a man met him, and asked him where he was going, and what he wanted. "I am going to try my luck in the world, and should like to begin by learning some art or trade," answered he.

"Then," said the man, "go with me, and I will teach you to become the cunningest thief that ever was."

"No," said the other, "that is not an honest calling, and what can one look to earn by it in the end but the gallows?"

"Oh!" said the man, "you need not fear the gallows; for I will only teach you to steal what will be fair game: I meddle with nothing but what no one else can get or care anything about, and where no one can find you out." So the young man agreed to follow his trade, and he soon showed himself so clever, that nothing could escape him that he had once set his mind upon.

The second brother also met a man, who, when he found out what he was setting out upon, asked him what craft he meant to follow. "I do not know yet," said he.

"Then come with me, and be a stargazer. It is a noble art, for nothing can be hidden from you, when once you understand the stars." The plan pleased him much, and he soon became such a skillful stargazer, that when he had served out his time, and wanted to leave his master, he gave him a glass, and said, "With this you can see all that is passing in the sky and on earth, and nothing can be hidden from you."

The third brother met a huntsman, who took him with him, and taught him so well all that belonged to hunting, that he became very clever in the craft of the woods; and when he left his master he gave him a bow, and said, "Whatever you shoot at with this bow you will be sure to hit."

The youngest brother likewise met a man who asked him what he wished to do. "Would not you like," said he, "to be a tailor?"

"Oh, no!" said the young man; "sitting cross-legged from morning to night, working backwards and forwards with a needle and goose, will never suit me."

"Oh!" answered the man, "that is not my sort of tailoring; come with me, and you will learn quite another kind of craft from that." Not knowing what better to do, he came into the plan, and learnt tailoring from the beginning; and when he left his master, he gave him a needle, and said, "You can sew anything with this, be it as soft as an egg or as hard as steel; and the joint will be so fine that no seam will be seen."

After the space of four years, at the time agreed upon, the four brothers met at the four crossroads; and having welcomed each other, set off towards their father's home, where they told him all that had happened to them, and how each had learned some craft.

Then, one day, as they were sitting before the house under a very high tree, the father said, "I should like to try what each of you can do in this way." So he looked up, and said to the second son, "At the top of this tree there is a chaffinch's nest; tell me how many eggs there are in it." The stargazer took his glass, looked up, and said, "Five."

"Now," said the father to the eldest son, "take away the eggs without letting the bird that is sitting upon them and hatching them know anything of what you are doing." So the cunning thief climbed up the tree, and brought away to his father the five eggs from under the bird; and it never saw or felt what he was doing, but kept sitting on at its ease. Then the father took the eggs, and put one on each corner of the table, and the fifth in the middle, and said to the huntsman, "Cut all the eggs in two pieces at one shot." The huntsman took up his bow, and at one shot struck all the five eggs as his father wished.

"Now comes your turn," said he to the young tailor; "sew the eggs and the young birds in them together again, so neatly that the shot shall have done them no harm." Then the tailor took his needle, and sewed the eggs as he was told; and when he had done, the thief was sent to take them back to the nest, and put them under the bird without its knowing it. Then she went on sitting, and hatched them: and in a few days they crawled out, and had only a little red streak across their necks, where the tailor had sewn them together.

"Well done, sons!" said the old man; "you have made good use of your time, and learnt something worth the knowing; but I am sure I do not know which ought to have the prize. Oh, that a time might soon come for you to turn your skill to some account!"

Not long after this there was a great bustle in the country; for the king's daughter had been carried off by a mighty dragon, and the king mourned over his loss day and night, and made it known that whoever brought her back to him should have her for a wife. Then the four brothers said to each other, "Here is a chance for us; let us try what we can do." And they agreed to see whether they could not set the princess free.

"I will soon find out where she is, however," said the stargazer, as he looked through his glass; and he soon cried out, "I see her afar off, sitting upon a rock in the sea, and I can spy the dragon close by, guarding her." Then he went to the king, and asked for a ship for himself and his brothers; and they sailed together over the sea, till they came to the right place. There they found the princess sitting, as the stargazer had said, on the rock; and the dragon was lying asleep, with his head upon her lap. "I dare not shoot at him," said the huntsman, "for I should kill the beautiful young lady also."

"Then I will try my skill," said the thief, and went and stole her away from under the dragon, so quietly and gently that the beast did not know it, but went on snoring.

Then away they hastened with her full of joy in their boat towards the ship; but soon came the dragon roaring behind them through the air; for he awoke and missed the princess. But when he got over the boat, and wanted to pounce upon them and carry off the princess, the huntsman took up his bow and shot him straight through the heart so that he fell down dead. They were still not safe; for he was such a great beast that in his fall he overset the boat, and they had to swim in the open sea upon a few planks. So the tailor took his needle, and with a few large stitches put some of the planks together; and he sat down upon these, and sailed about and gathered up all pieces of the boat; and then tacked them together so quickly that the boat was soon ready, and they then reached the ship and got home safe.

When they had brought home the princess to her father, there was great rejoicing; and he said to the four brothers, "One of you shall marry her, but you must settle amongst yourselves which it is to be."

Then there arose a quarrel between them; and the stargazer said, "If I had not found the princess out, all your skill would have been of no use; therefore she ought to be mine."

"Your seeing her would have been of no use," said the thief, "if I had not taken her away from the dragon; therefore she ought to be mine."

"No, she is mine," said the huntsman; "for if I had not killed the dragon, he would, after all, have torn you and the princess into pieces."

"And if I had not sewn the boat together again," said the tailor, "you would all have been drowned, therefore she is mine."

Then the king put in a word, and said, "Each of you is right; and as all cannot have the young lady, the best way is for neither of you to have her: for the truth is, there is somebody she likes a great deal better. But to make up for your loss, I will give each of you, as a reward for his skill, half a kingdom." So the brothers agreed that this plan would be much better than either quarrelling or marrying a lady who had no mind to have them. And the king then gave to each half a kingdom, as he had said; and they lived very happily the rest of their days, and took good care of their father; and somebody took better care of the young lady than to let either the dragon or one of the craftsmen have her again.

The Golden Goose

There was a man who had three sons, the youngest of whom was called Dummling, and was despised, mocked, and sneered at on every occasion.

It happened that the eldest wanted to go into the forest to hew wood, and before he went his mother gave him a beautiful sweet cake and a bottle of wine in order that he might not suffer from hunger or thirst.

When he entered the forest he met a little grey-haired old man who bade him good day, and said: "Do give me a piece of cake out of your pocket, and let me have a draught of your wine; I am so hungry and thirsty."

But the clever son answered: "If I give you my cake and wine, I shall have none for myself; be off with you," and he left the little man standing and went on.

But when he began to hew down a tree, it was not long before he made a false stroke, and the axe cut him in the arm, so that he had to go home and have it bound up. And this was the little grey man's doing.

After this the second son went into the forest, and his mother gave him, like the eldest, a cake and a bottle of wine. The little old grey man met him likewise, and asked him for a piece of cake and a drink of wine. But the second son, too, said sensibly enough: "What I give you will be taken away from myself; be off!" and he left the little man standing and went on. His punishment, however, was not delayed; when he had made a few blows at the tree he struck himself in the leg, so that he had to be carried home.

Then Dummling said: "Father, do let me go and cut wood."

The father answered: "Your brothers have hurt themselves with it, leave it alone, you do not understand anything about it."

But Dummling begged so long that at last he said: "Just go then, you will get wiser by hurting yourself." His mother gave him a cake made with water and baked in the cinders, and with it a bottle of sour beer.

When he came to the forest the little old grey man met him likewise, and greeting him, said: "Give me a piece of your cake and a drink out of your bottle; I am so hungry and thirsty."

Dummling answered: "I have only cinder cake and sour beer; if that pleases you, we will sit down and eat." So they sat down, and when Dummling pulled out his cinder cake, it was a fine sweet cake, and the sour beer had become good wine. So they ate and drank, and after that the little man said: "Since you have a good heart, and are willing to divide what you have, I will give you good luck. There stands an old tree; cut it down, and you will find something at the roots." Then the little man took leave of him.

Dummling went and cut down the tree, and when it fell there was a goose sitting in the roots with feathers of pure gold. He lifted her up, and taking her with him, went to an inn where he thought he would stay the night. Now the host had three daughters, who saw the goose and were curious to know what such a wonderful bird might be, and would have liked to have one of its golden feathers.

The eldest thought: "I shall soon find an opportunity of pulling out a feather," and as soon as Dummling had gone out she seized the goose by the wing, but her finger and hand remained sticking fast to it.

The second came soon afterwards, thinking only of how she might get a feather for herself, but she had scarcely touched her sister than she was held fast.

At last the third also came with the like intent, and the others screamed out: "Keep away; for goodness' sake keep away!" But she did not understand why she was to keep away. "The others are there," she thought, "I may as well be there too," and ran to them; but as soon as she had touched her sister, she remained sticking fast to her. So they had to spend the night with the goose.

The next morning Dummling took the goose under his arm and set out, without troubling himself about the three girls who were hanging on to it. They were obliged to run after him continually, now left, now right, wherever his legs took him.

In the middle of the fields the parson met them, and when he saw the procession he said: "For shame, you good-for-nothing girls, why are you running across the fields after this young man? Is that seemly?" At the same time he seized the youngest by the hand in order to pull her away, but as soon as he touched her he likewise stuck fast, and was himself obliged to run behind.

Before long the sexton came by and saw his master, the parson, running behind three girls. He was astonished at this and called out: "Hi! your reverence, whither away so quickly? Do not forget that we have a christening today!" and running after him he took him by the sleeve, but was also held fast to it.

Whilst the five were trotting thus, one behind the other, two labourers came with their hoes from the fields; the parson called out to them and begged that they would set him and the sexton free. But they had scarcely touched the sexton when they were held fast, and now there were seven of them running behind Dummling and the goose.

Soon afterwards he came to a city, where a king ruled who had a daughter who was so serious that no one could make her laugh. So he had put forth a decree that whosoever should be able to make her laugh should marry her. When Dummling heard this, he went with his goose and all her train before the king's daughter, and as soon as she saw the seven people running on and on, one behind the other, she began to laugh quite loudly, and as if she would never stop. Thereupon Dummling asked to have her for his wife; but the king did not like the son-in-law, and made all manner of excuses and said he must first produce a man who could drink a cellarful of wine. Dummling thought of the little grey man, who could certainly help him; so he went into the forest, and in the same place where he had felled the tree, he saw a man sitting, who had a very sorrowful face. Dummling asked him what he was taking to heart so sorely, and he answered: "I have such a great thirst and cannot quench it; cold water I cannot stand, a barrel of wine I have just emptied, but that to me is like a drop on a hot stone!"

"There, I can help you," said Dummling, "just come with me and you shall be satisfied."

He led him into the king's cellar, and the man bent over the huge barrels, and drank and drank till his loins hurt, and before the day was out he had emptied all the barrels. Then Dummling asked once more for his bride, but the king was vexed that such an ugly fellow, whom everyone called Dummling, should take away his daughter, and he made a new condition; he must first find a man who could eat a whole mountain of bread. Dummling did not think long, but went straight into the forest, where in the same place there sat a man who was tying up his body with a strap, and making an awful face, and saying: "I have eaten a whole overfull of rolls, but what good is that when one has such a hunger as I? My stomach remains empty, and I must tie myself up if I am not to die of hunger."

At this Dummling was glad, and said: "Get up and come with me; you shall eat yourself full." He led him to the king's palace where all the flour in the whole kingdom was collected, and from it he caused a huge mountain of bread to be baked. The man from the forest stood before it, began to eat, and by the end of one day the whole mountain had vanished. Then Dummling for the third time asked for his bride; but the king again sought a way out, and ordered a ship which could sail on land and on water. "As soon as you come sailing back in it," said he, "you shall have my daughter for wife."

Dummling went straight into the forest, and there sat the little grey man to whom he had given his cake. When he heard what Dummling wanted, he said: "Since you have given me to eat and to drink, I will give you the ship; and I do all this because you once were kind to me." Then he gave him the ship which could sail on land and water, and when the king saw that, he could no longer prevent him from having his daughter. The wedding was celebrated, and after the king's death, Dummling inherited his kingdom and lived for a long time contentedly with his wife.

Lily and the Lion

A merchant, who had three daughters, was once setting out upon a journey; but before he went he asked each daughter what gift he should bring back for her. The eldest wished for pearls; the second for jewels; but the third, who was called Lily, said, "Dear father, bring me a rose." Now it was no easy task to find a rose, for it was the middle of winter; yet as she was his prettiest daughter, and was very fond of flowers, her father said he would try what he could do. So he kissed all three, and bid them goodbye.

And when the time came for him to go home, he had bought pearls and jewels for the two eldest, but he had sought everywhere in vain for the rose; and when he went into any garden and asked for such a thing, the people laughed at him, and asked him whether he thought roses grew in snow. This grieved him very much, for Lily was his dearest child; and as he was journeying home, thinking what he should bring her, he came to a fine castle; and around the castle was a garden, in one half of which it seemed to be summertime and in the other half winter. On one side the finest flowers were in full bloom, and on the other everything looked dreary and buried in the snow. "A lucky hit!" said he, as he called to his servant, and told him to go to a beautiful bed of roses that was there, and bring him away one of the finest flowers.

This done, they were riding away well pleased, when up sprang a fierce lion, and roared out, "Whoever has stolen my roses shall be eaten up alive!" Then the man said, "I knew not that the garden belonged to you; can nothing save my life?"

"No!" said the lion, "nothing, unless you undertake to give me whatever meets you on your return home; if you agree to this, I will give you your life, and the rose too for your daughter." But the man was unwilling to do so and said, "It may be my youngest daughter, who loves me most, and always runs to meet me when I go home."

Then the servant was greatly frightened, and said, "It may perhaps be only a cat or a dog." And at last the man yielded with a heavy heart, and took the rose; and said he would give the lion whatever should meet him first on his return.

And as he came near home, it was Lily, his youngest and dearest daughter, that met him; she came running, and kissed him, and welcomed him home; and when she saw that he had brought her the rose, she was still more glad. But her father began to be very sorrowful, and to weep, saying, "Alas, my dearest child! I have bought this flower at a high price, for I have said I would give you to a wild lion; and when he has you, he will tear you in pieces, and eat you." Then he told her all that had happened, and said she should not go, let what would happen.

But she comforted him, and said, "Dear father, the word you have given must be kept; I will go to the lion, and soothe him: perhaps he will let me come safe home again."

The next morning she asked the way she was to go, and took leave of her father, and went forth with a bold heart into the wood. But the lion was an enchanted prince. By day he and all his court were lions, but in the evening they took their right forms again. And when Lily came to the castle, he welcomed her so courteously that she agreed to marry him. The wedding feast was held, and they lived happily together a long time. The prince was only to be seen as soon as evening came, and then he held his court; but every morning he left his bride, and went away by himself, she knew not whither, till the night came again.

After some time he said to her, "Tomorrow there will be a great feast in your father's house, for your eldest sister is to be married; and if you wish to go and visit her my lions shall lead you thither." Then she rejoiced much at the thoughts of seeing her father once more, and set out with the lions; and everyone was overjoyed to see her, for they had thought her dead long since. But she told them how happy she was, and stayed till the feast was over, and then went back to the wood.

Her second sister was soon after married, and when Lily was asked to go to the wedding, she said to the prince, "I will not go alone this time—you must go with me." But he would not, and said that it would be a very hazardous thing; for if the least ray of the torchlight should fall upon him his enchantment would become still worse, for he should be changed into a dove, and be forced to wander about the world for seven long years. However, she gave him no rest, and said she would take care no light should fall upon him. So at last they set out together, and took with them their little child; and she chose a large hall with thick walls for him to sit in while the wedding torches were lighted; but, unluckily, no one saw that there was a crack in the door. Then the wedding was held with great pomp, but as the train came from the church, and passed with the torches before the hall, a very small ray of light fell upon the prince. In a moment he disappeared, and when his wife came in and looked for him, she found only a white dove; and it said to her, "Seven years must I fly up and down over the face of the earth, but every now and then I will let fall a white feather, that will show you the way I am going; follow it, and at last you may overtake and set me free."

This said, he flew out at the door, and poor Lily followed; and every now and then a white feather fell, and showed her the way she was to journey. Thus she went roving on through the wide world, and looked neither to the right hand nor to the left, nor took any rest, for seven years. Then she began to be glad, and thought to herself that the time was fast coming when all her troubles should end; yet repose was still far off, for one day as she was travelling on she missed the white feather, and when she lifted up her eyes she could nowhere see the dove. "Now," thought she to herself, "no aid of man can be of use to me." So she went to the sun and said, "Thou shinest everywhere, on the hill's top and the valley's depth—hast thou anywhere seen my white dove?"

"No," said the sun, "I have not seen it; but I will give thee a casket—open it when thy hour of need comes."

So she thanked the sun, and went on her way till eventide; and when the moon arose, she cried unto it, and said, "Thou shinest through the night, over field and grove—hast thou nowhere seen my white dove?"

"No," said the moon, "I cannot help thee but I will give thee an egg—break it when need comes."

Then she thanked the moon, and went on till the night wind blew; and she raised up her voice to it, and said, "Thou blowest through every tree and under every leaf—hast thou not seen my white dove?"

"No," said the night wind, "but I will ask three other winds; perhaps they have seen it." Then the east wind and the west wind came, and said they too had not seen it, but the south wind said, "I have seen the white dove—he has fled to the Red Sea, and is changed once more into a lion, for the seven years are passed away, and there he is fighting with a dragon; and the dragon is an enchanted princess, who seeks to separate him from you."

Then the night wind said, "I will give thee counsel. Go to the Red Sea; on the right shore stand many rods—count them, and when thou comest to the eleventh, break it off, and smite the dragon with it; and so the lion will have the victory, and both of them will appear to you in their own forms. Then look round and thou wilt see a griffin, winged like bird, sitting by the Red Sea; jump on to his back with thy beloved one as quickly as possible, and he will carry you over the waters to your home. I will also give thee this nut," continued the night wind. "When you are halfway over, throw it down, and out of the waters will immediately spring up a high nut tree on which the griffin will be able to rest, otherwise he would not have the strength to bear you the whole way; if, therefore, thou dost forget to throw down the nut, he will let you both fall into the sea."

So our poor wanderer went forth, and found all as the night wind had said; and she plucked the eleventh rod, and smote the dragon, and the lion forthwith became a prince, and the dragon a princess again. But no sooner was the princess released from the spell, than she seized the prince by the arm and sprang on to the griffin's back, and went off carrying the prince away with her.

Thus the unhappy traveller was again forsaken and forlorn; but she took heart and said, "As far as the wind blows, and so long as the cock crows, I will journey on, till I find him once again." She went on for a long, long way, till at length she came to the castle whither the princess had carried the prince; and there was a feast got ready, and she heard that the wedding was about to be held. "Heaven aid me now!" said she; and she took the casket that the sun had given her, and found that within it lay a dress as dazzling as the sun itself. So she put it on, and went into the palace, and all the people gazed upon her; and the dress pleased the bride so much that she asked whether it was to be sold. "Not for gold and silver," said she, "but for flesh and blood." The princess asked what she meant, and she said, "Let me speak with the bridegroom this night in his chamber, and I will give thee the dress." At last the princess agreed, but she told her chamberlain to give the prince a sleeping draught, that he might not hear or see her. When evening came, and the prince had fallen asleep, she was led into his chamber, and she sat herself down at his feet, and said: "I have followed thee seven years. I have been to the sun, the moon, and the night wind, to seek thee, and at last I have helped thee to overcome the dragon. Wilt thou then forget me quite?" But the prince all the time slept so soundly, that her voice only passed over him, and seemed like the whistling of the wind among the fir trees.

Then poor Lily was led away, and forced to give up the golden dress; and when she saw that there was no help for her, she went out into a meadow, and sat herself down and wept. But as she sat she bethought herself of the egg that the moon had given her; and when she broke it, there ran out a hen and twelve chickens of pure gold, that played about, and then nestled under the old one's wings, so as to form the most beautiful sight in the world. And she rose up and drove them before her, till the bride saw them from her window, and was so pleased that she came forth and asked her if she would sell the brood. "Not for gold or silver, but for flesh and blood: let me again this evening speak with the bridegroom in his chamber, and I will give thee the whole brood."

Then the princess thought to betray her as before, and agreed to what she asked: but when the prince went to his chamber he asked the chamberlain why the wind had whistled so in the night. And the chamberlain told him all—how he had given him a sleeping draught, and how a poor maiden had come and spoken to him in his chamber, and was to come again that night. Then the prince took care to throw away the sleeping draught; and when Lily came and began again to tell him what woes had befallen her, and how faithful and true to him she had been, he knew his beloved wife's voice, and sprang up, and said, "You have awakened me as from a dream, for the strange princess had thrown a spell around me, so that I had altogether forgotten you; but heaven hath sent you to me in a lucky hour."

And they stole away out of the palace by night unawares, and seated themselves on the griffin, who flew back with them over the Red Sea. When they were halfway across Lily let the nut fall into the water, and immediately a large nut tree arose from the sea, whereon the griffin rested for a while, and then carried them safely home. There they found their child, now grown up to be comely and fair; and after all their troubles they lived happily together to the end of their days.

The Twelve Huntsmen

There was once a king's son who had a bride whom he loved very much. And when he was sitting beside her and very happy, news came that his father lay sick unto death, and desired to see him once again before his end. Then he said to his beloved: "I must now go and leave you, I give you a ring as a remembrance of me. When I am king, I will return and fetch you." So he rode away, and when he reached his father, the latter was dangerously ill, and near his death. He said to him: "Dear son, I wished to see you once again before my end, promise me to marry as I wish," and he named a certain king's daughter who was to be his wife.

The son was in such trouble that he did not think what he was doing, and said: "Yes, dear father, your will shall be done," and thereupon the king shut his eyes, and died.

When therefore the son had been proclaimed king, and the time of mourning was over, he was forced to keep the promise which he had given his father, and caused the king's daughter to be asked in marriage, and she was promised to him. His first betrothed heard of this, and fretted so much about his faithfulness that she nearly died. Then her father said to her: "Dearest child, why are you so sad? You shall have whatsoever you will."

She thought for a moment and said: "Dear father, I wish for eleven girls exactly like myself in face, figure, and size."

The father said: "If it be possible, your desire shall be fulfilled," and he caused a search to be made in his whole kingdom, until eleven young maidens were found who exactly resembled his daughter in face, figure, and size.

When they came to the king's daughter, she had twelve suits of huntsmen's clothes made, all alike, and the eleven maidens had to put on the huntsmen's clothes, and she herself put on the twelfth suit. Thereupon she took her leave of her father, and rode away with them, and rode to the court of her former betrothed, whom she loved so dearly. Then she asked if he required any huntsmen, and if he would take all of them into his service. The king looked at her and did not know her, but as they were such handsome fellows, he said: "Yes," and that he would willingly take them, and now they were the king's twelve huntsmen.

The king, however, had a lion which was a wondrous animal, for he knew all concealed and secret things. It came to pass that one evening he said to the king: "You think you have twelve huntsmen?"

"Yes," said the king, "they are twelve huntsmen."

The lion continued: "You are mistaken, they are twelve girls."

The king said: "That cannot be true! How will you prove that to me?"

"Oh, just let some peas be strewn in the antechamber," answered the lion, "and then you will soon see. Men have a firm step, and when they walk over peas none of them stir, but girls trip and skip, and drag their feet, and the peas roll about." The king was well pleased with the counsel, and caused the peas to be strewn.

There was, however, a servant of the king's who favoured the huntsmen, and when he heard that they were going to be put to this test he went to them and repeated everything, and said: "The lion wants to make the king believe that you are girls."

Then the king's daughter thanked him, and said to her maidens: "Show some strength, and step firmly on the peas." So next morning when the king had the twelve huntsmen called before him, and they came into the antechamber where the peas were lying, they stepped so firmly on them, and had such a strong, sure walk, that not one of the peas either rolled or stirred. Then they went away again, and the king said to the lion: "You have lied to me, they walk just like men."

The lion said: "They have been informed that they were going to be put to the test, and have assumed some strength. Just let twelve spinning wheels be brought into the antechamber, and they will go to them and be pleased with them, and that is what no man would do." The king liked the advice, and had the spinning wheels placed in the antechamber.

But the servant, who was well disposed to the huntsmen, went to them, and disclosed the project. So when they were alone the king's daughter said to her eleven girls: "Show some constraint, and do not look round at the spinning wheels."

And next morning when the king had his twelve huntsmen summoned, they went through the antechamber, and never once looked at the spinning wheels. Then the king again said to the lion: "You have deceived me, they are men, for they have not looked at the spinning wheels."

The lion replied: "They have restrained themselves." The king, however, would no longer believe the lion.

The twelve huntsmen always followed the king to the chase, and his liking for them continually increased. Now it came to pass that once when they were out hunting, news came that the king's bride was approaching. When the true bride heard that, it hurt her so much that her heart was almost broken, and she fell fainting to the ground. The king thought something had happened to his dear huntsman, ran up to him, wanted to help him, and drew his glove off. Then he saw the ring which he had given to his first bride, and when he looked in her face he recognized her. Then his heart was so touched that he kissed her, and when she opened her eyes he said: "You are mine, and I am yours, and no one in the world can alter that." He sent a messenger to the other bride, and entreated her to return to her own kingdom, for he had a wife already, and someone who had just found an old key did not require a new one. Thereupon the wedding was celebrated, and the lion was again taken into favour, because, after all, he had told the truth.

The Wedding of Mrs. Fox

First Story

There was once upon a time an old fox with nine tails, who believed that his wife was not faithful to him, and wished to put her to the test. He stretched himself out under the bench, did not move a limb, and behaved as if he were stone dead. Mrs. Fox went up to her room, shut herself in, and her maid, Miss Cat, sat by the fire, and did the cooking. When it became known that the old fox was dead, suitors presented themselves. The maid heard someone standing at the house door, knocking. She went and opened it, and it was a young fox, who said:

"What may you be about, Miss Cat?
Do you sleep or do you wake?"

She answered:

"I am not sleeping, I am waking,
Would you know what I am making?
I am boiling warm beer with butter,
Will you be my guest for supper?"

"No, thank you, miss," said the fox, "what is Mrs. Fox doing?"

The maid replied:

"She is sitting in her room,
Moaning in her gloom,
Weeping her little eyes quite red,
Because old Mr. Fox is dead."

"Do just tell her, miss, that a young fox is here, who would like to woo her."

"Certainly, young sir."

The cat goes up the stairs trip, trap,
The door she knocks at tap, tap, tap,
"Mistress Fox, are you inside?"
"Oh, yes, my little cat," she cried.
"A wooer he stands at the door out there."
"What does he look like, my dear?"

"Has he nine as beautiful tails as the late Mr. Fox?"

"Oh, no," answered the cat, "he has only one."

"Then I will not have him."

Miss Cat went downstairs and sent the wooer away. Soon afterwards there was another knock, and another fox was at the door who wished to woo Mrs. Fox. He had two tails, but he did not fare better than the first. After this still more came, each with one tail more than the other, but they were all turned away, until at last one came who had nine tails, like old Mr. Fox. When the widow heard that, she said joyfully to the cat:

"Now open the gates and doors all wide,
And carry old Mr. Fox outside."

But just as the wedding was going to be solemnized, old Mr. Fox stirred under the bench, and cudgelled all the rabble, and drove them and Mrs. Fox out of the house.

Second Story

When old Mr. Fox was dead, the wolf came as a suitor, and knocked at the door, and the cat who was servant to Mrs. Fox, opened it for him. The wolf greeted her, and said:

"Good day, Mrs. Cat of Kehrewit,
How comes it that alone you sit?
What are you making good?"

The cat replied:

"In milk I'm breaking bread so sweet,
Will you be my guest, and eat?"

"No, thank you, Mrs. Cat," answered the wolf. "Is Mrs. Fox not at home?"

The cat said:

"She sits upstairs in her room,
Bewailing her sorrowful doom,
Bewailing her trouble so sore,
For old Mr. Fox is no more."

The wolf answered:

"If she's in want of a husband now,
Then will it please her to step below?"
The cat runs quickly up the stair,
And lets her tail fly here and there,
Until she comes to the parlour door.
With her five gold rings at the door she knocks:
"Are you within, good Mistress Fox?
If you're in want of a husband now,
Then will it please you to step below?"

Mrs. Fox asked: "Has the gentleman red stockings on, and has he a pointed mouth?"

"No," answered the cat. "Then he won't do for me."

When the wolf was gone, came a dog, a stag, a hare, a bear, a lion, and all the beasts of the forest, one after the other. But one of the good qualities which old Mr. Fox had possessed, was always lacking, and the cat had continually to send the suitors away. At length came a young fox. Then Mrs. Fox said: "Has the gentleman red stockings on, and has a little pointed mouth?"

"Yes," said the cat, "he has."

"Then let him come upstairs," said Mrs. Fox, and ordered the servant to prepare the wedding feast.

"Sweep me the room as clean as you can,
Up with the window, fling out my old man!
For many a fine fat mouse he brought,
Yet of his wife he never thought,
But ate up every one he caught."

Then the wedding was solemnized with young Mr. Fox, and there was much rejoicing and dancing; and if they have not left off, they are dancing still.

Iron Hans

There was once upon a time a king who had a great forest near his palace, full of all kinds of wild animals. One day he sent out a huntsman to shoot him a roe, but he did not come back. "Perhaps some accident has befallen him," said the king, and the next day he sent out two more huntsmen who were to search for him, but they too stayed away. Then on the third day, he sent for all his huntsmen, and said: "Scour the whole forest through, and do not give up until you have found all three." But of these also, none came home again, none were seen again. From that time forth, no one would any longer venture into the forest, and it lay there in deep stillness and solitude, and nothing was seen of it, but sometimes an eagle or a hawk flying over it. This lasted for many years, when an unknown huntsman announced himself to the king as seeking a situation, and offered to go into the dangerous forest. The king, however, would not give his consent, and said: "It is not safe in there; I fear it would fare with you no better than with the others, and you would never come out again."

The huntsman replied: "Lord, I will venture it at my own risk, of fear I know nothing."

The huntsman therefore betook himself with his dog to the forest. It was not long before the dog fell in with some game on the way, and wanted to pursue it; but hardly had the dog run two steps when it stood before a deep pool, could go no farther, and a naked arm stretched itself out of the water, seized it, and drew it under. When the huntsman saw that, he went back and fetched three men to come with buckets and bale out the water. When they could see to the bottom there lay a wild man whose body was brown like rusty iron, and whose hair hung over his face down to his knees. They bound him with cords, and led him away to the castle. There was great astonishment over the wild man; the king, however, had him put in an iron cage in his courtyard, and forbade the door to be opened on pain of death, and the queen herself was to take the key into her keeping. And from this time forth everyone could again go into the forest with safety.

The king had a son of eight years, who was once playing in the courtyard, and while he was playing, his golden ball fell into the cage. The boy ran thither and said: "Give me my ball out."

"Not till you have opened the door for me," answered the man.

"No," said the boy, "I will not do that; the king has forbidden it," and ran away.

The next day he again went and asked for his ball; the wild man said: "Open my door," but the boy would not. On the third day the king had ridden out hunting, and the boy went once more and said: "I cannot open the door even if I wished, for I have not the key."

Then the wild man said: "It lies under your mother's pillow, you can get it there." The boy, who wanted to have his ball back, cast all thought to the winds, and brought the key. The door opened with difficulty, and the boy pinched his fingers. When it was open the wild man stepped out, gave him the golden ball, and hurried away. The boy had become afraid; he called and cried after him: "Oh, wild man, do not go away, or I shall be beaten!" The wild man turned back, took him up, set him on his shoulder, and went with hasty steps into the forest. When the king came home, he observed the empty cage, and asked the queen how that had happened. She knew nothing about it, and sought the key, but it was gone. She called the boy, but no one answered. The king sent out people to seek for him in the fields, but they did not find him. Then he could easily guess what had happened, and much grief reigned in the royal court.

When the wild man had once more reached the dark forest, he took the boy down from his shoulder, and said to him: "You will never see your father and mother again, but I will keep you with me, for you have set me free, and I have compassion on you. If you do all I bid you, you shall fare well. Of treasure and gold have I enough, and more than anyone in the world." He made a bed of moss for the boy on which he slept, and the next morning the man took him to a well, and said: "Behold, the gold well is as bright and clear as crystal, you shall sit beside it, and take care that nothing falls into it, or it will be polluted. I will come every evening to see if you have obeyed my order." The boy placed himself by the brink of the well, and often saw a golden fish or a golden snake show itself therein, and took care that nothing fell in. As he was thus sitting, his finger hurt him so violently that he involuntarily put it in the water. He drew it quickly out again, but saw that it was quite gilded, and whatsoever pains he took to wash the gold off again, all was to no purpose. In the evening Iron Hans came back, looked at the boy, and said: "What has happened to the well?"

"Nothing, nothing," he answered, and held his finger behind his back, that the man might not see it.

But he said: "You have dipped your finger into the water, this time it may pass, but take care you do not again let anything go in." By daybreak the boy was already sitting by the well and watching it. His finger hurt him again and he passed it over his head, and then unhappily a hair fell down into the well. He took it quickly out, but it was already quite gilded.

Iron Hans came, and already knew what had happened. "You have let a hair fall into the well," said he. "I will allow you to watch by it once more, but if this happens for the third time then the well is polluted and you can no longer remain with me."

On the third day, the boy sat by the well, and did not stir his finger, however much it hurt him. But the time was long to him, and he looked at the reflection of his face on the surface of the water. And as he still bent down more and more while he was doing so, and trying to look straight

into the eyes, his long hair fell down from his shoulders into the water. He raised himself up quickly, but the whole of the hair of his head was already golden and shone like the sun. You can imagine how terrified the poor boy was! He took his pocket handkerchief and tied it round his head, in order that the man might not see it. When he came he already knew everything, and said: "Take the handkerchief off." Then the golden hair streamed forth, and let the boy excuse himself as he might, it was of no use. "You have not stood the trial and can stay here no longer. Go forth into the world, there you will learn what poverty is. But as you have not a bad heart, and as I mean well by you, there is one thing I will grant you; if you fall into any difficulty, come to the forest and cry: "Iron Hans," and then I will come and help you. My power is great, greater than you think, and I have gold and silver in abundance."

Then the king's son left the forest, and walked by beaten and unbeaten paths ever onwards until at length he reached a great city. There he looked for work, but could find none, and he learnt nothing by which he could help himself. At length he went to the palace, and asked if they would take him in. The people about court did not at all know what use they could make of him, but they liked him, and told him to stay. At length the cook took him into his service, and said he might carry wood and water, and rake the cinders together. Once when it so happened that no one else was at hand, the cook ordered him to carry the food to the royal table, but as he did not like to let his golden hair be seen, he kept his little cap on. Such a thing as that had never yet come under the king's notice, and he said: "When you come to the royal table you must take your hat off."

He answered: "Ah, Lord, I cannot; I have a bad sore place on my head." Then the king had the cook called before him and scolded him, and asked how he could take such a boy as that into his service; and that he was to send him away at once. The cook, however, had pity on him, and exchanged him for the gardener's boy.

And now the boy had to plant and water the garden, hoe and dig, and bear the wind and bad weather. Once in summer when he was working alone in the garden, the day was so warm he took his little cap off that the air might cool him. As the sun shone on his hair it glittered and flashed so that the rays fell into the bedroom of the king's daughter, and up she sprang to see what that could be. Then she saw the boy, and cried to him: "Boy, bring me a wreath of flowers." He put his cap on with all haste, and gathered wild field flowers and bound them together. When he was ascending the stairs with them, the gardener met him, and said: "How can you take the king's daughter a garland of such common flowers? Go quickly, and get another, and seek out the prettiest and rarest."

"Oh, no," replied the boy, "the wild ones have more scent, and will please her better."

When he got into the room, the king's daughter said: "Take your cap off, it is not seemly to keep it on in my presence."

He again said: "I may not, I have a sore head." She, however, caught at his cap and pulled it off, and then his golden hair rolled down on his shoulders, and it was splendid to behold. He wanted to run out, but she held him by the arm, and gave him a handful of ducats. With these he departed, but he cared nothing for the gold pieces. He took them to the gardener, and said: "I present them to your children, they can play with them."

The following day the king's daughter again called to him that he was to bring her a wreath of field flowers, and then he went in with it, she instantly snatched at his cap, and wanted to take it away from him, but he held it fast with both hands. She again gave him a handful of ducats, but he would not keep them, and gave them to the gardener for playthings for his children. On the third day things went just the same; she could not get his cap away from him, and he would not have her money.

Not long afterwards, the country was overrun by war. The king gathered together his people, and did not know whether or not he could offer any opposition to the enemy, who was superior in strength and had a mighty army. Then said the gardener's boy: "I am grown up, and will go to the wars also, only give me a horse."

The others laughed, and said: "Seek one for yourself when we are gone, we will leave one behind us in the stable for you." When they had gone forth, he went into the stable, and led the horse out; it was lame of one foot, and limped hobblety jib, hobblety jib; nevertheless he mounted it, and rode away to the dark forest. When he came to the outskirts, he called "Iron Hans" three times so loudly that it echoed through the trees. Thereupon the wild man appeared immediately, and said: "What do you desire?"

"I want a strong steed, for I am going to the wars."

"That you shall have, and still more than you ask for." Then the wild man went back into the forest, and it was not long before a stable boy came out of it, who led a horse that snorted with its nostrils, and could hardly be restrained, and behind them followed a great troop of warriors entirely equipped in iron, and their swords flashed in the sun. The youth made over his three-legged horse to the stable boy, mounted the other, and rode at the head of the soldiers. When he got near the battlefield a great part of the king's men had already fallen, and little was wanting to make the rest give way. Then the youth galloped thither with his iron soldiers, broke like a hurricane over the enemy, and beat down all who opposed him. They began to flee, but the youth pursued, and never stopped, until there was not a single man left. Instead of returning to the king, however, he conducted his troop by byways back to the forest, and called forth Iron Hans. "What do you desire?" asked the wild man.

"Take back your horse and your troops, and give me my three-legged horse again." All that he asked was done, and soon he was riding on his three-legged horse. When the king returned to his palace, his daughter went to meet him, and wished him joy of his victory. "I am not the one who carried away the victory," said he, "but a strange knight who came to my assistance with his soldiers."

The daughter wanted to hear who the strange knight was, but the king did not know, and said: "He followed the enemy, and I did not see him again." She inquired of the gardener where his boy was, but he smiled, and said: "He has just come home on his three-legged horse, and the others have been mocking him, and crying: 'Here comes our hobblety jib back again!' They asked, too: 'Under what hedge have you been lying sleeping all the time?' So he said: 'I did the best of all, and it would have gone badly without me.' And then he was still more ridiculed."

The king said to his daughter: "I will proclaim a great feast that shall last for three days, and you shall throw a golden apple. Perhaps the unknown man will show himself." When the feast was announced, the youth went out to the forest, and called Iron Hans. "What do you desire?" asked he.

"That I may catch the king's daughter's golden apple."

"It is as safe as if you had it already," said Iron Hans. "You shall likewise have a suit of red armour for the occasion, and ride on a spirited chestnut horse." When the day came, the youth galloped to the spot, took his place amongst the knights, and was recognized by no one. The king's daughter came forward, and threw a golden apple to the knights, but none of them caught it but he, only as soon as he had it he galloped away.

On the second day Iron Hans equipped him as a white knight, and gave him a white horse. Again he was the only one who caught the apple, and he did not linger an instant, but galloped off with it. The king grew angry, and said: "That is not allowed; he must appear before me and tell his name." He gave the order that if the knight who caught the apple, should go away again they should pursue him, and if he would not come back willingly, they were to cut him down and stab him.

On the third day, he received from Iron Hans a suit of black armour and a black horse, and again he caught the apple. But when he was riding off with it, the king's attendants pursued him, and one of them got so near him that he wounded the youth's leg with the point of his sword. The youth nevertheless escaped from them, but his horse leapt so violently that the helmet fell from the youth's head, and they could see that he had golden hair. They rode back and announced this to the king.

The following day the king's daughter asked the gardener about his boy. "He is at work in the garden; the queer creature has been at the festival too, and only came home yesterday evening; he has likewise shown my children three golden apples which he has won."

The king had him summoned into his presence, and he came and again had his little cap on his head. But the king's daughter went up to him and took it off, and then his golden hair fell down over his shoulders, and he was so handsome that all were amazed. "Are you the knight who came every day to the festival, always in different colours, and who caught the three golden apples?" asked the king.

"Yes," answered he, "and here the apples are," and he took them out of his pocket, and returned them to the king. "If you desire further proof, you may see the wound which your people gave me when they followed me. But I am likewise the knight who helped you to your victory over your enemies."

"If you can perform such deeds as that, you are no gardener's boy; tell me, who is your father?"

"My father is a mighty king, and gold have I in plenty as great as I require."

"I well see," said the king, "that I owe my thanks to you; can I do anything to please you?"

"Yes," answered he, "that indeed you can. Give me your daughter to wife."

The maiden laughed, and said: "He does not stand much on ceremony, but I have already seen by his golden hair that he was no gardener's boy," and then she went and kissed him. His father and mother came to the wedding, and were in great delight, for they had given up all hope of ever seeing their dear son again. And as they were sitting at the marriage feast, the music suddenly stopped, the doors opened, and a stately king came in with a great retinue. He went up to the youth, embraced him and said: "I am Iron Hans, and was by enchantment a wild man, but you have set me free; all the treasures which I possess, shall be your property."

Snow White and Rose Red

There was once a poor widow who lived in a lonely cottage. In front of the cottage was a garden wherein stood two rose trees, one of which bore white and the other red roses. She had two children who were like the two rose trees, and one was called Snow White, and the other Rose Red. They were as good and happy, as busy and cheerful as ever two children in the world were, only Snow White was more quiet and gentle than Rose Red. Rose Red liked better to run about in the meadows and fields seeking flowers and catching butterflies; but Snow White sat at home with her mother, and helped her with her housework, or read to her when there was nothing to do.

The two children were so fond of one another that they always held each other by the hand when they went out together, and when Snow White said: "We will not leave each other," Rose Red answered: "Never so long as we live," and their mother would add: "What one has she must share with the other."

They often ran about the forest alone and gathered red berries, and no beasts did them any harm, but came close to them trustfully. The little hare would eat a cabbage leaf out of their hands, the roe grazed by their side, the stag leapt merrily by them, and the birds sat still upon the boughs, and sang whatever they knew.

No mishap overtook them; if they had stayed too late in the forest, and night came on, they laid themselves down near one another upon the moss, and slept until morning came, and their mother knew this and did not worry on their account.

Once when they had spent the night in the wood and the dawn had roused them, they saw a beautiful child in a shining white dress sitting near their bed. He got up and looked quite kindly at them, but said nothing and went into the forest. And when they looked round they found that they had been sleeping quite close to a precipice, and would certainly have fallen into it in the darkness if they had gone only a few paces further. And their mother told them that it must have been the angel who watches over good children.

Snow White and Rose Red kept their mother's little cottage so neat that it was a pleasure to look inside it. In the summer Rose Red took care of the house, and every morning laid a wreath of flowers by her mother's bed before she awoke, in which was a rose from each tree. In the winter Snow White lit the fire and hung the kettle on the hob. The kettle was of brass and shone like gold, so brightly was it polished. In the evening, when the snowflakes fell, the mother said: "Go, Snow White, and bolt the door," and then they sat round the hearth, and the mother took her spectacles and read aloud out of a large book, and the two girls listened as they sat and spun. And close by them lay a lamb upon the floor, and behind them upon a perch sat a white dove with its head hidden beneath its wings.

One evening, as they were thus sitting comfortably together, someone knocked at the door as if he wished to be let in. The mother said: "Quick, Rose Red, open the door, it must be a traveller who is seeking shelter." Rose Red went and pushed back the bolt, thinking that it was a poor man, but it was not; it was a bear that stretched his broad, black head within the door.

Rose Red screamed and sprang back, the lamb bleated, the dove fluttered, and Snow White hid herself behind her mother's bed. But the

bear began to speak and said: "Do not be afraid, I will do you no harm! I am half-frozen, and only want to warm myself a little beside you."

"Poor bear," said the mother, "lie down by the fire, only take care that you do not burn your coat." Then she cried: "Snow White, Rose Red, come out, the bear will do you no harm, he means well." So they both came out, and by and by the lamb and dove came nearer, and were not afraid of him. The bear said: "Here, children, knock the snow out of my coat a little"; so they brought the broom and swept the bear's hide clean; and he stretched himself by the fire and growled contentedly and comfortably. It was not long before they grew quite at home, and played tricks with their clumsy guest. They tugged his hair with their hands, put their feet upon his back and rolled him about, or they took a hazel switch and beat him, and when he growled they laughed. But the bear took it all in good part, only when they were too rough he called out:

"Leave me alive, children,
Snow White, Rose Red,
Will you beat your wooer dead?"

When it was bedtime, and the others went to bed, the mother said to the bear: "You can lie there by the hearth, and then you will be safe from the cold and the bad weather." As soon as day dawned the two children let him out, and he trotted across the snow into the forest.

Henceforth the bear came every evening at the same time, laid himself down by the hearth, and let the children amuse themselves with him as much as they liked; and they got so used to him that the doors were never fastened until their black friend had arrived.

When spring had come and all outside was green, the bear said one morning to Snow White: "Now I must go away, and cannot come back for the whole summer."

"Where are you going, then, dear bear?" asked Snow White.

"I must go into the forest and guard my treasures from the wicked dwarfs. In the winter, when the earth is frozen hard, they are obliged to stay below and cannot work their way through; but now, when the sun has thawed and warmed the earth, they break through it, and come out to pry and steal; and what once gets into their hands, and in their caves, does not easily see daylight again."

Snow White was quite sorry at his departure, and as she unbolted the door for him, and the bear was hurrying out, he caught against the bolt and a piece of his hairy coat was torn off, and it seemed to Snow White as if she had seen gold shining through it, but she was not sure about it. The bear ran away quickly, and was soon out of sight behind the trees.

A short time afterwards the mother sent her children into the forest to get firewood. There they found a big tree which lay felled on the ground, and close by the trunk something was jumping backwards and forwards in the grass, but they could not make out what it was. When they came nearer they saw a dwarf with an old, withered face and a snow white beard a yard long. The end of the beard was caught in a crevice of the tree, and the little fellow was jumping about like a dog tied to a rope, and did not know what to do.

He glared at the girls with his fiery red eyes and cried: "Why do you stand there? Can you not come here and help me?"

"What are you up to, little man?" asked Rose Red.

"You stupid, prying goose!" answered the dwarf: "I was going to split the tree to get a little wood for cooking. The little bit of food that we people get is immediately burnt up with heavy logs; we do not swallow so much as you coarse, greedy folk. I had just driven the wedge safely in, and everything was going as I wished; but the cursed wedge was too smooth and suddenly sprang out, and the tree closed so quickly that I could not pull out my beautiful white beard; so now it is tight and I cannot get away, and the silly, sleek, milk-faced things laugh! Ugh! how odious you are!"

The children tried very hard, but they could not pull the beard out, it was caught too fast. "I will run and fetch someone," said Rose Red.

"You senseless goose!" snarled the dwarf; "why should you fetch someone? You are already two too many for me; can you not think of something better?"

"Don't be impatient," said Snow White, "I will help you," and she pulled her scissors out of her pocket, and cut off the end of the beard.

As soon as the dwarf felt himself free he laid hold of a bag which lay amongst the roots of the tree, and which was full of gold, and lifted it up, grumbling to himself: "Uncouth people, to cut off a piece of my fine beard. Bad luck to you!" and then he swung the bag upon his back, and went off without even once looking at the children.

Some time afterwards Snow White and Rose Red went to catch a dish of fish. As they came near the brook they saw something like a large grasshopper jumping towards the water, as if it were going to leap in. They ran to it and found it was the dwarf. "Where are you going?" said Rose Red; "you surely don't want to go into the water?"

"I am not such a fool!" cried the dwarf; "don't you see that the accursed fish wants to pull me in?" The little man had been sitting there fishing, and unluckily the wind had tangled up his beard with the fishing line; a moment later a big fish made a bite and the feeble creature had not strength to pull it out; the fish kept the upper hand and pulled the dwarf towards him. He held on to all the reeds and rushes, but it was of little good, for he was forced to follow the movements of the fish, and was in urgent danger of being dragged into the water.

The girls came just in time; they held him fast and tried to free his beard from the line, but all in vain, beard and line were entangled fast together. There was nothing to do but to bring out the scissors and cut the beard, whereby a small part of it was lost. When the dwarf saw that he screamed out: "Is that civil, you toadstool, to disfigure a man's face? Was it not enough to clip off the end of my beard? Now you have cut off the best part of it. I cannot let myself be seen by my people. I wish you had been made to run the soles off your shoes!" Then he took out a sack of pearls which lay in the rushes, and without another word he dragged it away and disappeared behind a stone.

It happened that soon afterwards the mother sent the two children to the town to buy needles and thread, and laces and ribbons. The road led them across a heath upon which huge pieces of rock lay strewn about.

There they noticed a large bird hovering in the air, flying slowly round and round above them; it sank lower and lower, and at last settled near a rock not far away. Immediately they heard a loud, piteous cry. They ran up and saw with horror that the eagle had seized their old acquaintance the dwarf, and was going to carry him off.

The children, full of pity, at once took tight hold of the little man, and pulled against the eagle so long that at last he let his booty go. As soon as the dwarf had recovered from his first fright he cried with his shrill voice: "Could you not have done it more carefully! You dragged at my brown coat so that it is all torn and full of holes, you clumsy creatures!" Then he took up a sack full of precious stones, and slipped away again under the rock into his hole. The girls, who by this time were used to his ingratitude, went on their way and did their business in town.

As they crossed the heath again on their way home they surprised the dwarf, who had emptied out his bag of precious stones in a clean spot, and had not thought that anyone would come there so late. The evening sun shone upon the brilliant stones; they glittered and sparkled with all colours so beautifully that the children stood still and stared at them. "Why do you stand gaping there?" cried the dwarf, and his ashen-grey face became copper red with rage. He was still cursing when a loud growling was heard, and a black bear came trotting towards them out of the forest. The dwarf sprang up in a fright, but he could not reach his cave, for the bear was already close. Then in the dread of his heart he cried: "Dear Mr. Bear, spare me, I will give you all my treasures; look, the beautiful jewels lying there! Grant me my life; what do you want with such a slender little fellow as I? you would not feel me between your teeth. Come, take these two wicked girls, they are tender morsels for you, fat as young quails; for mercy's sake eat them!" The bear took no heed of his words, but gave the wicked creature a single blow with his paw, and he did not move again.

The girls had run away, but the bear called to them: "Snow White and Rose Red, do not be afraid; wait, I will come with you." Then they recognized his voice and waited, and when he came up to them suddenly his bearskin fell off, and he stood there a handsome man, clothed all in gold. "I am a king's son," he said, "and I was bewitched by that wicked dwarf, who had stolen my treasures; I have had to run about the forest as a savage bear until I was freed by his death. Now he has got his well-deserved punishment.

Snow White was married to him, and Rose Red to his brother, and they divided between them the great treasure which the dwarf had gathered together in his cave. The old mother lived peacefully and happily with her children for many years. She took the two rose trees with her, and they stood before her window, and every year bore the most beautiful roses, white and red.

The Six Swans

A King was once hunting in a large wood, and pursued his game so hotly that none of his courtiers could follow him. But when evening approached he stopped, and looking around him perceived that he had lost himself. He sought a path out of the forest but could not find one, and presently he saw an old woman, with a nodding head, who came up to him. "My good woman," said he to her, "can you not show me the way out of the forest?"

"Oh, yes, my lord King," she replied; "I can do that very well, but upon one condition, which if you do not fulfil, you will never again get out of the wood, but will die of hunger."

"What, then, is this condition?" asked the King.

"I have a daughter," said the old woman, "who is as beautiful as anyone you can find in the whole world, and well deserves to be your bride. Now, if you will make her your Queen, I will show you your way out of the wood." In the anxiety of his heart, the King consented, and the old woman led him to her cottage, where the daughter was sitting by the fire. She received the King as if she had expected him, and he saw at once that she was very beautiful, but yet she did not quite please him, for he

THE SIX SWANS
"THE SWANS CAME CLOSE UP TO HER WITH RUSHING WINGS, & STOOPED ROUND HER; SO THAT SHE COULD THROW THE SHIRTS OVER THEM."
SWAIN. SC

could not look at her without a secret shuddering. However, he took the maiden upon his horse, and the old woman showed him the way, and the King arrived safely at his palace, where the wedding was to be celebrated.

The King had been married once before, and had seven children by his first wife, six boys and a girl, whom he loved above everything else in the world. He became afraid, soon, that the stepmother might not treat his children very well, and might even do them some great injury, so he took them away to a lonely castle which stood in the midst of a forest. The castle was so entirely hidden, and the way to it was so difficult to discover, that he himself could not have found it if a wise woman had not given him a ball of cotton which had the wonderful property, when he threw it before him, of unrolling itself and showing him the right path. The King went, however, so often to see his dear children, that the Queen, noticing his absence, became inquisitive, and wished to know what he went to fetch out of the forest. So she gave his servants a great quantity of money, and they disclosed to her the secret, and also told her of the ball of cotton which alone could show her the way. She had now no peace until she discovered where this ball was concealed, and then she made some fine silken shirts, and, as she had learnt of her mother, she sewed within each a charm. One day soon after, when the King was gone out hunting, she took the little shirts and went into the forest, and the cotton showed her the path. The children, seeing someone coming in the distance, thought it was their dear father, and ran out full of joy. Then she threw over each of them a shirt, that, as it touched their bodies, changed them into Swans, which flew away over the forest. The Queen then went home quite contented, and thought she was free of her stepchildren; but the little girl had not met her with the brothers, and the Queen did not know of her.

The following day the King went to visit his children, but he found only the Maiden. "Where are your brothers?" asked he.

"Ah, dear father," she replied, "they are gone away and have left me alone"; and she told him how she had looked out of the window and seen them changed into Swans, which had flown over the forest; and then she showed him the feathers which they had dropped in the courtyard, and which she had collected together. The King was much grieved, but he did not think that his wife could have done this wicked deed, and, as he feared the girl might also be stolen away, he took her with him. She was, however, so much afraid of the stepmother, that she begged him not to stop more than one night in the castle.

The poor Maiden thought to herself, "This is no longer my place; I will go and seek my brothers"; and when night came she escaped and went quite deep into the wood. She walked all night long, and a great part of the next day, until she could go no further from weariness. Just then she saw a rough-looking hut, and going in, she found a room with six little beds, but she dared not get into one, so crept under, and laying herself upon the hard earth, prepared to pass the night there. Just as the sun was setting, she heard a rustling, and saw six white Swans come flying in at the window. They settled on the ground and began blowing one another until they had blown all their feathers off, and their swan's down slipped from them like a shirt. Then the Maiden knew them at once for her brothers, and gladly crept out from under the bed, and the brothers were not less glad to see their sister, but their joy was of short duration. "Here you must not stay," said they to her; "this is a robbers' hiding place; if they should return and find you here, they would murder you."

"Can you not protect me, then?" inquired the sister.

"No," they replied; "for we can only lay aside our swan's feathers for a quarter of an hour each evening, and for that time we regain our human form, but afterwards we resume our changed appearance."

Their sister then asked them, with tears, "Can you not be restored again?"

"Oh, no," replied they; "the conditions are too difficult. For six long years you must neither speak nor laugh, and during that time you must sew together for us six little shirts of starflowers, and should there fall a single word from your lips, then all your labour will be in vain." Just as the brothers finished speaking, the quarter of an hour elapsed, and they all flew out of the window again like Swans.

The little sister, however, made a solemn resolution to rescue her brothers, or die in the attempt; and she left the cottage, and, penetrating deep into the forest, passed the night amid the branches of a tree. The next morning she went out and collected the starflowers to sew together. She had no one to converse with and for laughing she had no spirits, so there up in the tree she sat, intent upon her work.

After she had passed some time there, it happened that the King of that country was hunting in the forest, and his huntsmen came beneath the tree on which the Maiden sat. They called to her and asked, "Who art thou?" But she gave no answer. "Come down to us," continued they; "we will do thee no harm." She simply shook her head, and when they pressed her further with questions, she threw down to them her gold necklace, hoping therewith to satisfy them. They did not, however, leave her, and she threw down her girdle, but in vain! and even her rich dress did not make them desist. At last the huntsman himself climbed the tree and brought down the Maiden, and took her before the King.

The King asked her, "Who art thou? What dost thou upon that tree?" But she did not answer; and then he questioned her in all the languages that he knew, but she remained dumb to all, as a fish. Since, however, she was so beautiful, the King's heart was touched, and he conceived for her a strong affection. Then he put around her his cloak, and, placing her before him on his horse, took her to his castle. There he ordered rich clothing to be made for her, and, although her beauty shone as the sunbeams, not a word escaped her. The King placed her by his side at table, and there her dignified mien and manners so won upon him, that he said, "This Maiden will I marry, and no other in the world"; and after some days he wedded her.

Now, the King had a wicked stepmother, who was discontented with his marriage, and spoke evil of the young Queen. "Who knows whence the wench comes?" said she. "She who cannot speak is not worthy of a King." A year after, when the Queen brought her firstborn into the world, the old woman took him away. Then she went to the King and complained that the Queen was a murderess. The King, however, would not believe it, and suffered no one to do any injury to his wife, who sat composedly sewing at her shirts and paying attention to nothing else. When a second child was born, the false stepmother used the same deceit, but the King again would not listen to her words, saying, "She is too pious and good to act so; could she but speak and defend herself, her innocence would come to light." But when again, the old woman stole away the third child, and then accused the Queen, who answered not a word to the accusation, the King was obliged to give her up to be tried, and she was condemned to suffer death by fire.

When the time had elapsed, and the sentence was to be carried out, it happened that the very day had come round when her dear brothers should be set free; the six shirts were also ready, all but the last, which yet wanted the left sleeve. As she was led to the scaffold, she placed the shirts upon her arm, and just as she had mounted it, and the fire was about to be kindled, she looked around, and saw six Swans come flying through the air. Her heart leapt for joy as she perceived her deliverers

approaching, and soon the Swans, flying towards her, alighted so near that she was enabled to throw over them the shirts, and as soon as she had done so, their feathers fell off and the brothers stood up alive and well; but the youngest was without his left arm, instead of which he had a swan's wing. They embraced and kissed each other, and the Queen, going to the King, who was thunderstruck, began to say, "Now may I speak, my dear husband, and prove to you that I am innocent and falsely accused"; and then she told him how the wicked woman had stolen away and hidden her three children. When she had concluded, the King was overcome with joy, and the wicked stepmother was led to the scaffold and bound to the stake and burnt to ashes. The King and Queen for ever after lived in peace and prosperity with their six brothers.

The Little Brother and Sister

There was once a little Brother who took his Sister by the hand, and said, "Since our own dear mother's death we have not had one happy hour; our stepmother beats us every day, and, when we come near her, kicks us away with her foot. Come, let us wander forth into the wide world." So all day long they travelled over meadows, fields, and stony roads. By the evening they came into a large forest, and laid themselves down in a hollow tree, and went to sleep. When they awoke the next morning, the sun had already risen high in the heavens, and its beams made the tree so hot that the little boy said to his Sister, "I am so very thirsty, that if I knew where there was a brook, I would go and drink. Ah! I think I hear one running"; and so saying, he got up, and taking his Sister's hand they went to look for the brook.

The wicked stepmother, however, was a witch, and had witnessed the departure of the two children: so, sneaking after them secretly, as is the habit of witches, she had enchanted all the springs in the forest.

Presently they found a brook, which ran trippingly over the pebbles, and the Brother would have drunk out of it, but the Sister heard how it said as it ran along, "Who drinks of me will become a tiger!" So the Sister exclaimed, "I pray you, Brother, drink not, or you will become a tiger, and tear me to pieces!"

So the Brother did not drink, although his thirst was very great, and he said, "I will wait till the next brook."

As they came to the second, the Sister heard it say, "Who drinks of me becomes a wolf!" The Sister ran up crying, "Brother, do not, pray do not drink, or you will become a wolf and eat me up!"

Then the Brother did not drink, saying, "I will wait until we come to the next spring, but then I must drink, you may say what you will; my thirst is much too great."

Just as they reached the third brook, the Sister heard the voice saying, "Who drinks of me will become a fawn—who drinks of me will become a fawn!" So the Sister said, "Oh, my Brother do not drink, or you will be changed into a fawn, and run away from me!" But he had already kneeled down, and he drank of the water, and, as the first drops passed his lips, his shape took that of a fawn.

At first the Sister wept over her little, changed Brother, and he wept too, and knelt by her, very sorrowful; but at last the maiden said, "Be still, dear little fawn, and I will never forsake you!" and, taking off her golden garter, she placed it around his neck, and, weaving rushes, made a girdle to lead him with. This she tied to him, and taking the other end in her hand, she led him away, and they travelled deeper and deeper into the forest. After they had gone a long distance they came to a little hut, and the maiden, peeping in, found it empty, and thought, "Here we can stay and dwell." Then she looked for leaves and moss to make a soft couch for the Fawn, and every morning she went out and collected roots and berries and nuts for herself, and tender grass for the Fawn. In the evening when the Sister was tired, and had said her prayers, she laid her head upon the back of the Fawn, which served for a pillow, on which she slept soundly. Had but the Brother regained his own proper form, their lives would have been happy indeed.

Thus they dwelt in this wilderness, and some time had elapsed when it happened that the King of the country had a great hunt in the forest; and now sounded through the trees the blowing of horns, the barking of dogs, and the lusty cry of the hunters, so that the little Fawn heard them, and wanted very much to join in. "Ah!" said he to his Sister, "let me go to the hunt, I cannot restrain myself any longer"; and he begged so hard that at last she consented.

"But," she told him, "return again in the evening, for I shall shut my door against the wild huntsmen, and, that I may know you, do you knock, and say, 'Sister, dear, let me in,' and if you do not speak I shall not open the door."

As soon as she had said this, the little Fawn sprang off quite glad and merry in the fresh breeze. The King and his huntsmen perceived the beautiful animal, and pursued him; but they could not catch him, and when they thought they certainly had him, he sprang away over the bushes, and got out of sight. Just as it was getting dark, he ran up to the hut, and, knocking, said, "Sister mine, let me in." Then she unfastened the little door, and he went in, and rested all night long upon his soft couch. The next morning the hunt was commenced again, and as soon as the little Fawn heard the horns and the tally-ho of the sportsmen he could not rest, and said, "Sister, dear, open the door; I must be off." The Sister opened it, saying, "Return at evening, mind, and say the words as before." When the King and his huntsmen saw him again, the Fawn with the golden necklace, they followed him, close, but he was too nimble and quick for them. The whole day long they kept up with him, but towards evening the huntsmen made a circle around him, and one wounded him slightly in the hinder foot, so that he could run but slowly. Then one of them slipped after him to the little hut, and heard him say, "Sister, dear, open the door," and saw that the door was opened and immediately shut behind him. The huntsman, having observed all this, went and told the King what he had seen and heard, and he said, "On the morrow I will pursue him once again."

The Sister, however, was terribly afraid when she saw that her Fawn was wounded, and, washing off the blood, she put herbs upon the foot, and said, "Go and rest upon your bed, dear Fawn, that your wound may heal." It was so slight, that the next morning he felt nothing of it, and when he heard the hunting cries outside, he exclaimed, "I cannot stop away—I must be there, and none shall catch me so easily again!" The Sister wept very much and told him, "Soon will they kill you, and I shall be here alone in this forest, forsaken by all the world: I cannot let you go."

"I shall die here in vexation," answered the Fawn, "if you do not, for when I hear the horn, I think I shall jump out of my skin." The Sister, finding she could not prevent him, opened the door, with a heavy heart, and the Fawn jumped out, quite delighted, into the forest. As soon as the King perceived him, he said to his huntsmen, "Follow him all day long till the evening, but let no one do him any harm." Then when the sun had set, the King asked his huntsman to show him the hut; and as they came to it he knocked at the door and said, "Let me in, dear Sister." Upon this the door opened, and, stepping in, the King saw a maiden more beautiful than he had ever beheld before. She was frightened when she saw not her Fawn, but a man enter, who had a golden crown upon his head.

But the King, looking at her with a kindly glance, held out to her his hand, saying, "Will you go with me to my castle, and be my dear wife?"

"Oh, yes," replied the maiden; "but the Fawn must go too: him I will never forsake."

The King replied, "He shall remain with you as long as you live, and shall never want."

The King took the beautiful maiden upon his horse, and rode to his castle, where the wedding was celebrated with great splendour and she became Queen, and they lived together a long time; while the Fawn was taken care of and played about the castle garden.

The wicked stepmother, however, on whose account the children had wandered forth into the world, had supposed that long ago the Sister had been torn into pieces by the wild beasts, and the little Brother in his Fawn's shape hunted to death by the hunters. As soon, therefore, as she heard how happy they had become, and how everything prospered with them, envy and jealousy were aroused in her wicked heart, and left her no peace; and she was always thinking in what way she could bring misfortune upon them.

Her own daughter, who was as ugly as night, and had but one eye, for which she was continually reproached, said, "The luck of being a Queen has never happened to me."

"Be quiet, now," replied the old woman, "and make yourself contented: when the time comes I will help and assist you." As soon, then, as the time came when the Queen gave birth to a beautiful little boy, which happened when the King was out hunting, the old witch took the form of a chambermaid, and got into the room where the Queen was lying, and said to her, "The bath is ready, which will restore you and give you fresh strength; be quick before it gets cold." Her daughter being at hand, they carried the weak Queen between them into the room, and laid her in the bath, and then, shutting the door, they ran off; but first they made up an immense fire in the stove, which must soon suffocate the poor young Queen.

When this was done, the old woman took her daughter, and, putting a cap upon her head, laid her in the bed in the Queen's place. She gave her, too, the form and appearance of the real Queen, as far as she was able; but she could not restore the lost eye, and, so that the King might not notice it, she turned her upon that side where there was no eye.

When midnight came, and everyone was asleep, the nurse, who sat by herself, wide awake, near the cradle, in the nursery, saw the door open and the true Queen come in. She took the child in her arms, and rocked it awhile, and then, shaking up its pillow, laid it down in its cradle, and covered it over again. She did not forget the Fawn, either, but going to the corner where he was, stroked his head, and then went silently out of the door. The nurse asked in the morning of the guards if anyone had passed into the castle during the night; but they answered, "No, we have not seen anybody." For many nights afterwards she came constantly, but never spoke a word; and the nurse saw her always, but she would not trust herself to speak about it to anyone.

When some time had passed away, the Queen one night began to speak, and said

"How fares my child! how fares my fawn?
Twice more will I come, but never again."

The nurse made no reply; but, when she had disappeared, went to the King, and told him. The King exclaimed, "Oh, mercy! what does this mean? The next night I will watch myself by the child." So in the evening he went into the nursery, and about midnight the Queen appeared, and said—

"How fares my child! how fares my fawn?
Once more will I come, but never again."

And she nursed the child, as she usually did, and then disappeared. The King dared not speak; but he watched the following night, and this time she said—

"How fares my child! how fares my fawn?
This time have I come, but never again."

At these words the King could hold back no longer, but, springing up, cried, "You can be no other than my dear wife!" Then she answered, "Yes, I am your dear wife"; and at that moment her life was restored by God's mercy, and she was again as beautiful and charming as ever. She told the King the fraud which the witch and her daughter had practised upon him, and he had them both tried, and sentence was pronounced against them. The little Fawn was disenchanted, and received once more his human form; and the Brother and Sister lived happily together to the end of their days.

The Three Spinsters

There was once a girl who was lazy and would not spin, and her mother could not persuade her to it, do what she would. At last the mother became angry and out of patience, and gave her a good beating, so that she cried out loudly. At that moment the Queen was going by; as she heard the crying, she stopped; and, going into the house, she asked the mother why she was beating her daughter, so that everyone outside in the street could hear her cries. The woman was ashamed to tell of her daughter's laziness, so she said, "I cannot stop her from spinning; she is forever at it, and I am poor and cannot furnish her with flax enough."

Then the Queen answered, "I like nothing better than the sound of the spinning wheel, and always feel happy when I hear its humming; let me take your daughter with me to the castle. I have plenty of flax, she shall spin there to her heart's content." The mother was only too glad of the offer, and the Queen took the girl with her.

When they reached the castle the Queen showed her three rooms which were filled with the finest flax as full as they could hold.

"Now you can spin me this flax," said she, "and when you can show it me all done you shall have my eldest son for bridegroom, you may be poor, but I make nothing of that—your industry is dowry enough." The girl was inwardly terrified, for she could not have spun the flax, even if she were to live to be a hundred years old, and were to sit spinning every day of her life from morning to evening. And when she found herself alone she began to weep, and sat so for three days without putting her hand to it. On the third day the Queen came, and when she saw that nothing had been done of the spinning she was much surprised; but the girl excused herself by saying that she had not been able to begin because of the distress she was in at leaving her home and her mother. The excuse contented the Queen, who said, however, as she went away, "Tomorrow you must begin to work."

When the girl found herself alone again she could not tell how to help herself or what to do, and in her perplexity she went and gazed out of the window. There she saw three women passing by, and the first of them had a broad flat foot, the second had a big underlip that hung down over her chin, and the third had a remarkably broad thumb. They all of them stopped in front of the window, and called out to know what it was that the girl wanted. She told them all her need, and they promised her their help, and said, "Then will you invite us to your wedding, and not be ashamed of us, and call us your cousins, and let us sit at your table; if you will promise this, we will finish off your flax-spinning in a very short time."

"With all my heart," answered the girl; "only come in now, and begin at once."

Then these same women came in, and she cleared a space in the first room for them to sit and carry on their spinning. The first one drew out the thread and moved the treddle that turned the wheel, the second moistened the thread, the third twisted it, and rapped with her finger on the table, and as often as she rapped a heap of yarn fell to the ground, and it was most beautifully spun. But the girl hid the three spinsters out of the Queen's sight, and only showed her, as often as she came, the heaps of well-spun yarn; and there was no end to the praises she received. When the first room was empty they went on to the second, and then to the third, so that at last all was finished. Then the three women took their leave, saying to the girl, "Do not forget what you have promised, and it will be all the better for you."

So when the girl took the Queen and showed her the empty rooms, and the great heaps of yarn, the wedding was at once arranged, and the bridegroom rejoiced that he should have so clever and diligent a wife, and praised her exceedingly.

"I have three cousins," said the girl, "and as they have shown me a great deal of kindness, I would not wish to forget them in my good fortune; may I be allowed to invite them to the wedding, and to ask them to sit at the table with us?" The Queen and the bridegroom said at once, "There is no reason against it."

So when the feast began in came the three spinsters in strange guise, and the bride said, "Dear cousins, you are welcome."

"Oh," said the bridegroom, "how come you to have such dreadfully ugly relations?" And then he went up to the first spinster and said, "How is it that you have such a broad flat foot?"

"With treading," answered she, "with treading." Then he went up to the second and said, "How is it that you have such a great hanging lip?"

"With licking," answered she, "with licking."

Then he asked the third, "How is it that you have such a broad thumb?"

"With twisting thread," answered she, "with twisting thread." Then the bridegroom said that from that time forward his beautiful bride should never touch a spinning wheel. And so she escaped that tiresome flax-spinning.

The Rabbit's Bride

There was once a woman who lived with her daughter in a beautiful cabbage garden; and there came a rabbit and ate up all the cabbages. At last said the woman to her daughter, "Go into the garden, and drive out the rabbit."

"Shoo! shoo!" said the maiden; "don't eat up all our cabbages, little rabbit!"

"Come, maiden," said the rabbit, "sit on my tail and go with me to my rabbit hutch."

But the maiden would not. Another day, back came the rabbit, and ate away at the cabbages, until the woman said to her daughter, "Go into the garden, and drive away the rabbit."

"Shoo! shoo!" said the maiden; "don't eat up all our cabbages, little rabbit!"

"Come, maiden," said the rabbit, "sit on my tail and go with me to my rabbit hutch." But the maiden would not. Again, a third time back came the rabbit, and ate away at the cabbages, until the woman said to her daughter, "Go into the garden, and drive away the rabbit."

"Shoo! shoo!" said the maiden; "don't eat up all our cabbages, little rabbit!"

"Come, maiden," said the rabbit, "sit on my tail and go with me to my rabbit hutch." And then the girl seated herself on the rabbit's tail, and the rabbit took her to his hutch. "Now," said he, "set to work and cook some bran and cabbage; I am going to bid the wedding guests." And soon they were all collected. Would you like to know who they were? Well, I can only tell you what was told to me; all the hares came, and the crow who was to be the parson to marry them, and the fox for the clerk, and the altar was under the rainbow.

But the maiden was sad, because she was so lonely. "Get up! get up!" said the rabbit, "the wedding folk are all merry." But the bride wept and said nothing, and the rabbit went away, but very soon came back again. "Get up! get up!" said he, "the wedding folk are waiting." But the bride said nothing, and the rabbit went away. Then she made a figure of straw, and dressed it in her own clothes, and gave it a red mouth, and set it to watch the kettle of bran, and then she went home to her mother. Back again came the rabbit, saying, "Get up! get up!" and he went up and hit the straw figure on the head, so that it tumbled down.

And the rabbit thought that he had killed his bride, and he went away and was very sad.

The Drummer

A young drummer went out quite alone one evening into the country, and came to a lake on the shore of which he perceived three pieces of white linen lying. "What fine linen," said he, and put one piece in his pocket. He returned home, thought no more of what he had found, and went to bed. Just as he was going to sleep, it seemed to him as if someone was saying his name. He listened, and was aware of a soft voice which cried to him: "Drummer, drummer, wake up!" As it was a dark night he could see no one, but it appeared to him that a figure was hovering about his bed. "What do you want?" he asked. "Give me back my dress," answered the voice, "that you took away from me last evening by the lake."

"You shall have it back again," said the drummer, "if you will tell me who you are."

"Ah," replied the voice, "I am the daughter of a mighty King; but I have fallen into the power of a witch, and am shut up on the glass mountain. I have to bathe in the lake every day with my two sisters, but I cannot fly back again without my dress. My sisters have gone away, but I have been forced to stay behind. I entreat you to give me my dress back."

"Be easy, poor child," said the drummer. "I will willingly give it back to you." He took it out of his pocket, and reached it to her in the dark. She snatched it in haste, and wanted to go away with it. "Stop a moment, perhaps I can help you."

"You can only help me by ascending the glass mountain, and freeing me from the power of the witch. But you cannot come to the glass mountain, and indeed if you were quite close to it you could not ascend it."

"When I want to do a thing I always can do it," said the drummer, "I am sorry for you, and have no fear of anything. But I do not know the way which leads to the glass mountain."

"The road goes through the great forest, in which the maneaters live," she answered, "and more than that, I dare not tell you." And then he heard her wings quiver, as she flew away.

By daybreak the drummer arose, buckled on his drum, and went without fear straight into the forest. After he had walked for a while without seeing any giants, he thought to himself, I must waken up the sluggards, and he hung his drum before him, and beat such a reveille, that the birds flew out of the trees with loud cries. It was not long before a giant who had been lying sleeping among the grass, rose up, and was as tall as a fir tree. "Wretch!" cried he, "what art thou drumming here for, and wakening me out of my best sleep?"

"I am drumming," he replied, "because I want to show the way to many thousands who are following me."

"What do they want in my forest?" demanded the giant. "They want to put an end to thee, and cleanse the forest of such a monster as thou art!"

"Oh!" said the giant, "I will trample you all to death like so many ants."

"Dost thou think thou canst do anything against us?" said the drummer; "if thou stoopest to take hold of one, he will jump away and hide himself; but when thou art lying down and sleeping, they will come forth from every thicket, and creep up to thee. Every one of them has a hammer of steel in his belt, and with that they will beat in thy skull."

The giant grew angry and thought, If I meddle with the crafty folk, it might turn out badly for me. I can strangle wolves and bears, but I cannot protect myself from these earthworms. "Listen, little fellow," said he, "go back again, and I will promise you that for the future I will leave you and your comrades in peace, and if there is anything else you wish for, tell me, for I am quite willing to do something to please you."

"Thou hast long legs," said the drummer, "and canst run quicker than I; carry me to the glass mountain, and I will give my followers a signal to go back, and they shall leave thee in peace this time."

"Come here, worm," said the giant; "seat thyself on my shoulder, I will carry thee where thou wishest to be." The giant lifted him up, and the drummer began to beat his drum up aloft to his heart's delight. The giant thought, "That is the signal for the other people to turn back." After a while, a second giant was standing in the road, who took the drummer from the first, and stuck him in his buttonhole. The drummer laid hold of the button, which was as large as a dish, held on by it, and looked merrily around. Then they came to a third giant, who took him out of the buttonhole, and set him on the rim of his hat. Then the drummer walked backwards and forwards up above, and looked over the trees, and when he perceived a mountain in the blue distance, he thought, "That must be the glass mountain," and so it was. The giant only made two steps more, and they reached the foot of the mountain, where the giant put him down. The drummer demanded to be put on the summit of the glass mountain, but the giant shook his head, growled something in his beard, and went back into the forest.

And now the poor drummer was standing before the mountain, which was as high as if three mountains were piled on each other, and at the same time as smooth as a looking glass, and did not know how to get up it. He began to climb, but that was useless, for he always slipped back again. "If one was a bird now," thought he, but what was the good of wishing, no wings grew for him. Whilst he was standing thus, not knowing what to do, he saw, not far from him, two men who were struggling fiercely together. He went up to them and saw that they were disputing about a saddle which was lying on the ground before them, and which both of them wanted to have. "What fools you are," said he, "to quarrel about a saddle, when you have not a horse for it!"

"The saddle is worth fighting about," answered one of the men, "whosoever sits on it, and wishes himself in any place, even if it should be the very end of the earth, gets there the instant he has uttered the wish. The saddle belongs to us in common. It is my turn to ride on it, but that other man will not let me do it."

"I will soon decide the quarrel," said the drummer, and he went to a short distance and stuck a white rod in the ground. Then he came back and said: "Now run to the goal, and whoever gets there first, shall ride first." Both put themselves into a trot, but hardly had they gone a couple of steps before the drummer swung himself on the saddle, wished himself on the glass mountain, and before anyone could turn round, he was there. On the top of the mountain was a plain; there stood an old stone house, and in front of the house lay a great fishpond, but behind it was a dark forest. He saw neither men nor animals; everything was quiet; only the wind rustled amongst the trees, and the clouds moved by quite close above his head. He went to the door and knocked. When he had knocked for the third time, an old woman with a brown face and red eyes opened the door. She had spectacles on her long nose, and looked sharply at him; then she asked what he wanted. "Entrance, food, and a bed for the night," replied the drummer.

"That thou shalt have," said the old woman, "if thou wilt perform three services in return."

"Why not?" he answered, "I am not afraid of any kind of work, however hard it may be." The old woman let him go in, and gave him some food and a good bed at night. The next morning when he had had his sleep out, she took a thimble from her wrinkled finger, reached it to the drummer, and said: "Go to work now, and empty out the pond with this thimble; but thou must have it done before night, and must have sought out all the fishes which are in the water and laid them side by side, according to their kind and size."

"That is strange work," said the drummer, but he went to the pond, and began to empty it. He baled the whole morning; but what can anyone do to a great lake with a thimble, even if he were to bale for a thousand years? When it was noon, he thought, "It is all useless, and whether I work or not it will come to the same thing." So he gave it up and sat down. Then came a maiden out of the house who set a little basket with food

before him, and said: "What ails thee, that thou sittest so sadly here?" He looked at her, and saw that she was wondrously beautiful. "Ah," said he, "I cannot finish the first piece of work, how will it be with the others? I came forth to seek a king's daughter who is said to dwell here, but I have not found her, and I will go farther."

"Stay here," said the maiden, "I will help thee out of thy difficulty. Thou art tired, lay thy head in my lap, and sleep. When thou awakest again, thy work will be done." The drummer did not need to be told that twice. As soon as his eyes were shut, she turned a wishing ring and said: "Rise, water. Fishes, come out." Instantly the water rose on high like a white mist, and moved away with the other clouds, and the fishes sprang on the shore and laid themselves side by side each according to his size and kind. When the drummer awoke, he saw with amazement that all was done. But the maiden said: "One of the fish is not lying with those of its own kind, but quite alone; when the old woman comes tonight and sees that all she demanded has been done, she will ask thee: What is this fish lying alone for? Then throw the fish in her face, and say: This one shall be for thee, old witch." In the evening the witch came, and when she had put this question, he threw the fish in her face. She behaved as if she did not remark it, and said nothing, but looked at him with malicious eyes.

Next morning she said: "Yesterday it was too easy for thee, I must give thee harder work. Today thou must hew down the whole of the forest, split the wood into logs, and pile them up, and everything must be finished by the evening." She gave him an axe, a mallet, and two wedges. But the axe was made of lead, and the mallet and wedges were of tin. When he began to cut, the edge of the axe turned back, and the mallet and wedges were beaten out of shape. He did not know how to manage, but at midday the maiden came once more with his dinner and comforted him. "Lay thy head on my lap," said she, "and sleep; when thou awakest, thy work will be done." She turned her wishing ring, and in an instant the whole forest fell down with a crash, the wood split, and arranged itself in heaps, and it seemed just as if unseen giants were finishing the work.

When he awoke, the maiden said: "Dost thou see that the wood is piled up and arranged, one bough alone remains; but when the old woman comes this evening and asks thee about that bough, give her a blow with it, and say: That is for thee, thou witch." The old woman came: "There thou seest how easy the work was!" said she, "but for whom hast thou left that bough which is lying there still?"

"For thee, thou witch," he replied, and gave her a blow with it. But she pretended not to feel it, laughed scornfully, and said: "Early tomorrow morning thou shalt arrange all the wood in one heap, set fire to it, and burn it." He rose at break of day, and began to pick up the wood, but how can a single man get a whole forest together? The work made no progress. The maiden, however, did not desert him in his need. She brought him his food at noon, and when he had eaten, he laid his head on her lap, and went to sleep. When he awoke, the entire pile of wood was burning in one enormous flame, which stretched its tongues out into the sky. "Listen to me," said the maiden, "when the witch comes, she will give thee all kinds of orders; do whatever she asks thee without fear, and then she will not be able to get the better of thee, but if thou art afraid, the fire will lay hold of thee, and consume thee. At last when thou hast done everything, seize her with both thy hands, and throw her into the midst of the fire." The maiden departed, and the old woman came sneaking up to him. "Oh, I am cold," said she, "but that is a fire that burns; it warms my old bones for me, and does me good! But there is a log lying there which won't burn, bring it out for me. When thou hast done that, thou art free, and mayst go where thou likest, come; go in with a good will!" The drummer did not reflect long; he sprang into the midst of the flames, but they did not hurt him, and could not even singe a hair of his head. He carried the log out, and laid it down. Hardly, however, had the wood touched the earth than it was transformed, and the beautiful maiden who had helped him in his need stood before him, and by the silken and shining golden garments which she wore, he knew right well that she was the King's daughter. But the old woman laughed venomously, and said: "Thou thinkest thou hast her safe, but thou hast not got her yet!" Just as she was about to fall on the maiden and take her away, the youth seized the old woman with both his hands, raised her up on high, and threw her into the jaws of the fire, which closed over her as if it were delighted that an old witch was to be burnt.

Then the King's daughter looked at the drummer, and when she saw that he was a handsome youth and remembered how he had risked his life to deliver her, she gave him her hand, and said: "Thou hast ventured everything for my sake, but I also will do everything for thine. Promise to be true to me, and thou shalt be my husband. We shall not want for riches, we shall have enough with what the witch has gathered together here." She led him into the house, where there were chests and coffers crammed with the old woman's treasures. The maiden left the gold and silver where it was, and took only the precious stones. She would not stay any longer on the glass mountain, so the drummer said to her: "Seat thyself by me on my saddle, and then we will fly down like birds."

"I do not like the old saddle," said she, "I need only turn my wishing ring and we shall be at home."

"Very well, then," answered the drummer, "then wish us in front of the town gate." In the twinkling of an eye they were there, but the drummer said: "I will just go to my parents and tell them the news, wait for me outside here, I shall soon be back."

"Ah," said the King's daughter, "I beg thee to be careful. On thy arrival do not kiss thy parents on the right cheek, or else thou wilt forget everything, and I shall stay behind here outside, alone and deserted."

"How can I forget thee?" said he, and promised her to come back very soon, and gave his hand upon it. When he went into his father's house, he had changed so much that no one knew who he was, for the three days which he had passed on the glass mountain had been three years. Then he made himself known, and his parents fell on his neck with joy, and his heart was so moved that he forgot what the maiden had said, and kissed them on both cheeks. But when he had given them the kiss on the right cheek, every thought of the King's daughter vanished from him. He emptied out his pockets, and laid handfuls of the largest jewels on the table. The parents had not the least idea what to do with the riches. Then the father built a magnificent castle all surrounded by gardens, woods, and meadows as if a prince were going to live in it, and when it was ready, the mother said: "I have found a maiden for thee, and the wedding shall be in three days." The son was content to do as his parents desired.

The poor King's daughter had stood for a long time without the town waiting for the return of the young man. When evening came, she said: "He must certainly have kissed his parents on the right cheek, and has forgotten me." Her heart was full of sorrow, she wished herself into a solitary little hut in a forest, and would not return to her father's court. Every evening she went into the town and passed the young man's house; he often saw her, but he no longer knew her. At length she heard the people saying: "The wedding will take place tomorrow." Then she said: "I will try if I can win his heart back." On the first day of the wedding ceremonies, she turned her wishing ring, and said: "A dress as bright as the sun." Instantly the dress lay before her, and it was as bright as if it had been woven of real sunbeams. When all the guests were assembled, she entered the hall. Everyone was amazed at the beautiful dress, and the bride most of all, and as pretty dresses were the things she had most delight in, she went to the stranger and asked if she would sell it to her. "Not for money," she answered, "but if I may pass the first night outside the door of the room where your betrothed sleeps, I will give it up to you." The bride could not overcome her desire and consented, but she mixed a sleeping draught with the wine her betrothed took at night, which made him fall into a deep sleep. When all had become quiet, the King's daughter crouched down by the door of the bedroom, opened it just a little, and cried:

"Drummer, drummer, I pray thee hear!
Hast thou forgotten thou heldest me dear?
That on the glass mountain we sat hour by hour?
That I rescued thy life from the witch's power?
Didst thou not plight thy troth to me?
Drummer, drummer, hearken to me!"

But it was all in vain, the drummer did not awake, and when morning dawned, the King's daughter was forced to go back again as she came. On the second evening she turned her wishing ring and said: "A dress as silvery as the moon." When she appeared at the feast in the dress which was as soft as moonbeams, it again excited the desire of the bride, and the King's daughter gave it to her for permission to pass the second night also, outside the door of the bedroom. Then in the stillness of the night, she cried:

"Drummer, drummer, I pray thee hear!
Hast thou forgotten thou heldest me dear?
That on the glass mountain we sat hour by hour?
That I rescued thy life from the witch's power?
Didst thou not plight thy troth to me?
Drummer, drummer, hearken to me!"

But the drummer, who was stupefied with the sleeping draught, could not be aroused. Sadly next morning she went back to her hut in the forest. But the people in the house had heard the lamentation of the stranger maiden, and told the bridegroom about it. They told him also that it was impossible that he could hear anything of it, because the maiden he was going to marry had poured a sleeping draught into his wine. On the third evening, the King's daughter turned her wishing ring, and said: "A dress glittering like the stars." When she showed herself therein at the feast, the bride was quite beside herself with the splendour of the dress, which far surpassed the others, and she said: "I must, and will have it." The maiden gave it as she had given the others for permission to spend the night outside the bridegroom's door. The bridegroom, however, did not drink the wine which was handed to him before he went to bed, but poured it behind the bed, and when everything was quiet, he heard a sweet voice which called to him:

"Drummer, drummer, I pray thee hear!
Hast thou forgotten thou held me dear?

That on the glass mountain we sat hour by hour?
That I rescued thy life from the witch's power?
Didst thou not plight thy troth to me?
Drummer, drummer, hearken to me!"

Suddenly, his memory returned to him. "Ah," cried he, "how can I have acted so unfaithfully; but the kiss which in the joy of my heart I gave my parents, on the right cheek, that is to blame for it all, that is what stupefied me!" He sprang up, took the King's daughter by the hand, and led her to his parents' bed. "This is my true bride," said he, "if I marry the other, I shall do a great wrong." The parents, when they heard how everything had happened, gave their consent. Then the lights in the hall were lighted again, drums and trumpets were brought, friends and relations were invited to come, and the real wedding was solemnized with great rejoicing. The first bride received the beautiful dresses as a compensation, and declared herself satisfied.

Little One-Eye, Two-Eyes and Three-Eyes

Once upon a time there was a Woman, who had three daughters, the eldest of whom was named One-Eye, because she had but a single eye, and that placed in the middle of her forehead; the second was called Two-Eyes, because she was like other mortals; and the third, Three-Eyes, because she had three eyes, and one of them in the centre of her forehead, like her eldest sister. But, because her second sister had nothing out of the common in her appearance, she was looked down upon by her sisters, and despised by her mother. "You are no better than common folk," they would say to her; "you do not belong to us"; and then they would push her about, give her coarse clothing, and nothing to eat but their leavings, besides numerous other insults as occasion offered.

Once it happened that Two-Eyes had to go into the forest to tend the goat; and she went very hungry, because her sisters had given her very little to eat that morning. She sat down upon a hillock, and cried so much that her tears flowed almost like rivers out of her eyes! By and by she looked up and saw a Woman standing by, who asked, "Why are you weeping, Two-Eyes?"

"Because I have two eyes like ordinary people," replied the maiden, "and therefore my mother and sisters dislike me, push me into corners, throw me their old clothes, and give me nothing to eat but what they leave. Today they have given me so little that I am still hungry."

"Dry your eyes, then, now," said the wise Woman; "I will tell you something which shall prevent you from being hungry again. You must say to your goat:

"'Little kid, milk
Table, appear!'

"and immediately a nicely filled table will stand before you, with delicate food upon it, of which you can eat as much as you please. And when you are satisfied, and have done with the table, you must say:

"'Little kid, milk
Table, depart!'

"and it will disappear directly."

With these words the wise Woman went away, and little Two-Eyes thought to herself she would try at once if what the Woman said were true, for she felt very hungry indeed.

"Little kid, milk
Table, appear!"

said the maiden, and immediately a table covered with a white cloth stood before her, with a knife and fork, and silver spoon; and the most delicate dishes were ranged in order upon it, and everything as warm as if they had been just taken away from the fire. Two-Eyes said a short grace, and then began to eat; and when she had finished she pronounced the words which the wise Woman had told her:

"Little kid, milk
Table, depart!"

and directly the table and all that was on it quickly disappeared. "This is capital housekeeping," said the maiden, in high glee; and at evening she went home with her goat, and found an earthen dish which her sisters had left her filled with their leavings. She did not touch it; and the next morning she went off again without taking the meagre breakfast which was left out for her. The first and second time she did this the sisters thought nothing of it; but when she did the same the third morning their attention was roused, and they said, "All is not right with Two-Eyes, for she has left her meals twice, and has touched nothing of what was left for her; she must have found some other way of living." So they determined that One-Eye should go with the maiden when she drove the goat to the meadow and pay attention to what passed, and observe whether anyone brought her to eat or to drink.

When Two-Eyes, therefore, was about to set off, One-Eye told her she was going with her to see whether she took proper care of the goat and fed her sufficiently. Two-Eyes, however, divined her sister's object, and drove the goat where the grass was finest, and then said, "Come, One-Eye, let us sit down, and I will sing to you." So One-Eye sat down, for she was quite tired with her unusual walk and the heat of the sun.

"Are you awake or asleep, One-Eye?
Are you awake or asleep?"

sang Two-Eyes, until her sister really went to sleep. As soon as she was quite sound, the maiden had her table out, and ate and drank all she needed; and by the time One-Eye woke again the table had disappeared, and the maiden said to her sister, "Come, we will go home now; while you have been sleeping the goat might have run about all over the world." So they went home, and after Two-Eyes had left her meal untouched, the mother inquired of One-Eye what she had seen, and she was obliged to confess that she had been asleep.

The following morning the mother told Three-Eyes that she must go out and watch Two-Eyes, and see who brought her food, for it was certain that someone must. So Three-Eyes told her sister that she was going to accompany her that morning to see if she took care of the goat and fed her well; but Two-Eyes saw through her design, and drove the goat again to the best feeding place. Then she asked her sister to sit down and she would sing to her, and Three-Eyes did so, for she was very tired with her long walk in the heat of the sun. Then Two-Eyes began to sing as before:

"Are you awake, Three-Eyes?"

but, instead of continuing as she should have done,

"Are you asleep, Three-Eyes?"

she said by mistake,

"Are you asleep, Two-Eyes?"

and so went on singing:

"Are you awake, Three-Eyes?"
"Are you asleep, Two-Eyes?"

By and by Three-Eyes closed two of her eyes, and went to sleep with them; but the third eye, which was not spoken to, kept open. Three-Eyes, however, cunningly shut it too, and feigned to be asleep, while she was really watching; and soon Two-Eyes, thinking all safe, repeated the words:

"Little kid, milk
Table, appear!"

and as soon as she was satisfied she said the old words:

"Little kid, milk
Table, depart!"

Three-Eyes watched all these proceedings; and presently Two-Eyes came and awoke her, saying, "Ah, sister! you are a good watcher, but come, let us go home now." When they reached home Two-Eyes again ate nothing; and her sister told her mother she knew now why the haughty hussy would not eat their victuals. "When she is out in the meadow," said her sister, "she says:

"'Little kid, milk
Table, appear!'

"and, directly, a table comes up laid out with meat and wine, and everything of the best, much better than we have; and as soon as she has had enough she says:

"'Little kid, milk
Table, depart!'

"and all goes away directly, as I clearly saw. Certainly she did put to sleep two of my eyes, but the one in the middle of my forehead luckily kept awake!"

"Will you have better things than we?" cried the envious mother; "then you shall lose the chance"; and so saying, she took a carving knife and killed the goat dead.

As soon as Two-Eyes saw this she went out, very sorrowful, to the old spot and sat down where she had sat before to weep bitterly. All at once the wise Woman stood in front of her again, and asked why she was crying. "Must I not cry," replied she, "when the goat which used to furnish me every day with a dinner, according to your promise, has been killed by my mother, and I am again suffering hunger and thirst?"

"Two-Eyes," said the wise Woman, "I will give you a piece of advice. Beg your sisters to give you the entrails of the goat, and bury them in the earth before the house door, and your fortune will be made." So saying, she disappeared, and Two-Eyes went home, and said to her sisters, "Dear sisters, do give me some part of the slain kid; I desire nothing else—let me have the entrails." The sisters laughed and readily gave them to her; and she buried them secretly before the threshold of the door, as the wise Woman had bidden her.

The following morning they found in front of the house a wonderfully beautiful tree, with leaves of silver and fruits of gold hanging from the boughs, than which nothing more splendid could be seen in the world. The two elder sisters were quite ignorant how the tree came where it stood; but Two-Eyes perceived that it was produced by the goat's entrails, for it stood on the exact spot where she had buried them. As soon as the mother saw it she told One-Eye to break off some of the fruit. One-Eye went up to the tree, and pulled a bough toward her, to pluck off the fruit; but the bough flew back again directly out of her hands; and so it did every time she took hold of it, till she was forced to give up, for she could not obtain a single golden apple in spite of all her endeavors. Then the mother said to Three-Eyes, "Do you climb up, for you can see better with your three eyes than your sister with her one."

Three-Eyes, however, was not more fortunate than her sister, for the golden apples flew back as soon as she touched them. At last the mother got so impatient that she climbed the tree herself; but she met with no more success than either of her daughters, and grasped the air only when she thought she had the fruit. Two-Eyes now thought she would try, and said to her sisters, "Let me get up, perhaps I may be successful."

"Oh, you are very likely indeed," said they, "with your two eyes: you will see well, no doubt!" So Two-Eyes climbed the tree, and directly she touched the boughs the golden apples fell into her hands, so that she plucked them as fast as she could, and filled her apron before she went down. Her mother took them of her, but returned her no thanks; and the two sisters, instead of treating Two-Eyes better than they had done, were only the more envious of her, because she alone could gather the fruit—in fact, they treated her worse.

One morning, not long after the springing up of the apple tree, the three sisters were all standing together beneath it, when in the distance a young Knight was seen riding toward them. "Make haste, Two-Eyes!" exclaimed the two elder sisters; "make haste, and creep out of our way, that we may not be ashamed of you"; and so saying, they put over her in great haste an empty cask which stood near, and which covered the golden apples as well, which she had just been plucking. Soon the Knight came up to the tree, and the sisters saw he was a very handsome man, for he stopped to admire the fine silver leaves and golden fruit, and presently asked to whom the tree belonged, for he should like to have a branch off it. One-Eye and Three-Eyes replied that the tree belonged to them; and they tried to pluck a branch off for the Knight. They had their trouble for nothing, however, for the boughs and fruit flew back as soon as they touched them. "This is very wonderful," cried the Knight, "that this tree should belong to you, and yet you cannot pluck the fruit!" The sisters, however, maintained that it was theirs; but while they spoke Two-Eyes rolled a golden apple from underneath the cask, so that it travelled to the feet of the Knight, for she was angry, because her sisters had not spoken the truth. When he saw the apple he was astonished, and asked where it came from; and One-Eye and Three-Eyes said they had another sister, but they dared not let her be seen, because she had only two eyes, like common folk! The Knight, however, would see her, and called, "Two-Eyes, come here!" and soon she made her appearance from under the cask.

The Knight was bewildered at her great beauty, and said, "You, Two-Eyes, can surely break off a bough of this tree for me?" "Yes," she replied, "that I will, for it is my property"; and climbing up, she easily broke off a branch with silver leaves and golden fruit, which she handed to the Knight. "What can I give you in return, Two-Eyes?" asked the Knight. "Alas! if you will take me with you I shall be happy, for now I suffer hunger and thirst, and am in trouble and grief from early morning to late evening; take me, and save me!" Thereupon the Knight raised Two-Eyes upon his saddle, and took her home to his father's castle. There he

gave her beautiful clothes, and all she wished for to eat or to drink; and afterward, because his love for her had become so great, he married her, and a very happy wedding they had.

Her two sisters, meanwhile, were very jealous when Two-Eyes was carried off by the Knight; but they consoled themselves by saying, "The wonderful tree remains still for us; and even if we cannot get at the fruit, everybody that passes will stop to look at it, and then come and praise it to us. Who knows where our wheat may bloom?" The morning after this speech, however, the tree disappeared, and with it all their hopes; but when Two-Eyes that same day looked out of her chamber window, behold, the tree stood before it, and there remained!

For a long time after this occurrence Two-Eyes lived in the enjoyment of the greatest happiness; and one morning two poor women came to the palace and begged an alms. Two-Eyes, after looking narrowly at their faces, recognized her two sisters, One-Eye and Three-Eyes, who had come to such great poverty that they were forced to wander about, begging their bread from day to day. Two-Eyes, however, bade them welcome, invited them in, and took care of them, till they both repented of their evil which they had done to their sister in the days of their childhood.

The Miller and the Water Sprite

There was once upon a time a Miller who lived with his wife in great contentment. They had money and land, and their prosperity increased year by year more and more. But ill luck comes like a thief in the night, as their wealth had increased so did it again decrease, year by year, and at last the Miller could hardly call the mill in which he lived his own. He was in great distress, and when he lay down after his day's work, found no rest, but tossed about in his bed, full of care. One morning he rose before daybreak and went out into the open air, thinking that perhaps there his heart might become lighter. As he was stepping over the milldam the first sunbeam was just breaking forth, and he heard a rippling sound in the pond. He turned round and perceived a beautiful woman, rising slowly out of the water. Her long hair, which she was holding off her shoulders with her soft hands, fell down on both sides, and covered her white body. He soon saw that she was the Water Sprite of the millpond, and in his fright did not know whether he should run away or stay where he was. But the Water Sprite made her sweet voice heard, called him by his name, and asked him why he was so sad. The Miller was at first struck dumb, but when he heard her speak so kindly, he took heart, and told her how he had formerly lived in wealth and happiness,

but that now he was so poor that he did not know what to do. "Be easy," answered the Water Sprite, "I will make thee richer and happier than thou hast ever been before, only thou must promise to give me the young thing which has just been born in thy house."

"What else can that be," thought the Miller, "but a young puppy or kitten?" and he promised her what she desired. The Water Sprite descended into the water again, and he hurried back to his mill, consoled and in good spirits. He had not yet reached it, when the maidservant came out of the house, and cried to him to rejoice, for his wife had given birth to a little boy. The Miller stood as if struck by lightning; he saw very well that the cunning Water Sprite had been aware of it, and had cheated him. Hanging his head, he went up to his wife's bedside and when she said, "Why dost thou not rejoice over the fine boy?" he told her what had befallen him, and what kind of a promise he had given to the Water Sprite. "Of what use to me are riches and prosperity?" he added, "if I am to lose my child; but what can I do?" Even the relations, who had come thither to wish them joy, did not know what to say. In the meantime prosperity again returned to the Miller's house. All that he undertook succeeded, it was as if presses and coffers filled themselves of their own accord, and as if money multiplied nightly in the cupboards. It was not long before his wealth was greater than it had ever been before. But he could not rejoice over it untroubled, for the bargain which he had made with the Water Sprite tormented his soul. Whenever he passed the millpond, he feared she might ascend and remind him of his debt. He never let the boy himself go near the water. "Beware," he said to him, "if thou dost but touch the water, a hand will rise, seize thee, and draw thee down." But as year after year went by and the Water Sprite did not show herself again, the Miller began to feel at ease. The boy grew up to be a youth and was apprenticed to a huntsman. When he had learnt everything, and had become an excellent huntsman, the lord of the village took him into his service. In the village lived a beautiful and truehearted maiden, who pleased the huntsman, and when his master perceived that, he gave him a little house, the two were married, lived peacefully and happily, and loved each other with all their hearts.

One day the huntsman was chasing a roe; and when the animal turned aside from the forest into the open country, he pursued it and at last shot it. He did not notice that he was now in the neighbourhood of the dangerous millpond, and went, after he had disembowelled the stag, to the water, in order to wash his blood-stained hands. Scarcely, however, had he dipped them in than the Water Sprite ascended, smilingly wound her dripping arms around him, and drew him quickly down under the waves, which closed over him. When it was evening, and the huntsman did not return home, his wife became alarmed. She went out to seek him, and as he had often told her that he had to be on his guard against the snares of the Water Sprite, and dared not venture into the neighbourhood of the millpond, she already suspected what had happened. She hastened to the water, and when she found his hunting pouch lying on the shore, she could no longer have any doubt of the misfortune. Lamenting her sorrow, and wringing her hands, she called on her beloved by name, but in vain. She hurried across to the other side of the pond, and called him anew; she reviled the Water Sprite with harsh words, but no answer followed. The surface of the water remained calm, only the crescent moon stared steadily back at her. The poor woman did not leave the pond. With hasty steps, she paced round and round it, without resting a moment, sometimes in silence, sometimes uttering a loud cry, sometimes softly sobbing. At last her strength came to an end, she sank down to the ground and fell into a heavy sleep. Presently a dream took possession of her. She was anxiously climbing upwards between great masses of rock; thorns and briars caught her feet, the rain beat in her face, and the wind tossed her long hair about. When she had reached the summit, quite a different sight presented itself to her; the sky was blue, the air soft, the ground sloped gently downwards, and on a green meadow, gay with flowers of every colour, stood a pretty cottage. She went up to it and opened the door; there sat an old woman with white hair, who beckoned to her kindly. At that very moment, the poor woman awoke, day had already dawned, and she at once resolved to act in accordance with her dream. She laboriously climbed the mountain; everything was exactly as she had seen it in the night. The old woman received her kindly, and pointed out a chair on which she might sit. "Thou must have met with a misfortune," she said, "since thou hast sought out my lonely cottage." With tears, the woman related what had befallen her.

"Be comforted," said the old woman, "I will help thee. Here is a golden comb for thee. Tarry till the full moon has risen, then go to the millpond, seat thyself on the shore, and comb thy long black hair with this comb. When thou hast done, lay it down on the bank, and thou wilt see what will happen."

The woman returned home, but the time till the full moon came passed slowly. At last the shining disc appeared in the heavens, then she went out to the millpond, sat down and combed her long black hair with the golden comb, and when she had finished, she laid it down at the water's edge. It was not long before there was a movement in the depths, a wave rose, rolled to the shore, and bore the comb away with it. In not more than the time necessary for the comb to sink to the bottom, the surface of the water parted, and the head of the huntsman arose. He did not speak, but looked at his wife with sorrowful glances. At the same instant, a second wave came rushing up, and covered the man's head. All had vanished, the millpond lay peaceful as before, and nothing but the face of the full moon shone on it. Full of sorrow, the woman went back, but again the dream showed her the cottage of the old woman. Next morning she again set out and complained of her woes to the wise woman. The old woman gave her a golden flute, and said, "Tarry till the full moon comes again, then take this flute; play a beautiful air on it, and when thou hast finished, lay it on the sand; then thou wilt see what will happen." The wife did as the old woman told her. No sooner was the flute lying on the sand than there was a stirring in the depths, and a wave rushed up and bore the flute away with it. Immediately afterwards the water parted, and not only the head of the man, but half of his body also arose. He stretched out his arms longingly towards her, but a second wave came up, covered him, and drew him down again. "Alas, what does it profit me?" said the unhappy woman, "that I should see my beloved, only to lose him again!" Despair filled her heart anew, but the dream led her a third time to the house of the old woman. She set out, and the wise woman gave her a golden spinning wheel, consoled her and said, "All is not yet fulfilled, tarry until the time of the full moon, then take the spinning wheel, seat thyself on the shore, and spin the spool full, and when thou hast done that, place the spinning wheel near the water, and thou wilt see what will happen."

The woman obeyed all she said exactly; as soon as the full moon showed itself, she carried the golden spinning wheel to the shore, and span industriously until the flax came to an end, and the spool was quite filled with the threads. No sooner was the wheel standing on the shore than there was a more violent movement than before in the depths of the pond, and a mighty wave rushed up, and bore the wheel away with it. Immediately the head and the whole body of the man rose into the air, in a waterspout. He quickly sprang to the shore, caught his wife by the hand and fled. But they had scarcely gone a very little distance, when the whole pond rose with a frightful roar, and streamed out over the open country. The fugitives already saw death before their eyes, when the woman in her terror implored the help of the old woman, and in an instant they were transformed, she into a toad, he into a frog. The flood which had overtaken them could not destroy them, but it tore them apart and carried them far away. When the water had dispersed and they both touched dry land again, they regained their human form, but neither knew where the other was; they found themselves among strange people, who did not know their native land. High mountains and deep valleys lay between them. In order to keep themselves alive, they were both obliged to tend sheep. For many long years they drove their flocks through field and forest and were full of sorrow and longing. When spring had once more broken forth on the earth, they both went out one day with their flocks, and as chance would have it, they drew near each other. They met in a valley, but did not recognize each other; yet they rejoiced that they were no longer so lonely. Henceforth they each day drove their flocks to the same place; they did not speak much, but they felt comforted. One evening when the full moon was shining in the sky, and the sheep were already at rest, the shepherd pulled the flute out of his pocket, and played on it a beautiful but sorrowful air. When he had finished he saw that the shepherdess was weeping bitterly. "Why art thou weeping?" he asked.

"Alas," answered she, "thus shone the full moon when I played this air on the flute for the last time, and the head of my beloved rose out of the water." He looked at her, and it seemed as if a veil fell from his eyes, and he recognized his dear wife, and when she looked at him, and the moon shone in his face she knew him also. They embraced and kissed each other, and no one need ask if they were happy.

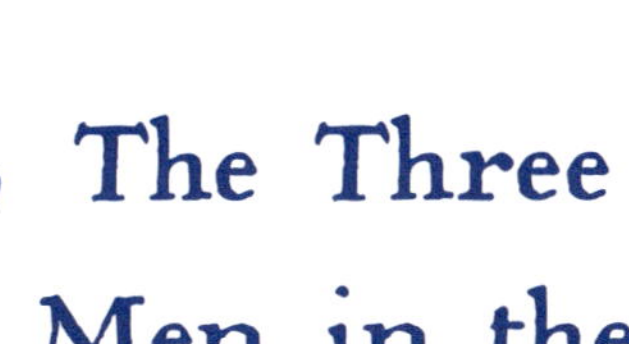

The Three Little Men in the Wood

There was once a man, whose wife was dead, and a woman, whose husband was dead; and the man had a daughter, and so had the woman. The girls were acquainted with each other, and used to play together sometimes in the woman's house. So the woman said to the man's daughter, "Listen to me, tell your father that I will marry him, and then you shall have milk to wash in every morning and wine to drink, and my daughter shall have water to wash in and water to drink." The girl went home and told her father what the woman had said.

The man said, "What shall I do! Marriage is a joy, and also a torment." At last, as he could come to no conclusion, he took off his boot, and said to his daughter, "Take this boot, it has a hole in the sole; go up with it into the loft, hang it on the big nail and pour water in it. If it holds water, I will once more take to me a wife; if it lets out the water, so will I not."

The girl did as she was told, but the water held the hole together, and the boot was full up to the top. So she went and told her father how it was. And he went up to see with his own eyes, and as there was no mistake about it, he went to the widow and courted her, and then they had the wedding.

The next morning, when the two girls awoke, there stood by the bedside of the man's daughter milk to wash in and wine to drink, and by the bedside of the woman's daughter there stood water to wash in and water to drink. On the second morning there stood water to wash in and water to drink for both of them alike. On the third morning there stood water to wash in and water to drink for the man's daughter, and milk to wash in and wine to drink for the woman's daughter; and so it remained ever after. The woman hated her stepdaughter, and never knew how to treat her badly enough from one day to another. And she was jealous because her stepdaughter was pleasant and pretty, and her real daughter was ugly and hateful.

Once in winter, when it was freezing hard, and snow lay deep on hill and valley, the woman made a frock out of paper, called her stepdaughter, and said, "Here, put on this frock, go out into the wood and fetch me a basket of strawberries; I have a great wish for some."

"Oh dear," said the girl, "there are no strawberries to be found in winter; the ground is frozen, and the snow covers everything. And why should I go in the paper frock? it is so cold out of doors that one's breath is frozen; the wind will blow through it, and the thorns will tear it off my back!"

"How dare you contradict me!" cried the stepmother, "be off, and don't let me see you again till you bring me a basket of strawberries." Then she gave her a little piece of hard bread, and said, "That will do for you to eat during the day," and she thought to herself, "She is sure to be frozen or starved to death out of doors, and I shall never set eyes on her again."

So the girl went obediently, put on the paper frock, and started out with the basket. The snow was lying everywhere, far and wide, and there was not a blade of green to be seen. When she entered the wood she saw a little house with three little men peeping out of it. She wished them good day, and knocked modestly at the door. They called her in, and she came into the room and sat down by the side of the oven to warm herself and eat her breakfast. The little men said, "Give us some of it."

"Willingly," answered she, breaking her little piece of bread in two, and giving them half. They then said, "What are you doing here in the wood this winter time in your little thin frock?"

"Oh," answered she, "I have to get a basket of strawberries, and I must not go home without them." When she had eaten her bread they gave her a broom, and told her to go and sweep the snow away from the back door. When she had gone outside to do it the little men talked among themselves about what they should do for her, as she was so good and pretty, and had shared her bread with them. Then the first one said, "She shall grow prettier every day." The second said, "Each time she speaks a piece of gold shall fall from her mouth." The third said, "A king shall come and take her for his wife."

In the meanwhile the girl was doing as the little men had told her, and had cleared the snow from the back of the little house, and what do you suppose she found? fine ripe strawberries, showing dark red against the snow! Then she joyfully filled her little basket full, thanked the little men, shook hands with them all, and ran home in haste to bring her stepmother the thing she longed for. As she went in and said, "Good evening," a piece of gold fell from her mouth at once. Then she related all that had happened to her in the wood, and at each word that she spoke gold pieces fell out of her mouth, so that soon they were scattered all over the room.

"Just look at her pride and conceit!" cried the stepsister, "throwing money about in this way!" but in her heart she was jealous because of it, and wanted to go too into the wood to fetch strawberries. But the mother said, "No, my dear little daughter, it is too cold, you will be frozen to death." But she left her no peace, so at last the mother gave in, got her a splendid fur coat to put on, and gave her bread and butter and cakes to eat on the way.

The girl went into the wood and walked straight up to the little house. The three little men peeped out again, but she gave them no greeting, and without looking round or taking any notice of them she came stumping into the room, sat herself down by the oven, and began to eat her bread and butter and cakes.

"Give us some of that," cried the little men, but she answered, "I've not enough for myself; how can I give away any?" Now when she had done with her eating, they said, "Here is a broom, go and sweep all clean by the back door."

"Oh, go and do it yourselves," answered she; "I am not your housemaid." But when she saw that they were not going to give her anything, she went out to the door. Then the three little men said among themselves, "What shall we do to her, because she is so unpleasant, and has such a wicked jealous heart, grudging everybody everything?" The first said, "She shall grow uglier every day." The second said, "Each time she speaks a toad shall jump out of her mouth at every word." The third said, "She shall die a miserable death."

The girl was looking outside for strawberries, but as she found none, she went sulkily home. And directly she opened her mouth to tell her mother what had happened to her in the wood a toad sprang out of her mouth at each word, so that everyone who came near her was quite disgusted.

The stepmother became more and more set against the man's daughter, whose beauty increased day by day, and her only thought was how to do her some injury. So at last she took a kettle, set it on the fire, and scalded some yarn in it. When it was ready she hung it over the poor girl's shoulder, and gave her an axe, and she was to go to the frozen river and break a hole in the ice, and there to rinse the yarn. She obeyed, and went and hewed a hole in the ice, and as she was about it there came by a splendid coach, in which the king sat. The coach stood still, and the king said, "My child, who art thou, and what art thou doing there?"

She answered, "I am a poor girl, and am rinsing yarn." Then the king felt pity for her, and as he saw that she was very beautiful, he said, "Will you go with me?"

"Oh yes, with all my heart," answered she; and she felt very glad to be out of the way of her mother and sister.

So she stepped into the coach and went off with the king; and when they reached his castle the wedding was celebrated with great splendour, as the little men in the wood had foretold.

At the end of a year the young Queen had a son; and as the stepmother had heard of her great good fortune she came with her daughter to the castle, as if merely to pay the king and queen a visit. One day, when the king had gone out, and when nobody was about, the bad woman took the queen by the head, and her daughter took her by the heels, and dragged her out of bed, and threw her out of the window into a stream that flowed beneath it. Then the old woman put her ugly daughter in the bed, and covered her up to her chin.

When the king came back, and wanted to talk to his wife a little, the old woman cried, "Stop, stop! she is sleeping nicely; she must be kept quiet today." The king dreamt of nothing wrong, and came again the next morning; and as he spoke to his wife, and she answered him, there jumped each time out of her mouth a toad instead of the piece of gold as heretofore. Then he asked why that should be, and the old woman said it was because of her great weakness, and that it would pass away.

But in the night, the boy who slept in the kitchen saw how something in the likeness of a duck swam up the gutter, and said,

"My King, what mak'st thou?
Sleepest thou, or wak'st thou?"

But there was no answer. Then it said,

"What cheer my two guests keep they?"

So the kitchen boy answered,

"In bed all soundly sleep they."

It asked again,

"And my little baby, how does he?"

And he answered,

"He sleeps in his cradle quietly."

Then the duck took the shape of the Queen and went to the child, and gave him to drink, smoothed his little bed, covered him up again, and then, in the likeness of a duck, swam back down the gutter. In this way she came two nights, and on the third she said to the kitchen boy, "Go and tell the king to brandish his sword three times over me on the threshold!" Then the kitchen boy ran and told the king, and he came with his sword and brandished it three times over the duck, and at the third time his wife stood before him living, and hearty, and sound, as she had been before.

The king was greatly rejoiced, but he hid the queen in a chamber until the Sunday came when the child was to be baptized. And after the baptism he said, "What does that person deserve who drags another out of bed and throws him in the water?"

And the old woman answered, "No better than to be put into a cask with iron nails in it, and to be rolled in it down the hill into the water."

Then said the king, "You have spoken your own sentence"; and he ordered a cask to be fetched, and the old woman and her daughter were put into it, and the top hammered down, and the cask was rolled down the hill into the river.